DEADLY REVENGE

DEADLY REVENGE

A Novel

JOHNSON
ADEYANJU
MD

iUniverse, Inc.
New York Lincoln Shanghai

DEADLY REVENGE

iUniverse books may be ordered through booksellers or by contacting:

iUniverse
2021 Pine Lake Road, Suite 100
Lincoln, NE 68512
www.iuniverse.com
1-800-Authors (1-800-288-4677)

ISBN: 978-0-595-45831-8 (pbk)
ISBN: 978-0-595-90131-9 (ebk)

Printed in the United States of America

For my dearly loved family,

Chris, Matthew, Justin and Shannon

And to the rest of my beloved family everywhere

CHAPTER 1

There were only fifteen of them left in this particular building of the prison yard. Solid brick prison walls of about five thousand square feet enclosed them. Except for the welded rectangular door that stood at the main entrance of the building, no other major outlet existed. The four small windows that were closely divided with hard iron bars on each side of the walls, allowed air to come in slowly from the surrounding yard. Because the nature of the crime of the prisoners in this building was extremely serious, it was tagged "The Red Building." It stood in isolation from the other buildings which numbered up to about three or four in the prison yard and which contained over one-hundred men prisoners; serving various terms in jail.

All the men in the red building were desperate criminals. They wore red uniforms to distinguish them from others, and their building was also painted red to distinguish it from the remaining buildings around. Apart from an occasional supply of newspapers and a one in hundred gift to a few of them by friendly warders, they seemed to be infinitely isolated from worldly events. They are all hardened criminals who see no good thing in living a normal daily life except to steal, kill, and destroy to attain a stupendous state of enjoyment.

Inside the red building stood about two dozens of double Decker beds with mattresses that were stuffed with hard grasses. The hallway is lit by two flickering florescent light bulbs that cast a dim shadow on the inmates. The only toilet at the end of the hallway emanates a treacherous odor that greats the prisoners every time the bathroom door creaks open. Only about six months ago, the building was so crowded that about four or five men were sharing a bed. Now, with a drastic reduction in the number of men being released at the completion of their various prison terms, the remaining fifteen men in the building found it convenient to occupy available beds without much hindrance. This, did not in any event, implies that the building would not be filled up within the next few weeks or so.

In one corner of the building was the bed of the oldest occupant in the prison. His name was Bobinson Okoye, simply known to his inmates as Bob. He was around thirty, serving a five-year stretch for forgery and impersonation. His head was completely covered by a growth of low-cut hair that slightly protruded to the middle of his forehead. His fiercely penetrating eyes rested on his twisted nose and massive jaw. His broad chest and muscular arms flank his firm belly and set upon his rough thick legs. He was an inch to six feet in height, with a hard oblong face that revealed more of his ruthlessness whenever he wasn't smiling. He had been there now for over four years, nursing a burning and vicious wound that had been more than permanent on his mind.

Although about two years or so after coming to the prison, Bob had almost forgotten what brought him there. The bundle of vindictiveness that lay on his conscience began to withdraw gradually as he took to the prison's life and absorbed the diverse knowledge of prison humiliations that was being shared by his co-prisoners. Though his term in the prison was now running to an end, never for once did he forget how he suffered in his early days. He would, sometimes, recollect the time he was being ordered to perform several unwanted assignments. He had endured being kicked, spat upon, carried prisoner's waste and danced to the tune of overfed prison lords. All these excluded the heavy labor, when together with others, he would be sent out to clear a portion supposed to be worked on by a bulldozer in the prison farm. There was always a stubborn tree to uproot, a large pit to dig to enclose the prisoners' wastes and so many bricks to carry from one end of the farm to the other. He dared not refuse. He knew if he did, he would be buried alive by the warders and the guards who were always around with their fierce, hungry looking dogs to take care of every stubborn prisoner.

Cautiously, Bob had taken all these treatments like a man, and accepted them as the refugees accept their initial sufferings. He knew it was hard to survive at the Central Maximum prison. He knew the prison to be one of the toughest maximum prisons in the country and probably the toughest in the city of Lagos. To come out of the prison alive, he just had to abide by whatever type of treatment he was given.

Just like a society or an organization, the prisoners in the red building had a way of administering themselves. Their affairs were usually vested on three persons who must have won themselves their positions after victories in several forms of violent incidents. The toughest of the three persons was usually designated the first in command, followed by the second and third in command respectively.

The job of the first in command was to fight against all forms of injustice that were to be sanctioned against the prisoners. He was also responsible for preventing any undue hostility among inmates, and he had the final say in all disputes.

The second in command was to apportion jobs and punishments in the building and the prison farm. He was also responsible for whether or not the prisoners accept or reject any job given by the prison guards.

The third in command was assigned the job of providing information to all the prisoners. He keeps the tab of any secret plan within the building, inside the prison, or any outside information that could benefit or put the prisoners in danger. Whether he liked it or not, he must make all facts known to his superiors before any action is carried out. How he was to do this was nobody's business. As such, the third in command always found himself at the mercy of the guards and other prisoners in order to inform his superiors about what was going on in the prison.

At the completion of his third year, Bobinson Okoye had won himself the position of the third in command. But rather than concentrating on the job that was handed over to him, he immediately began a leadership tussle for the position of the second in command. The law was if you could fight and wrestle your immediate boss to submission, then his position automatically became yours. Bob waited impatiently for the day he would have the chance of challenging the second in command to a duel.

His chance did come on one Friday morning when all the prisoners were in the prison farm. The men from Bob's building had just started working. They were cutting some grasses and removing some trees, a little away from the rest of the prisoners. None of the prison guards or their dogs was near enough. Seeing the free atmosphere that surrounded them, Bob deliberately picked up a lump of hard soil and threw it at Baro, the second in command, who was busy removing a particle of dirt the wind had blown in his eyes. The lump scattered into pieces as it landed on the Baro's face.

Baro looked wildly around, wiping his face and turned to face Bob as soon as he realized that he was the one who threw the dirt. He was so saturated with rage that he picked up an axe lying close to a freshly cut wood and went for Bob with the aim of chopping off his head.

Bob waited and watched studiously as Baro came with the axe in a sudden rush; aiming its glowing blade at his head. He ducked as the axe came within reach. Before Baro could regain balance, Bob gave him a terrible kick on the elbow that sent the axe in his hands flying into space. Then he descended on him with karate chops that sent the breath out of him.

From that day, Bob became the second in command, and barely four weeks after his victory over the second in command, the first in command, Alexis Ogungbe, a man whose reputation was greater than he looked and whom Bob didn't know he would later meet for a crucial assignment after leaving the prison, was released from the Central Maximum at the end of his sixth year. This was when Bob's term was three years and nine months, so he was automatically made the first in command of the prison lords.

As soon as he became the prisoners' first in command, Bob immediately set about the task of becoming the friend of Mr. Kunle Williams, the Chief Superintendent and the oldest guard in the prison. He liked his ability to comprehend prisoners' problems. He respected his wit and valued his sense of judgment.

Mr. Williams himself had dealt with so many criminals in the prison that he could tell what sort of trade a new intake had as soon as brought in. He had endured the lawless activities of those prisoners whose rudeness and insubordination could have forced him to poison himself, but he had kept to the job simply because he enjoyed it and looked forward to his long awaited retirement. Mr. Williams believed strongly in reforming a prisoner, no matter how stubborn. He treated all the prisoners with respect and has always won their admiration. As a result, he enjoyed a tremendous support from the prisoners and many ugly incidents that could have destroyed the prison were often avoided because of him.

Now that Bob was in a position to ease him from the prison punishments, he wanted to know more about the man than his prison assignments. Though he scarcely saw him more than once or twice a week, he usually make sure he made the best of the little time he had whenever they met in the prison farm or whenever he came to the prison to address them. Bob would tell him that now that he was the leader and spokesman of the red building, he had been doing everything possible to keep all troubles at bay.

Mr. Williams knew if there wasn't any problem in the red building, then there wouldn't be problems in the rest of the buildings. He knew if the red building suddenly became dangerous, then the whole prison would be dangerous. He therefore saw it wise in thanking and commending Bob for his excellent job in maintaining order at the red building whenever they met.

On the exact day that Bob had been at the Central Maximum for four years, a new prisoner was brought into the red building. Bob thought instinctively that this new man would up stir some trouble in the building as soon as he was pushed in. As it turned out, Bob couldn't think of the best friend he could have had in the prison other than this man. Eddy, whose real name was Edward Atuga, was sentenced to one year imprisonment for killing two people and wounding two policemen in a riot that started after a political rally. He was a reckless political thug, backing and serving as the right hand man of one of the leading politicians in the country. Had it not occurred that some of the politicians quickly waded into his case to possibly free him of the offense, he would have bagged more years than the term he was given.

Bob knew he was dangerous, but he wanted him as a friend. To make sure he got what he wanted, he asked for information about Eddy, and in a day or two, he not only knew that Eddy was a political assassin, but he also got as far as knowing that both of them were to be released from the prison on the same day.

Bob had been looking for someone to confide in. Someone tough and trustworthy, who could survive difficult jobs and who will not crumbled when things are complicated.

The people he had been testing were either too weak to keep secret, or too rough to carry out a careful plan. With only a year left in the prison, he knew he was getting late. He had to find someone quick. He needed a reliable companion to help him on his desired plan. He knew if he couldn't find someone in this prison, he hardly would be able to find someone after his release. For good three months after Eddy came in, Bob decidedly kept away from him and watched his character from a distance. Eddy hardly spoke to any of the prisoners, and when he did, he was always wild and mean. At the end of the third month, Bob could no longer keep his detachment from him. One day, on a bright shining afternoon, when the prisoners were scheduled for a job on the cornfield, he concluded that he would carry out his plan to fight Eddy in order to judge his strength before offering him his friendship.

After the prisoner had taken their lunch, they assembled in front of their individual building. Then there was a roll call, which was swiftly done by one of the senior warders. The prisoners were marched to their respective positions in the field. The guards and their dogs stood in front and behind, as the prisoners lumbered in their short knickers and gowns with their heads dressed in battered bowl caps.

The prisoners from each building formed a long row of laborer's line and began to work. The heat from the sun was too much, so the guards and their dogs found a place to stay under the shade of a nearby tree. From time to time, they strutted around in their black uniforms and their duck peak caps with batons in hands.

Soon after the prisoners from the red building began to work, a guard came over to where Bob was standing and demanded that he should order two of his men to remove a tree stump near them.

"You mean the one over there," Bob said, pointing to the stump and thinking here was his chance to embroil Eddy.

"Sure," the guard replied, looking steadily at his dark forehead.

"That's too little for two men," Bob said as the guard started to go. "One man can handle that."

"Just make sure it is removed. I don't want to know how many men it takes," the guard replied without looking back.

Then Bob went over to where Eddy was working and tapped him gently on the shoulder. Eddy stood up and looked inquiringly at him.

"Look man," Bob said, staring back with reproach, "It's time you do a big job with your fat hands. Can you see what's left of the tree over there," he went on, pointing at the stump, "Get it removed from the ground before we go. Understand?"

Eddy stared at him for what seemed a long testy second, but finally he shrugged his shoulders and nodded in approval.

Bob knew quite well that he had hit him right and that a few more words like that would throw them both into a fierce combat. He waited for about five minutes, making sure everyone was busy and making doubly sure Eddy had started on the work he gave him. He went over to where Eddy was working, looked for sometime at what he was doing and said, "Why have you purposely decided to do this job the way you like? Instead of digging deep on the ground around the wood and then cutting the roots with your cutlass, you keep fooling around and messing up with the soil. Do you have to spend all the day on this job that doesn't even require more than ten minutes?"

"Ten minutes?" Eddy asked surprisingly, "two guys cannot finish this job in thirty minutes!"

"Rubbish!" Bob said, pretending to be offended. "Who the hell do you think you are? I give you a job and tell you to finish it in time, and you have the gut to raise your voice and scowl at me. Nonsense, will you bend down and work?"

"Look man," Eddy said, suddenly cares less of what might happen, "you are a prisoner in this joint like me. The fact that you have been here longer shouldn't give you the right to misuse your leadership. If you've got something against me why don't you right out say it."

Bob folded his fists and pointed his right index finger at his face.

"Shut up and start digging."

"I am doing nothing till I get some help." Eddy said. "Let me warn you man, don't get the idea you can try those dirty punishments of yours on me. If you do, then I'll make sure you regret … et."

Before he could finish the last statement, Bob grabbed the neck of his gown, pulled him roughly against his large chest and shoved him off. Eddy staggered and fell over a pile of hard soil behind him. Sitting on a mound, with his hands stretched out he cursed himself for giving Bob such a chance. He sat down for a while looking at Bob above his eyes and suddenly grinned.

Bob was expecting a rush; instead Eddy slowly stood up and advanced towards him like a prizefighter. As they met, the two men held themselves with such a surprising strength that they remained motionless for about thirty seconds. Then with a quick movement that baffled Bob, Eddy went under him, got hold of his waist and lifted him off the ground. As he spun wildly, trying to throw him off with all his strength, Bob twisted his right foot doggedly around Eddy's leg. With such a foot grip, Eddy knew there was nothing he could do except to drop him back on the ground and start all over again. Before he could finish thinking through, Bob's hands were already on his throat, his fingers exploring his neck pit. Eddy quickly dropped him and pushed him off. Bob had scarcely moved about two steps backward when Eddy came out with a fast offensive fist. Bob saw it and ducked. The blow swayed across his face and chapped his nose as it went past. Probably because Eddy's weight was all in the blow, he swerved to the left. And as he did, Bob caught his wrist, threw it up and bent down to absorb his belly on his back. Then with all his strength, he threw him into the open field. Eddy landed with such a force that he was completely covered with the dust. Without thinking of what had happened, he rolled himself over, and rose to face Bob again.

Two of the guards who had spotted what was happening came running towards them. They were in time to stop Eddy as he posed for another show down, and then descended on him with their batons. Bob ran forward, took hold of their uniforms from the back and shoved them to a standstill.

"Hey!" he cried as he released them, "you don't have to beat him like that! We are only stretching our muscles."

Annoyingly, the two warders turned to look at him. "Do you think you are free to exercise your power in this prison as you please?" One of them said, looking at him peevishly. "You are doing all this in the auspices of Mr. Williams, and I'll have to report you to the governor when he comes."

The guard who had spoken readjusted his shirt, and then started off with his colleague in the direction of the other guards who were coming to meet them, leaving the rest prisoners who had dropped their tools, staring at them.

Bob knew Eddy was disappointed at the intervention of the guards. He saw the look of contempt in his eyes, but caring less about the way he felt, he went to where he was standing and offered him his hand.

"Forget about the fight, man," he said as Eddy took his hand reluctantly, "It's one of those things that happen between men at times."

"You better don't let it happen between us again," Eddy said frankly. "If we are to become friends, I think its better we avoid fighting. I could be tricky at it sometimes."

Both men looked at each other for some seconds. Bob liked the look of confidence in him, and thought convincingly that this was the man he had been looking for.

Back inside the red building, they soon forgot their differences. Their friendship began to grow. A sort of candid association developed between them. The inmates soon saw that their friendship was reliable. No one tried to drive a wedge of deceit between them. Bob knew they that were both scheduled to be released from the prison around the same time. He decided it would be better to tell Eddy about his plan a few weeks before his prison term is over.

Apart from Eddy, there was another person Bob wanted as an acquaintance in the red building. Ibrahim Kamal, a young medical undergraduate, who came in when Bob's had about eight months left in the prison. Kamal was spending twelve months for Criminal Abortion. He had the kind of intelligence Bob envied. He thought he was responsible and learned, unlike most of the remaining inmates who were downright illiterate.

Unlike Kamal, Bob only had a basic education. He never made it through University. He had spent most of his time in Lagos, mixing freely with the street boys and following Masquerades all around during the annual Egungu festivals. At seven, he lost his father, and it was then he realized he would have to do something for himself if he was to get anywhere in life. His mother, doing a petty trade at a local flea market, put him in a primary school until he obtained his first school certificate. He fended himself through a Grammar school, taught as a teacher for some time and then sat for a public examination which earned him a diploma in banking. He decided to abandon teaching and call it quit for the banks. After several unsuccessful attempts, he was finally employed as a clerk at the Joint Arena Bank in Lagos.

Two years after Bob's employment at the bank, he discovered a way of forging checks and falsifying customers' accounts. He successfully did this for half a year, but luck ran against him when he met a young businessman called Charles Aduwo. Out of sheer gesture and friendliness, Charles unknowingly entered into a trap set up by Bob. He falsified Charles account and surreptitiously withdrew over N800, 000.00 from his bank statement. Unfortunately for Bob, Charles got an inside tip and appeared at the time one of Bob accomplices came to collect part of the money. Before Bob could realize what was happening, he was already in police hands. It was soon discovered that he was responsible for the catalogue of frauds that had once thrown the bank into confusion and public ridicule. He was handed over to the no nonsense police detectives, who coaxed and tormented him to evolve all the tricks of his criminal deceptions.

To worsen Bob's punishment, Charles' brother was one of the police officers in charge of his offense. When he realized this, he knew only luck could save him from death in his punishment cell. By the time he was dragged to the court, he was almost dead from the beatings he received in the cell. The judge was merciless in his ruling. All the money in his account was returned to the Bank He received five years of hard labor and three weeks of corporal punishment. He will receive twelve strokes of cane every morning of his first three weeks' in the prison.

Bob's first few weeks in the prison were memories of pain. Apart from the twelve strokes of cane he received each morning, there were several unpleasant assignments. He vowed that only his dead body would come back to the Central Maximum prison if he was ever let out. Up to the end of the eighth week, his body was still sore with wounds. He found life a boring state of unimaginable things and silently prayed that death would come over him. All the time this was happening, his mind ached for Charles. He felt like holding his head on his hands and breaking it to pieces on a standing rock. He wanted him as bad as a lion wanted his prey at the climax of his hunger. Insomuch was his mind filled with vengeance against Charles that he found it difficult to sleep without dreaming of killing him. For almost every night of his first three months in prison, he had to fight over the nightmares of goring dismemberment of the man he hated so much.

Bob's nightmares soon lessen as his term ran out, but whenever he thought about his life in retrospect, he couldn't see how Charles could remain alive as soon as he was freed from his bondage. He had spent several uncountable hours thinking about how to do this. He decided that for his plan to succeed, he needed to team up with someone. Now that Eddy had become part of him, and with only a few months left for them in the prison, he felt if he didn't begin to get his plan ready now, it might be too late when he was out.

One evening, after an overtiring day on the prison farm, Bob lay on his bed staring at the white roof of the red building. He was smoking a half-cigar stick he got from one of the guards. Over the pillow that supported his clean-shaven head, he turned and looked to his left. He saw Eddy jumping down from his bed and sauntered toward him. Just as the tip of the cigarette on his hand was burning up, Eddy came over and snatched it from him.

"I've been tired of this deadly hole since the first day I walked in," Eddy said as he blew off the last smoke on the cigarette and extinguished the butt with a foot stamp.

Bob put on a tight smile and tapped his teeth with his forefinger. "I'll rather die than come here again," he said.

"The same with me," Eddy said, "I'd break the jail if I had been given more than a year."

"No way," Bob said, lowering his voice to the minimum. "Have you seen the security outside? No one can break it. I have thought about that idea once, but I quickly dropped it when I saw the set up."

"Breaking jail isn't a problem for me," Eddy said, "I'll do it if I want, only it needs planning but that isn't included in my plan now. I have been yearning for something bigger than breaking a jail."

"What is it you are yearning for?" Bob asked, suddenly interested in what Eddy was having in mind.

"Best unknown to nobody else," Eddy replied.

"Couldn't I share from it?" Bob asked.

"Not now," Eddy said.

"Why skipping it now," Bob said, "you know we have less than six months to spend in this joint, and that's not too early to start knowing about each other's plan?"

"Did you say each other's plan?" Eddy asked interestingly.

"Yes," Bob said.

"Then it means you are yearning for something too."

"I don't believe in yearning for something, "Bob said, "I believe in planning for things, and I've been planning for this one I have in mind for years."

"What is it?" Eddy asked, somewhat puzzled.

"It's something more important than to be discussed here. As a matter of fact, I have already decided to brief you about it. I'm just waiting for a convenient time," Bob said.

"Then let's postpone it until we both have a sufficient time. We can't afford to leak our secrets here. The walls have ears," Eddy said.

"Sure," Bob said.

Just then, Kamal came to join them; whistling softly, and shaking his head as he settled one of his legs on the lower deck of Bob's bed.

"What's happening men? What's all this hush-hush stuff?"

Bob suddenly sat upright on the bed and said to Kamal, "Boy, would you care telling me the ugly things you did to that pregnant girl before you were thrown here?"

"I was beginning to wonder why you haven't asked me that question," Kamal said. "You see," he went on expressively with his head jerked aside, "I've really gone tough since I got to this place, so I wouldn't be ashamed to share my confession with you."

"Right, fine, carry on," Eddy said. "We are listening."

"You see," Kamal began, "It seems there is a special kind of mysterious charm in women that always makes men give them a fair treatment," he paused, raising his eyebrow and looking up at the same time. "It's a sort of challenging part of a man's' lives that turn them into clinging dogs of sickly sociable gallivant. Somehow, I find it difficult to explain why a man should be so selfish, or why on earth a man should be so foolish and forget to give a woman all the respect she deserves. Whatever it is, a woman is one of the most intricate beings created by the supreme one. Although she is very flexible and highly susceptible to persuasion, she also has a beautiful mind and the brain to disarm man of all his powerful capacities. I knew early on in life that the woman also has a delicate body that requires tender love and care. She is the one that bears fruit. Ever since my teenage years, I wanted to pursue an area in Medicine that will protect a woman's delicate body and the precious fruit she bears,"

He paused for a while looking at Bob.

"During my second year in training, I saw a lot of ugly things being done to young pregnant girls by our local men with butcher knives in hands. I vowed I will never be like one of these back alley idiots. I also knew there is a lot of money to be made in back alley abortions. As a young medical student in training, I have no right by law to touch anything like that but I needed the money and I felt I could do better than the grotesque jobs some of the guys out there were doing. I knew how to do D and C. All I needed was a private place."

"What's D and C?" Eddy asked.

"It is a fancy word for opening and cleaning stuff out of a woman's womb," Kamal replied.

"Within the field of medical treatment," he continued, "there are certain things that are beyond my reach while in training, but I took a risk by engaging myself in removing unwanted pregnancies. I started doing this so call D and C for young girls and ladies in a private apartment I rented outside the campus. In less than six months that I started this job, I was reeling in money. I bought myself a small car and a lot of good things. Before I would be back from school, the entrance to my apartment would be filled with girls waiting for me to come and do the job for them. I was good at it, and I charged them lower prices than most doctors do. So they always came to my apartment, even if I was out of town."

A large insect with annoying buzzing sound continued to circle above Kamal's head. Without looking up, he scooped it with his right hand, squeezed it and threw the remnant across the hallway.

"Do you guys want to be bored with all the medical terms of what I did?"

"Carry on!" Bob exclaimed. "We are not interested in your medical jargons," Eddy fixed himself up on the bed and sat looking at Kamal.

"You see," Kamal continued, "On this particular day I was to meet my waterloo, I was in the class listening to a lecture when a student came to inform me that someone wanted to see me at home for a very urgent matter. Unfortunately for me, the lecture was not all that important, so I took an excuse and went out. I got home to find this girl and her boyfriend waiting for me. She was in a lot of pain. I took her to my private room where I have all the equipment. She was sweating profusely as she lay down on the exam table. I took one look at her private part and found two small towels stacked there. The towels were totally soaked in blood. I yelled at the boyfriend to come right into the room but no one answered. Before anything could be done, she went pale, passed out and never regained consciousness. She was dead on my hands."

He paused for a few seconds to let the look of disappointment on his friends' faces disappeared.

"It so happened that the father of the girl was very important in town that I felt utterly miserable to run away when I realized what had happened to his daughter. When the boyfriend fled, I was faced with a police case. The matter took a new turn when the police learnt I was not a qualified doctor. I was dragged to the court, and the judge was unruly about what my lawyer put up to defend me. He gave me twelve months. It was later that I learnt the girl had earlier tried to abort herself with a tooth brush before she came to see me."

"Tooth brush?" Bob cried, gripping his pillow tightly.

"Yes. She screwed her womb with it. She had already lost a lot blood before she came to me. The way she had it covered it up surprised me."

"Maybe her boyfriend did it for her," Eddy said. "She must have had nerves like steel."

"Who knows what the heck they did to themselves," Kamal said? "It's my bad luck."

"We all take risks," Bob said, clasping his hands on a mosquito that was hovering over his head. "Those that take the overbearing ones that land in trouble."

"Ay, just like us," Kamal said. "When next I come into this world, I'll make sure I take the trouble-free risks."

That night, after they've gone to bed, they all dreamed about what brought them to the prison. Bob dreamed he was chasing Charles around a lonely road, and as he was about to hammer Charles's head with a club, he was splashed all over with mud by a speeding truck. Eddy dreamed he saw the ghost of the two men he killed in the political riot, beckoning him to come for another fight. Kamal dreamt of seeing the ghost of the dead girl and her boyfriend, kissing each other in a deserted alley.

CHAPTER 2

Lagos state once boasts the capital of Nigeria. Located in the western part of the country, the state sits along the coast of the Atlantic Ocean with a current estimate of 9 million populations. Although considered the smallest of the Nigerian 36 states, it's the nation's largest urban center with a strong geographical influence on the entire country.

Lagos is where every aspiring job seeker, worker, politician and ruler in the country wants to be. It is where to find someone from every tribe in the country and where most immigrants like to work, dine and intermingle with the natives. It is one of the nation's centers of excellence, where foreigners from different parts of the world converge and partake in the structural and economic development of the country.

Lagos houses archeological landmarks including the National Theater, one of the country's historic monuments. You can find practically anything in the street of Lagos, from the most expensive diamond import from South Africa to the latest technologically advanced electronic gadget from Japan. The native medicine man can easily pick up a human skull with the right contact in the city and the archbishop can easily gather the nation's faithful with the stroke of a bell.

Transportation medium ranges from the state municipal bus to local commercial vehicles using mini-vans, utility vehicles, taxis and popular motorcycle riders known as 'Okadas'. Traveling within the metropolitan area can be quite an adventure. Passengers ride in city buses with tight fitting space and banged up vehicles that proudly display their religious banners. Some people hitchhike on private motorists to their destination. People cross the road all the time in the middle of traffic. Drivers can be quite reckless as they juggle for space and maneuver between people and other motorists.

Lagos is known for its elite socialite life. Party starts on Friday night from local disc jockey to the most beloved music band on Sunday night. Whether it a funeral for the loved one or just out there to have fun, party goers spend most of their savings on the most expensive garments, dancing and drinking till the bar is empty.

Despite its wealth and affluence, poverty and joblessness abound. Brilliant university graduates of social study, law, history, philosophy and political science roam the street looking for a never existing job. The urban epitome of the state also attracts typical large city wastes and overcrowding. Unemployment provides a magnate for its share of violent and vicious crime.

In the city of Lagos, one of the most restless and disquiet areas was Mushin. Located in the city's mainland, and surrounded by other suburban districts, the area carried an unparalleled reputation for wanton lawlessness and unthinkable brutality. Some of the areas were controlled by a group of reckless and barbaric hooligans, who sometimes attacked and struck innocent residents without reason. The atrocities and lack of sheer human feelings by these groups of heartless thugs outweighed the goodness and hospitality of a large number of decent people living in the area. As a result, the area was dared, feared and given several forms of unwelcome appellations by Lagosians living outside the district.

In the early to mid seventies, you dared not visit Mushin at night, most especially when there was no light. If you did, then you would probably experience something you've never savored from your birth. As soon as you set foot on the narrow road along Mushin bus station, the stony and the fearsome faces of the loitering miscreants there would begin to stare at you. Their terrible and glittering eyes would likely force you to miss your steps. You'd feel your guts rise from the bottom of your belly into your mouth. The smoke from the hemp on their mouths would follow your path and intrude your senses. You might lose your breath and begin to hyperventilate in an instant of flickering nervousness. You'd better run, otherwise, someone might descend on you like a wild renegade.

Every now and then, you could be mercilessly attacked by a group of drugged or narcotized teens. These vagabonds may come out of the blue, hitch you up and desensitize your body with blows. Mindlessly, you lay on the ground, feeling cheated and nursing a chunk of skin and soft tissue swelling smacked all over your body by the evil hands. When you regained consciousness, you found all your belongings gone. As you started to look wildly around, huge laughter, followed simultaneously by flying stones, would make you get up so fast and put on a kind of race that if critically considered would have smashed the 100 meters Olympic record.

Not until the late seventies, when the Lagos state police command carried, out its operation keep Lagos clean, that most of the undesirable elements in the area were wiped out.

Somewhere between Idioro and the end of Olorunsogo along Agege motor road, stood a large film and racket building known as the Central Casino. The Casino was owned by a large overfed gambler who could best be described as a potbelly man with a large square head supported by an overhanging jaw. He had two small dark eyebrows and a bowl moustache that opened occasionally to show his tobacco-stained teeth. His hair, which he regarded as his asset, was plastered unevenly to his head and as it stretched to the back, it carved out in the middle, a bald and shining space that eventually earned him the name 'Channel Ten'. This nickname, which completely overshadowed his real name, Dona Rangie, was procured in the likeness of what was observed when the Nigeria Television Authority suddenly came into live with the word 'Channel Ten' conspicuously written on a bald screen.

Dona considered money before anything in life. So when he successfully persuaded a ragged old man who had been looking for money to part with a small bungalow surrounded by a long stretch of land, he immediately pulled down the bungalow and converted the whole place to the only building that now stood as the largest and most famous Casino in the area. The Casino is a two-story building. The lower floor consisted of two large halls. One hall is equipped with assorted forms of slot machines, gambling equipment and a racketeering office. The second hall is more or less like a movie theater or a Cinema with an operating room set up with a large film projector. It has a large open space packed with long benches made of steel and scattered wood chairs to accommodate the crowd.

The music and the entertainment center were located at the back of the Casino with a broad pavement that yielded a large dancing floor.

The upper floor had six rooms serving as a resting inn with two small offices and a large gym.

The Central Casino had a gang, known as the 'Felony Boys'.

In reality, the gang consisted of a number of cruel and dreadful men whom Dona regarded as his staff. The men were nothing short of a pack of hogs and sadists whose rashness and nihilistic terrorism had thrown Mushin and its surroundings into a fierce and chaotic habitat. Although Dona himself had a little to do with the gang, however, he was responsible for its protection and finances. The boys regarded him as the sleeping boss because he has no role in controlling their actions or say how their operations are carried out.

The brain behind the whole organization, the man whom the whole people of Mushin and its suburbs dreaded most was Augustine Pappillo. The people around knew him as Pappy. He was a willful and bellicose sadist who struck with brutal indifference. Working with him were six tough and violent men who together with him completed the Felony circle.

Two of these men, Fatai Bello and Shamsondeen Sharafa, manned the gambling halls. Dele Idris, the only social guy among them, manned the music joint, while the Cinema job was shared by both Isiaka Afolabi and Rasheed Amusa. For all drag out, beat ups and general discipline among stubborn or rebellious customers was Alexis Ogungbe. Fresh from Central Maximum prison, he was nicknamed Hercules, partly because of his brute strength and wholly because of his wild and untamed attitude. Pappy considered him his second best.

Apart from the Felony Boys, always present at the club were street boys loitering around to give a helping hand.

On most evenings, the club would be filled with assorted scamps and wastrels, smoking hemp and idling around, staring with bulging eyes and whistling with croaked threatening voices. Neither the obvious wickedness of the Felony Boys nor the callous attitude of the street boys did in any way disturb the numerous customers that were always present at the club.

The Felony Boys always tried as much as they could to avoid anything that might block the flow of money from the customers to their Boss. However, they put on a rueful show for those who acted beyond the boundary of the expected behavior.

Among all his staff, the only person Dona trusted was Folorunsho Taiwo; his appointed manager. Folly, as Dona fondly called him, abhorred trouble and hated quarrels. He was the only person with a little bit of conscience among Dona's staff. He was faithful, honest, efficient and serious. Dona never for once mistrusted him or worried about any work he handled. Dona depended on him for the progress of the club, and cared less about the indifference attitude of the Felony Boys. He knew the club had not been running on loss because Folly was there. He often assured himself that as long as Folly was there, he had no problems concerning how money would come in.

Although Folly was always ready to help any of the Felony Boys whenever they needed help, he distanced himself from any of their perfidious and treacherous activities. The Felony Boys on the other hand knew his ways of life contrast theirs, so for most of the time, he was left alone and avoided them whenever necessary.

With this kind of life by his men, and with a lot of money and women to fondle with, Dona only came to the club once in a while, talked with his manager and his staff on how the club was progressing, and then returned to his house at Ikeja, where he owned a luxurious one story building with a lot of maids to do his domestic work. Most people didn't know that the Casino belonged to him. Instead, people thought Folly and the Felony Boys jointly owned it.

Nothing in the history of this Casino was hidden from Edward Atuga, the prisoner who shared the same building with Bobinson Okoye in the Central Maximum prison. It was here that he had in mind when he was telling Bob that he was yearning for something big. He was once with the Felony Boys before he quit, joining his favorite political party. It was while he was with the party that he turned himself into a vicious political thug, which eventually landed him behind the hard Iron bars of the Central Maximum prison.

Right from the moment he was Imprisoned, he had been thinking of where to go after been released. He had come to the conclusion that he would have to return to the Casino at Mushin. He had spent a lot of time with the Felony Boys. He liked them, fancied their ways of life and valued Dona all the more. He had no doubt that Dona and the boys would accept him whenever he appeared and offered to join them again.

Since Bob told him he wanted to brief him about something he had been planning for years, he had waited impatiently to hear what Bob had in mind. He had on several occasions tried to guess about what it could possibly be. He had told himself that before someone could be thrown into the Central Maximum prison for five years, he must have done something evil. Maybe he killed someone, or he had stolen a lot of money hidden somewhere. If Bob was planning to dig out some hidden treasure somewhere outside the prison, he would like to know about it. It would be nice to get rich and invest in something profitable when out of prison. He knew Bob had taken to him. In turn, with the few months they have spent together, he had grown to like Bob. Eddy thought that if he wanted to get anywhere in life he had to throw away his die-hard ideology of mistrusting everybody.

Although sometimes he had noticed Bob to be somewhat indifferent, overall, he considered him to be very straightforward and completely determined to achieve his goal. Few good months had now passed and Bob hadn't mentioned anything about his desired plan. The last time he spoke about it was that night he said he would postpone it to a convenient time. They now had two weeks to leave the prison and yet Bob hadn't said anything. Had the convenient time not arrived yet? What was Bob waiting for? Was he waiting for him to make the initiative? Or had he completely forgotten about it? No. Someone like Bob would be the last to forget something like that. As all these thoughts went through Eddy's mind within his last fourteen days at the Central Maximum prison without a suitable answer, he finally concluded that he would have to talk to Bob on their last night in prison if he didn't say anything before then. If it was something that could land him big money when he was out, then he could as well abandon the idea of going back to the Casino.

A week before they were to be released from the prison. Bob unfolded his plan to Eddy. They were in the prison farm. Both men were sitting together on the stem of a large tree, a little away from the other prisoners who seemed tired to lay their hands on any other job for the day. Earlier in the day, Kamal was taken to the prison clinic to receive treatment for a viral illness he caught from some of the other inmates. He had not returned yet and thinking this was a chance from being disturbed, Bob called Eddy, telling him it was time to reveal what he had been keeping in mind since he came to the prison.

"Since you've come to this yard, have you ever heard me mentioning the name of a man called Charles Aduwo to you?" Bob inquired.

Eddy shook his head.

"No," He said.

"That name is very precious to me," Bob said. "That's why I don't want every Dick and Harry to know about it. After I have settled my scores with the man who owns the name, then the name would become as filthy as a dirty rag."

"Why is the name so precious to you at present and what scores have you to settle with him?" Eddy asked inquiringly.

"You need not hurry. Just listen to my story," Bob said. He stared for some seconds at the open field, focusing his eyes on the huge amount of corns planted on the prison farm and thinking back to how it all started.

"About seven years ago," he said, not looking at Eddy. "I started working as a clerk with the Joint Arena Bank in Lagos. Two years later I was transferred to the Credit Control department of the bank and it was here I had access to so many things including the accounts of many wealthy customers. After about, two or three detected frauds; carried out by some people who were interested in getting rich overnight and who didn't think of how best to lay their plans before being rounded up, I decided to carry out a systematic research on fabricating documents. I was very influential with most of the clerks at the bank. I was friendly with the sectional heads and get along well with the Manager. So to get at authentic documents wasn't a problem for me. After obtaining the necessary documents I needed, I would make their photocopies and return the originals to where I took them. Then I would begin a cautious study on the copies with me. I had an outside connection. I knew a lot of guys that were quick at business. With some help, I managed to obtain some forged checks and a tiny microscopic machine for forging signatures. That was how it all began. All I had to do was obtained the lists of' our customers, most especially the big companies and the rich individuals, laid my hands by one way or the other on their accounts, forged some checks and did all the necessary paperwork and endorsements. Usually, I would give the checks to some of my friends outside the bank to cash the money for me. Sometimes it would require a little bit of pressure, sometimes the promise of a big reward, but as the thing became regular, moving steadily and raising no alarm, most of my acquaintance regarded the job as something to be done and get tipped. I got more money than I needed, visited friends, and spent lavishly at parties. I bought a nice Mercedes Benz but never drove it to work because my colleagues at the bank might start wondering where an ordinary clerk like me with small salary would get money for such a thing."

At this junction, two warders were coming toward them. Eddy, hearing the noise of their patrolling feet, looked up and tapped Bob gently on the shoulder.

"Your men are coming," he whispered.

Bob looked up and saw the two guards. They appeared not to bother him. He shifted his buttocks, sat upright and crossed his legs.

"They won't disturb us," he said, "however, let's change the subject until they are gone."

The two men started talking about the type of job they would do when out of prison. The two warders, Alonge Gabriel and Cyril Elemba, walked toward them with short heavy steps, slinging their batons stylishly as they came to where the two men were sitting.

"If not because you two have only a week left here, I would have bet you were planning a jail break," Cyril said, smiling brightly at them.

"If that was possible, I wouldn't have been long gone," Bob said.

"And you guards would have had your spines blown to bits if ever we had tried that," Eddy added.

"Not a thing would touch my hair," Alonge said. "Do you think I eat with all my fingers?"

"Baba Osun!" Eddy shouted, raising his hands to hail him. "We know you people can kill three birds with one stone."

"Look at you," Alonge continued, "you don't know anything. Do you think we are safe here without personal security? That's why we are crying for a pay rise. When you people get out of this place, there are chances you can find a good job. With the kind of pay we receive here only luck can help."

"Why can't you resign and look for a better Job?" Eddy asked.

"It's not easy to get a nice job with little or any academic background," Cyril said. "That's why we are still here."

"Sure. At least, man must whack," Bob said, uncrossing his legs. He began to pick his ear with the nail on the tip of his smallest left finger.

Finding a way to dismiss them and pointing to a short banana tree that stood where some of the prisoners were working.

"Oga, the banana tree over there is ripe enough to eat. I think it's time you instruct our boys to pluck it," Eddy said.

"That tree was planted by Mr. Williams, so the bananas on it belong to nobody but him," Cyril said, shaking his head.

"That doesn't mean you shouldn't get it for him," Eddy replied, trying to control his rising voice.

"Forget about banana or no banana," Alonge cut in. "What are you guys going to do when you leave us?"

"That's what we were discussing before you came here. I'll appreciate it if you can leave us to decide on it before we come and tell you," Bob said in a flat cold voice.

Sensing how important the moment was for the two men and thinking they would soon be leaving the prison to take a new life, Cyril grabbed Alonge on the wrist.

"Let's leave and allow them to concentrate on how to plan their future," Cyril said. The two guards walked away.

"Could you please remind me of where I stopped?" Bob asked Eddy.

"You were saying something about the way you were throwing money around," Eddy said, scratching the back of his head.

"You see," Bob continued, "I was really enjoying life. With plenty of money, and with lots of friends around, I felt on top of the world. Then, just when I was thinking of how to stop this lavish spending, create some more money and quit the bank for a bigger business, this man called Charles Aduwo suddenly appeared. A friend in the bank introduced him to me. I found out he smuggled precious metals and fine gems into the country in the pretext of an importer and exporter merchant. I didn't tell my friend I was interested in his money. I got at his identity in the bank and decided to withdraw about N800, 000.00 from his bank account. I was thinking this attempt would be my last fraud in the bank before I resigned. The very day one of my friends was to collect this money, Charles came to the bank. I was practically unaware of his presence. To make the situation worse, I didn't know he was an intimate friend of the bank Manager. As soon as he came to the bank, he went to the Manager's office and asked to see his bank account. The Manager told him that the bank has just received a slip to withdraw the sum of N800, 000.00 from his account. Charles said he knew nothing of such transaction."

Bob paused for a while, looking at Eddy's attentive eyes.

"That was how the whole thing started," He continued. "My friend was rounded up. In order to free him, I told the police he knew nothing about what had happened. So I was alone faced with the case and that was what brought me here." He paused for a moment, tightening the muscles on his face.

"Now," Bob said, raising his forefinger, "I would have accepted the punishment for what happened. I would have paid my prison due to the society for being a thief and a rogue without a question. As it would be and to this day, it is now otherwise because of certain things I hate to remember in life. The first was when I was in the punishment cell. I would have died there except for the timely intervention of the court order. A young corporal among the secret police responsible for my punishment told me that the officer in charge of my ordeal was Charles's brother, and that he had instructed them to kill me before I could have the chance of appearing in court. It was really a horrible time for me in the punishment cell. I was bumped, clawed, maimed, and mercilessly beaten. I had to spend two weeks in the hospital before I was transferred here. I had some money in my account before I was caught. During my trial, the judge was so furious that he ordered that my bank account should be frozen up, I lost about N900, 000.00 to the bank, and I was left with nothing. When I was brought here with five years ahead, I felt utterly miserable about everything.

The morning of my first three weeks in the prison was greeted with 12 strokes of cane that sore my back and left scars for my children and grandchildren to see. For every stroke and every bit of painful memory, I see Charles face. I vowed I would not let him live. If he is dead before I leave the prison, I will find his grave and desecrate it."

He stopped and looked down at his gown pocket. He dipped two of his fingers into it and bought out a small piece of paper that was torn out of a newspaper."

"Look," he said, holding up the paper in front of Eddy. "This paper has been with me for the past 24 months. There was a day Mr. Williams forgot one of his newspaper on the farm. I was running through it when I saw his adverts. I had to remove the whole page and cut out this portion from it. Since then, it has been my only document in this yard."

He gave it to Eddy who spread it and looked thoughtfully at the adverts. Written on the piece of paper was:

Charles Aduwo and Co.
Gold and Trinket Magnate,
Exporter and Importer of Precious Gems,
For full Information, visit us at 7452D,
Broad Street, Lagos.

"You think this will lead you to him?" Eddy asked, looking once more at the contents of the paper.

"If it can't, then nothing will," Bob replied. "That was why I told you that the name is very important to me, and anything that can lead me to its owner is as important as a wedding ring is to a bride."

"Right now," he continued, getting the piece of paper back from Eddy and folding it into his pocket, "I have nothing else to live for. I don't care if I went out today and died; in as much as Charles could go down with me, there is no problem. The only person I valued in life was my mother. I got the information she died about two years ago, so I only need to take care of Charles and myself and everything will end."

Charles sighed and looked at Eddy who was staring at the ground ruefully.

Eddy was deeply touched. He felt sorry for his friend, so when Bob had finished, he pulled himself up and began his own life history. He told Bob of how he had started a boring and uninteresting life at Mushin after he had abandoned his primary school education in elementary four. He said his mother told him he had no father and she too died when he was twelve. After his mother's death, he found life so miserable he had turn into a bus boy running errands in commercial vehicles living with different masters.

At eighteen, Eddy learned how to drive. He drove the 'Molues' and 'Danfos' for about three years before he found his way to the Central Casino. He told Bob everything he knew about the club, keeping nothing back about Dona and the Felony Boys. He said if there was any gang that could track Charles and go free with whatever happened to him, it was the Casino's gang. He boasted of the gang's reputation with such an unbridled confidence that Bob thought half his problems was solved if the gang could help him. Eddy said he regretted having left the club for the political party. What he was planning now was to go back to the Casino and began a new life there. He briefed Bob about how the Felony Boys always carry out their operation and told him of where to get quick money from the Casino.

After what seemed to be a length discussion, they both agreed to go to the Casino after leaving the prison. Eddy said he would introduce Bob to Dona and the boys, and that if there were any job he could do, they would certainly employ him.

A week later, Bob and Eddy were released from the Central Maximum Prison. Early in the morning of the day they were to be released, there was a general roll call. Mr. Jibade, a thin tall warder with thin lips, stood in front of the prisoners and announced to them that both men would be going out on that day. He specifically told the two men to submit the prison's belongings at their disposal to the discharging officer. After the roll call, the two men followed the warder; waving to the rest of the prisoners as they left.

Beside the prison gate, about five minutes walk from the prison buildings, stood a row of office buildings where the guards and other prison officials exchanged duties.

In one of the offices, Mr. Williams, usually called chief by the guards, sat behind a Formica topped table with his hair-covered legs crossed beneath. His black duty cap, rested on one corner of the table. With a few gray hairs between the lumps of dark hair on his head, a well-set folklore moustache on his upper lip, and thick-rimmed glasses placed on the bridge of his square nose, he stared intently at the front page of the newspaper between his hands. A knock came on the door. He looked above the rim of his glasses before saying, "Yes, come in."

Followed by Bob and Eddy, Mr. Jibade opened the door. As the three men came in, Mr. Williams removed his glasses and looked up at them.

"You've brought them," he said, lowering the glasses on the table.

"Yes, sir," the warder replied, giving a half salute.

The chief pushed the newspaper on his hands further into the table and sat back on the chair. He looked past the warder to the two men behind him.

"Have you been told you are going out today?" He said.

"Yes sir," Both men answered simultaneously.

"At twelve o'clock this afternoon, you'll be released," the chief said authoritatively, brushing his moustache aside with his finger.

"You are to discharge all our belongings at your disposal to Mr. Shehu who in turn will give you your properties. Mr. Jibade will take you to our branch police headquarter in front of the prison gate where you will sign off before leaving finally for home," he paused and leaned on the table.

"Mr. Okoye," he said with his eyes fixed on Bob. "I think I've given you all the necessary advice I could in this yard. Make sure you find a better work to occupy your hands. Anytime you need my help, I have told you of where to find me, so I will really appreciate it if you take to my words.

Then he shifted his eyes to Eddy and said, "And you, do make sure you don't tamper with anything that can bring you here again. You've seen how awful this place is and I am sure you won't like to come here again. Be of good behavior and allow your body to enjoy the sweetness of life. I wish both of you a successful and trouble free living."

Then he picked up a desk diary on his table, flicked through the pages, and removed a N200 note half way through. He gave the money to Bob and told the two men to share it as a transport fare to their homes. Two fast drops of salty water came from Bob's eyes as he accepted the money and thanked him for his fatherly disposition. Eddy didn't know what to say. He didn't know what to do either. He wanted to prostrate, but it escaped his memory. Disturbed by the man's generosity, he faltered out,

"Than ... k ... you, sir."

"Don't mention," the old man replied. He bid them farewell and told the warder to take them away.

At exactly twelve-noon, the iron gate of the Central Maximum prison was opened by an elderly security guard. Bob and Eddy, already changed to their own clothes, stepped into the deserted road in front of the prison, feeling the warming breeze of the city they had long departed. Followed by Mr. Jibade, they headed fast to the basement of Sandstone Police Station opposite the prison. As soon as they came into view, two armed police security guards with dogs in hands suddenly appeared behind a tree.

The dogs opened their large mouths and barked at the men. Mr. Jibade waved to them, and the two guards returned to shade with their dogs.

Sergeant Eric Chiddy, the desk sergeant at Sandstone Police station was drinking a cup of hot cocoa when the three men came in. He knew exactly what Mr. Jibade wanted whenever he appeared in this manner. He stood up and shook hands with him as soon as he came in with the other two.

"As usual?" He asked.

"Yes. Is any police van around to convey these men to the town?"

"Hum ... right, one of our boys is planning to go out now, and they can follow him," he said hesitantly. Then he stood up and went over to the table at his back, pulled out a drawer and brought out a large brown notebook. He came back to the desk with the book, obtained the names of the two men, checked through the book, and then went to an inner office for their files.

Five minutes later, Bob and Eddy had completed all the documents they were expected to sign before leaving the prison and headed to the waiting police van. As Bob approached the waiting van, he looked across the road and once again spelt out the fading letters of the prison name as he did about five years ago when he was about to enter the prison. "Well," he said to himself, "no coming back. Rather than being corrected here again, I'll kill myself."

As if reading his thoughts, the police constable behind the driving wheel of the police van pressed his horn repeatedly to hasten the two men. Both men quickened their steps, reached the van, and climbed in at the back. They had barely entered when the constable engaged gear and drove off.

Fifteen minutes of fast driving brought them into the city. The driver was kind enough. He was going to Sabo police station, but he decided to carry them to Yaba, where he dropped them and went back. Unaware of the curious faces that were staring at them because they had just alighted from a police van, the two men joined the waiting crowd at the bus stop. They looked gravely and mean. They were terribly reduced in weight. The large and hot floor of the bus terminal took their steps with little or no effort. The two men tried the first three buses without success. The fourth was a long municipal bus, which they managed to enter after a lot of struggling. The seats were already occupied, so they had to stand on the narrow passage of the bus with the remaining passengers. The bus stopped in the first two stations, dropping and picking passengers as it went. As the bus began its journey to the third station, a child at the back of a woman seating beside where Eddy was standing began to cry. At first, the little boy was making a little noise, but after a while, it suddenly turned to a squeal. Some people in the bus began to shout at the woman to take care of her child. Eddy looked down at the woman as she began to nestle the child at her back. His eyes shifted from her to the little boy and suddenly stopped when he saw blood dripping from where the boy was thrusting one of his legs at her mother's back. He quickly tapped the woman and drew her attention to what he had seen. The woman spun around; looked wildly at her back and poignantly unfolded her child's support. She unclimbed the baby boy, heaved him to her laps and exclaimed when she saw the deep knife cut on his leg. Apparently, a pickpocket who mistook the position of her child's leg for money must have inflicted the cut. There was confusion as the boy began to cry innocently. A young man came out with a carefully folded tissue paper and placed it gently on the child's wound. Surprised by the clarion of the whole event, some people in the bus began to look at their pockets. An old man and a young lady found out that their money had gone. And when Bob looked at his shirt pocket, he found out that the N200 given to him by the chief guard and the piece of paper containing Charles address, had both disappeared.

CHAPTER 3

The first three weeks at the Central Casino were weeks of empirical disappointments for Bob. There were series of frustrating ordeals aggravated by people of acrimonious characters. Many of the people eccentric and irregular behavior had turned the Casino into an obnoxious jungle. Together with Eddy, he had spent the first three days in the Casino without seeing Dona Rangit. Eddy did all the preliminary introductions to Folorunsho Taiwo and the Felony Boys. Bob had been glad when Eddy introduced him to Folly; telling him some of his past activities in the bank before going to the prison, and ending it with a bogus statement of a framed fraud by his former employer. Folly appeared to have a great interest in Bob, thinking he could help him in the preparation of the club's financial statement, which had been untouched for sometime. He promised Bob he would speak to Dona on his possibility of being employed.

But something kept worrying Bob. He thought Pappy hated his presence in the club. When Eddy took him to Pappy for introduction, he had scanned him with cold uninviting eyes, and only nodded in reply to all what Eddy had said about him. After the introduction, Bob called Eddy and told him he didn't like the way Pappy reacted to the formal greetings. Eddy replied that Pappy wouldn't like him until he was satisfied he could withstand a lot of trouble. How this was to be done, he didn't tell him. With the exception of Pappy, he was getting along well with the rest of the Felony Boys, and it appeared he knew some of them in the past.

As far as taking care of himself, Eddy knew what to do. Twice since they arrived, he had gone out as a bus conductor with some of his old friends who were running the commercial vehicles. He always came back to the club with some money and shared whatever he had with Bob. In the night, he would help the boys in the Cinema hall and buy tickets from the man at the gate of the Cinema to resell them above the normal price to the curious film lovers who were always anxious to get in whenever the crowd was unusually large.

Twice also, Bob had tried to help the boys in the racket halls, but Pappy had caught him and threatened to tear off his shoulders from his body if he ever tried it again. He would have tried a scene, but he had already decided to avoid any violent engagement until he had been fully initiated into the club. "Maybe this bully would try and understand me," he kept telling himself whenever Pappy barged past him.

But this, Pappy hated. Whenever a new guy arrived, he would try as much as possible to know how reliable such a guy was by constantly disturbing and threatening with his raucous voice until such a person would be forced to bark back. It was when this was done that he would estimate how great the strength of the person was by putting up an intimidating show of boisterous indignation that could render either of them a quick passenger of a hospital ambulance. So far Bob hadn't replied to his threats, talk less of barking back.

Bob hadn't quite forgotten his ordeal in the passenger bus they boarded when they were coming to the Casino. He was completely flabbergasted when he discovered that both the money and the piece of paper in his pocket had gone. How could he be so gullible and foolishly unaware? Is he getting infinitely retarded or had his stay in the prison completely robbed him of his astuteness? He was brooding over all of this when the bus conductor passed him. The conductor too was so wondered by the whole event that he didn't remember to collect money from almost half the passengers, Bob and Eddy had got down from the bus before they remembered they hadn't paid for the journey. Bob told Eddy he knew the contents of the stolen piece of paper as he knew the back of his hands. Later in the day, while trying to sleep, he remembered and jotted the address in the piece of paper down on a match-box.

On the early hours of Thursday evening, the fourth day of Bob and Eddy's arrival at the Casino, Dona Rangit came to the club. It was around 5 P.M. and his Mercedes car was parked outside the club. He walked past a group of boys who were staring at the posters on the boards at the entrance of the club, turned and walked up the stair case. He was unaware of the two men who were staring curiously at him as he clamed the stairs. Folly was planning to come downstairs when he met him in the passage. Both men shook hands and Folly followed him back to his office.

Dona's office wasn't much of an office, but it was averagely furnished to please his taste.

"How is everything?" Dona asked Folly who went to the window and opened it.

"Fine, sir," Folly said. "I thought you would be here yesterday."

"Yes, I told Pappillo I was coming when I saw him on his way from the Secretariat yesterday. But I ran into an old friend who kept me from coming, so I had to postpone my coming here till today."

Ever since Pappy knew how to drive, he had been driving with a fake diver license. Dona advised him just of recent to obtain a valid one. At first, he was obstinate, but at the insistence of his boss, he decided to get one. He thought he might meet a rebellious cop who would stop at nothing from taking him to court if he was caught without a driving license. He hadn't a N10, 000 fines to pay in the court and he wouldn't like the alternative of spending six months in jail if he couldn't pay the fine. So, yesterday, he went to the State Secretariat to see a friend who had promised him one.

It was when he was coming that Dona saw him and told him he would be coming to the club, which he didn't.

"I have been having a hell of problems in collecting the ticket sales from some of our boys these days," Folly said as he came to sit on the chair facing Dona.

"Lately," he continued, "we've been having some nice movies and the crowd is always more than we expected. So what most of the boys do now is to re-cut used tickets after they've sold the ones given to them, sell the extra, and pocket the money. If I asked them for the surplus, or complained about their attitude, they always threatened to cut my throat."

"Who are the boys in charge of the Cinema?" Dona asked in a tone, which seemed he was very concerned about any attempt to cheat the club. "Isiaka and Rasheed. They take turns in operating the machines and cutting the tickets."

"Who are those assisting them if the crowd is large?"

"Alex and some boys in the town do, but most of the boys are to keep the crowd in order and prevent the lines from falling out."

"But why can't you order sufficient number of tickets?" Dona asked raising his eyebrow.

"Mr. Oladele said he couldn't give us more than the present supply, which could run out of supply if we didn't manage."

"You mean the supplier; that man with marks?"

"Yes. He said that about a week ago."

"Okay, when next you see him, tell him I want a word with him."

"Yes, sir," Folly said, nodding his head.

"How about our machines, are they functioning well?"

"They are all doing fine I've recently installed two automatic electric bulbs in each hall to help our night customers."

"That's all right, any other development?" Dona asked, beginning to arrange the ledger cards on his table.

"Yes," Folly said. "I've been trying to see you about a guy who called himself Bobinson Okoye. He came here on Monday with Eddy."

"Who is Eddy?" Dona asked surprisingly.

Expecting this, Folly said, "Edward Atuga, sir. He was the guy who was jailed a year ago for knocking off Stephen and Sapara. He was working here before he went away with the politicians. Remember that?"

"Yeah!" Dona cried excitedly. "That man with a scrubby chin. I thought he was hanged for that."

"No," Folly said, rubbing his nose. "His boss knew a lot of powerful people and also got a nice lawyer who put a lot of pressure on the judge. He got a year at the Central Maximum."

"Bastard!" He must have been born lucky. Where is he?"

"He should be somewhere around," Folly said. "He came here with this man I was telling you about. They want to join the club."

"Well, let's see them. If the other guy is as good as Eddy, then there is nothing preventing us from employing him.

As Folly stood up and made his way to the door. Dona asked, "Where is Pappillo?"

"I think he should be somewhere downstairs," Folly answered unsurely, his hands already on the door.

"Tell him to come here with Hercules in fifteen minutes time. I will like to talk to them on this ticket issue."

Five minutes later, Dona was canceling a figure in one of the ledger cards on the table when he heard a knock on the door. The door clicked open and Folly came in, followed by Bob and Eddy.

Bob waited and closed the door before joining the other two who were already sitting in two of the three chairs in front of Dona. Bob, although frenzied, was staring at the rounded portion of Dona's flabby head as his hand touched the third chair. He thought it looked like a rounded pebble. From his head, his eyes came down on the huge tobacco pipe inside the ash-tray on the table. As he stared at it, he thought it had a mouth like the rim of a teacup with a pipe like the handle of a spectacles frame.

Bob wondered how a man could derive pleasure in smoking from such a huge pipe.

Satisfied he had erased the erring figure on the ledger he was correcting; Dona dropped the pen and looked up at the three men sitting in front of him.

"Quite an age he said to Eddy, offering his hand, and withdrawing it to shake Bob's.

"I am happy to see you again, sir," Eddy said and then introduced his friend who was saying, "I am pleased to meet you, sir."

"Folly was telling me a few minutes ago about you and your friend, Eddy. He said you wanted to join the club again," Dona said.

"That's right, sir," Eddy grinned widely. "I have nowhere else to go. That's why I come here with my friend."

"Well, I think you've come at the right time," Dona said. "But I only know you; I know nothing about your friend. Maybe you'll care to tell me about him, or perhaps if he prefers to talk himself, that is equally welcome."

Both men looked at each other and Bob quickly jerked his head aside; signaling to Eddy to carry on.

Dona took out a lighter from his jacket's pocket, picked up the pipe on the table and lighted it. With the bowl of the pipe on his palm and the stem on his mouth, he began to smoke; drawing in and letting out the smoke at regular intervals as Eddy began to speak.

Eddy started by telling Dona of how he met Bob in the prison, and how they had both formed an ever-growing friendship right within the core of the same building in the prison till now that circumstances had brought them to his presence. He spoke of what led Bob to the prison, keeping back his criminal deception about forging bank documents and stealing money from customers account. He told Dona that Bob was framed just like he had told Folly.

With this kind of record and his background as a banker, Dona was thinking Bob was looking for somewhere to work until he can get back on his feet and regain his demeaned image. He thought he would go away after he had successfully mixed with the society again.

Dona guessed wrong. Bob was neither there to retouch his life nor regain his demeaned image. He was there for only one thing. And that was to satisfy his growing vindictiveness for Charles. As soon as he came to the Casino, he had quickly studied and surveyed the whole surrounding, noting every character and keeping in mind the savage and unmerciful activities of the endemic men in the club. He had come to the conclusion that he had come to the right place and that his unflinching ache of vengeance against Charles could only be satisfied at this joint. All he wanted now was for Dona to give him the go ahead in any job and then he would wait for the right time to carry out his plot. So far, Eddy had talked without mentioning Charles. That satisfied him. He looked at Dona's expressionless face, expecting him to say he wasn't satisfied with what Eddy had said about him.

"Mr. Okoye, since when have you been living in Lagos?" Dona asked.

Bob answered optimistically that he had been living in Lagos all his life.

"Then you should know all the nooks and corners of this city like a taxi driver." Dona said, letting out smoke from his nostrils as he spoke.

"Yes, sir," Bob replied.

"If you work with my boys, how am I sure you will not run away after a few months?"

"I won't, sir." Bob said casually, not preparing for that question.

"If you won't run away after a short while, and if you can abide by our laws here, which I am sure the boys will explain to you after you've accepted our terms, then you and your friend can work here," Dona said.

"I am grateful for your support, sir," Eddy said as he rose from the chair. Together with his Bob, they left the office, leaving Folly with his master.

"Sir, what do you think of Mr. Okoye's record?" Folly asked as soon as he heard the door shut.

"I think Eddy kept back a little of it." Dona said, removing his tobacco pipe from the mouth, putting it on the ash-tray on the table. "I don't believe his entire story. He couldn't have landed himself five years for being framed. Something kept telling me he tried his hands on forged checks, probably on a very large amount belonging to somebody else. He overplayed his cards and got caught."

He paused and sat back on the chair.

"Anyway," he went on, raising his hands expressively, "we can still employ him. After all, there are lots of boys with filthier records than that at this club. The idea with us is that we don't employ on the basis of merit. Our kind of job is the type that requires people like them, rough, tough and vicious with nothing to fear."

"Do you mean we can employ both of them?" Folly asked, a little animated.

"Yes," Dona said. "There are lots of Jobs they can do here. This man called Okoye can work with you, and Eddy, as usual could work with the boys."

Folly liked the idea. He had been hoping that Dona would employ someone with a monetary experience to assist him in his office work. To collect money in bulk; to buy receipts and issue them out; to write and keep amount of vouchers, tickets, memos and all the likes and then to draw a gradual weekly-expenses sheet of sales for the club's account, were all seemingly exhaustible to him. He alone had been coping with all these. The Felony Boys were to him nothing but a sheer provision of human waste. He found it difficult to collect the sales they made on behalf of the club from them. They offered no help or assistance with his job.

"That's very good," Folly said, still suppressing his satisfaction. "If our new man could now assist me, I think I would be able to see well to other things going on around the club. In case of Eddy, I'll suggest he's assigned to collect our movies from the warehouse with the delivery van, so that the problem of waiting for the boys from the warehouse will be solved. He can also help the boys in the racketeering office at the peak of business."

"That's alright," Dona said. "But what other jobs do you have for Bob apart from helping you in keeping the club's account."

Folly's brain worked quickly.

"He's also to take care of all wear and tear materials in the building. I will make sure he sees to all replacement of outdated things and inform me of their covering expenses."

Dona nodded in approval. He regarded how his brain worked and envied his ability to coordinate the boys to various assignments. His sense of devotion to duty satisfied him. The club was progressing and its current annual income showed some profit.

On the face of it all, everything seemed alright with the club, except for the infernal cruelty of the Felony Boys. Dona knew the club was sunk in depravity, he knew there was nothing he could do about the dragon net that was fast turning the club into a depot of depraved persons. Sooner or later, he told himself, Bob and Eddy were certainly going to enter the Felony circle. Their composition would now form a reliable squadron for the club, and any external aggression from any group of Lagos underworld men could now be forestalled and reduce to ashes.

Concerning the two men about the underworld, Dona knew he couldn't bring Folly into that. He had lived well enough with him to know that such matters disturbed him. Perturbing and nasty operations were negative to his nature. This was where Pappy would have to come in. He would have to test Bob before he could be initiated into the underworld. As for Eddy, Dona knew he was good. He was Pappy's second best before he went away, and now that another man had occupied that position, he'd probably need a broken neck before he can regain it. Right now, Dona told himself that was none of his concern. That was a problem to be settled among the Felony Boys themselves.

After he had accepted Folly's decision on the job Bob and Eddy were to do, he fixed a salary, which Folly agreed was suitable for the two men.

"I don't think it is necessary for the two men to come here again," Dona said, as Folly was about to leave.

"Tell them they can start their jobs right away."

"Okay, sir," Folly said and left the office.

Left alone, Dona rang for Pappy and Hercules. There were only four telephones in the club: one in Dona's office, one in Folly's office, one in the hallway at the top floor where most of the Felony Boys hang out and the last one hung somewhere in the passage on the lower floor. Dele Idris, the boy in charge of the music joint, was passing when he heard the telephone ringing. He went to the phone, listened to the message and ran downstairs to deliver it.

Five minutes later. Pappy waddled to the door of Dona's office. He rammed on the door twice, carrying the noise he was making with his clenched fist to Dona's ears. Dona's reply to the knock concurred with the sound of the door as it opened and Pappy walked in. The two men looked at each other for some seconds. Dona saw that the whitish portions on Pappy's pupils had turned red and the black transparent lenses were staring at him ruggedly. He had just taken the hemp, Dona concluded thoughtfully. As Pappy opened his mouth to say something, there came another bang on the door and Hercules sauntered into the office. His eyes met Pappy's gaze before going past to meet Dona's.

These two thugs are certainly a disgrace to human decency, Dona thought as he stared at the two muscular men before him. The two sat to face him.

Pappy began to fondle with the hair on his cheeks; moving his fingers gently down to his aggressive jaw before running them up to his fuzzed eyes. He rubbed his hairless brow with his fingers and cleaned the water that emerged under his eyelids with the back of his hand.

Hercules rested his thick muscular body on the chair, disturbing his rotund face by raising his furrow. He picked the scratches that covered his beardless chin as he looked past the window at the airplane that was flying over. About five feet ten, he was an inch shorter than Pappy.

Both men seemed to look like brothers whenever they sat together to discuss how to deal with their enemies.

"Have you seen our new men?" Dona asked, using the word new to include Eddy in order to hear what Pappy would say.

"Eddy is not new to me," Pappy replied, knowing that Dona was aware of that, "only the other guy whom he introduced to us as Bob."

"The other guy is not new to me either," Hercules put in. "We both spent some time together in the prison before I left him there."

"Are you telling me you met that burly at the Central Maximum?" Dona asked surprisingly.

"That's what he told me," Pappy said.

"Well, he's going to be working with us," Dona said, "and when I mean working with us, you know what I mean."

"Yes," Pappy said. "But I do not trust him until I am sure he's good. As far as Eddy is concerned, he's alright."

"That guy has a lot of strength in him, Pappy," Hercules said. "The little time I spent with him in the prison told me he could withstand a lot of pressure."

"The fact that you've met him somewhere doesn't mean we shouldn't test him. He could beat up the whole men at Central Maximum without being able to handle the least powerful among our boys."

"Suppose you call Eddy and ask him how reliable he is." Hercules said, determined to defend Bob at all cost.

"Eddy isn't the boss of the Felony Boys. He can't tell me what I want. What I am telling you is I'm going to decide how good this guy is and how I do it isn't anybody's business."

"Okay, does what pleases you," Hercules said defenselessly.

Dona knew Pappy like his ways in this kind of issue, so he too agreed with him, but, he told him to mind how he did it because Bob was too fresh from prison than to be wounded by some jobless boys and sent to the hospital where he would be stared at by 'who did this to you nurses.'

Pappy knew it was after he was satisfied with Bob's test that he would be fully regarded as a member of the club. And if you were Dona's staff and Pappy didn't certify you as fit for the underworld, then you could as well know that your existence in the club was as shaky as a chair with wobble legs.

After the three men had made their feelings known about the new men, there was a short silence in the office; a silence, which Dona knew Pappy, would soon break with his unavoidable war of nerves. But instead of the silence in the office being broken by any of the three men, it was broken by sudden cries and yelling of people down in the lower floor of the building. The commotion down was so great that the angry cries of the crowd outside echoed in the ears of the three men. Hercules was the first to stand up. He was about to dart out when Pappy grabbed his wrist and shoved him back to his seat.

"Remember, man!" He bawled. "We are not the only guys here. Eddy, Bob, and the rest of the boys should be able to take care of the situation."

Were it not for Dona who quickly waded in, Hercules was so furious he wanted to remove the hand that held his wrist and slammed it on the edge of the wooden chair between his legs.

"I don't fancy your ways at time," Hercules said with reproach.

"Keep that language for your old man," Pappy replied mockingly.

"The trouble with you is you have a tongue as bad as your manners," Hercules said.

"And the problem with you is you have manners as bad as that of the ape," Pappy replied.

"Can't both of you stop behaving like kids?" Dona snapped. "I didn't call you here to quarrel."

"Let's see what's happening downstairs," Pappy looked at Hercules.

After about a minute or so, Hercules stood up and followed him, leaving Dona to stare at the blue door of his office as he jammed the door violently behind him. Noting that the disorderliness outside had been quelled and thinking of what to do, he closed his drawer, gathered the ledger cards and the sheets on the table into the filing tray, and reached for the telephone to tell Folly he was leaving. As his hand touched the receiver, he remembered fussily that he had not even mentioned what Folly said about the tickets to two men before they left.

The last show of the night was just over. The noise of the people who were pushing themselves violently as they rushed out at the end of the movie had died down. Except for about two or three men who were still trying their lucks in front of the slot machine and some hungry taxi drivers, who were cooling their guts in front of the kiosk behind the club's building, everywhere appeared to be silent. It was around twelve midnight and the club's night guards were already lying on the mats they spread on the pavement outside the building.

It was his sixth day at the club. Bob at the back of the club, a little away from some of the customers, waiting for Eddy to close for the day. He had just come downstairs; tired of Folly's pile of jobs, but satisfied of the plate of food the man ordered for him after completing his work. Any moment from now, Rasheed was bound to appear. Together with Eddy, they could then follow the boy to his rented room in the street at the back of the club. The last four nights had been spent in Rashid's room; the first two having been spent oh the pavement with the guards. Rasheed had agreed to accommodate them until they would be able to find a place for themselves. Although they were both anxious to find an apartment they could rent around the club, Bob knew it could take them three or four months to get one if they didn't know anybody to help.

As Bob sat there waiting for Eddy, Pappy came out of the club through the back exit. He walked past some of the guards, entered into a small studio at back of the club and shut himself in. The studio was like a small cell with several peepholes. It was attached to the club's main building and couldn't take more than three people at a time. Whoever is there had the advantage of watching every activity going on in the back the building without being seeing.

Tonight, Pappy decided to see how reliable Bob was in standard physical combat and murderous attacks. Before he had gone inside the studio, he had instructed four strong boys to draw Bob into a fight and had informed the

Felony Boys and the guards of his plan. The four boys he selected were from the list of vagabonds he usually kept with him. The boys were grown up ragamuffins who always partook in every attempt to ransack and terrorize the local inhabitants. One of the boys was a little taller than Bob, one a little below his height, and the other two of same height. The tallest of the boys was carrying a knife he had been instructed to bring out at a signal from Pappy during the fight. Apart from being one of the best knife jugglers in the club, the boy was a ruthless local butcher who could cut up his assailants as if cutting a piece of meat. He didn't give a damn to whatever happened to whom he stabbed; in as much as the knife kept finding a flesh to expose, it satisfied him. The rest of the boys were to fight Bob with bare hands. So as soon as Pappy had shut himself into the studio, and the boys had acknowledged the go-ahead signal; the tallest boy, who had been leaning on the kiosk beside the club, straightened himself and picked up an empty bottle of beer he had reserved for the occasion. Out of the corners of his eyes, he looked at Bob where he was sitting. After a short hesitation, he moved up a few steps and threw the bottle across.

Bob was just planning to stand up when a bottle landed on the floor beside him. The bottle scattered into pieces, and part of the broken fragments that rebounded landed at the back of his hand, giving him a tiny cut as it did. His eyes ran surprisingly over the broken bottle and then looked up almost immediately at where the bottle had come. The boy who threw the bottle was standing a few feet away, and he grinned ruefully at Bob as he looked at him.

"What's the matter with you?" Bob retorted. "Are you blind or what?"

The boy didn't answer. Instead, he looked disdainfully at him, turned his back and walked few steps away. Bob was so furious he didn't notice the blood that was beginning to form from the cut on his hand. He ran to the boy and turned him aside from the shoulder. The boy jerked off his hand with a sudden blow and pushed him off. Bob was taken back by the boy's action. His invitation to fight was so obvious that the first thing he thought was whether the boy had been sent to fight him in order to rid him of his existence at the club. He was surprised too that the guards were only looking at them and had to shift their eyes when he looked at them. His mind suddenly recalled Pappy's threats of fight as he thought of what this might be. Could this be the boy Pappy had sent to estimate his strength? He wondered. Was that son of Mermaid so foolish as to send this ignoramus son of Judas he could strangle to death to come and fight him? He was forced to ask himself if he could afford to spoil his plan in a bid to impress the Felony Boys. If that frigid and irrational criminal succeeded in sending him back to prison out of a sheer recklessness that could result in the death of this boy he had sent to fight him, would he be ready to liquidate Charles for him? No, he wouldn't fight the boy because Pappy was merely interested in knowing how well he could fight. If he wanted that, he would have to fight him himself.

Bob had nearly shrugged off what the boy did to him when Eddy's words rang silently in his ears that he would have to prove himself worthy before the underworld could accept any proposition from him. The Casino gang was great and highly regarded. Before you could count yourself as a member of the gang, you had to be feared, indomitable, bullish and respected. He hadn't done anything in the Casino to show he could be adored with any of these attributes. Here was a chance he could use to demonstrate his absolute strength. If cruelty was what gave the boys their dignities, then he could as well show them that he possessed a genuine one.

Cautiously, Bob stepped backward a few feet, spaced his legs evenly as he came to a standstill and beckoned the boy to come toward him with his left hand. As the boy advanced towards him, he noticed out of the corners of his eyes that three other hefty boys were also moving spirally towards him. With certainty, he knew without being told that Pappy, Eddy, and the rest of the Felony Boys were hanging around to watch the fight.

CHAPTER 4

"Ouch!" Bob yelped. "Gently please."

"Sorry man," Rasheed replied sympathetically. "You'll soon get over it."

Bob stretched his left arms at length, opened his eyes, closed them again, and then rested his head on the edge of the armchair. Sweats were running down his head to his flat hairy chest. He was naked except for the pants on his waist.

Again, Rasheed dipped the soft small towel on his hands into the hot water in the pail, brought it up and down intermittently, waited for the vapor to dissipate and strained the towel. He quickly shook off the water that burned his palms and placed the towel on Bob's left arm in one swift movement.

Bob moaned softly, turned his head aside and gnawed at his nails discontentedly. The wound on the muscles of his upper arm was deep. It was inflicted on him with a butcher knife by one of the four boys who fought him yesterday. The fight had been gruesome. Two of the boys had to retire in the middle of the fight. They had their noses punched out of order with swollen faces that would take them weeks to repair. The shortest boy was a torn in flesh for Bob. Stumpy and muscular with a hairless head, he gave Bob a lot of heavy punches and kneeling kicks that nearly put him off the fight. Bob had to remove two of his frontal teeth with a terrific blow that heaved him out of the fight. Pappy, who had come out of the hiding by then, signaled to the tallest boy to bring out the knife as soon as he observed that all the other boys were down. Bob saw a knife come out of the boy's groin and moved fast into his hand. He watched as the boy changed it from one hand to the other with professional agility. The movement of the knife was so fast Bob found it difficult to know which hand the boy was going to use.

Bob knew he would have to be very tactful in approaching the boy or else the boy could easily inflict him with a fatal wound. The boy had earlier received a stabbing blow on his jaw and had also suffered a severe kick on his private part, so he was not only determined to make Bob suffer for what he had done to him, but also make him regret for what he had done to his colleagues. Bob had already been soaked with rains of blows and kicks from the four boys, so he was determined not to let this last one go unpunished. Remorselessly determined, he began a systematic display of skills; bending left and right and showing some boxing footwork he inherited in his youthful days.

The boy too was watchful. He had regained his energy, and then with a gleam of confidence, he began to move cautiously toward Bob, half bending his body with a raised furrow and extending his hands at an angle proportional to his body. This time, the tip of the knife had nosed downward and the base of glaring blade held firmly with his palm. As he approached Bob with a glaringly set eyes; aiming at where to strike him, he suddenly took three long strides, changed the knife to the other hand and trusted it forward. The knife was almost an inch away from Bob's belly before he jumped back, creating a wider space between them as he did. The boy ran forward and charged again with the knife. Again, Bob jumped to another side, but this time he missed his steps and fell backward. The boy closed up, bent over him, and aimed the knife at his shoulder. Bob shot out a hand for his wrist and covered his chest with the other hand. The boy cleverly slipped through his defense and slashed his left biceps muscle with the butcher knife. Bob's determination to subdue the boy completely bereaved him of the knife's effect. He trusted his right arm forward, grabbed the boy and pulled him down. His hand found his throat and he squeezed it grimly, forcing the boy to drop the knife. He held his grip until he went limp. He pushed off the boy, stood up, and kicked him so viciously the boy retched. The boy rolled over and squirmed to one side on the floor. As blood tricked down his shirt, Bob turned to look around and found all the Felony Boys standing and waving at him from the back of the building. He was right all along. He knew this was a test.

After the fight, all the Felony Boys gave him a warm handshake.

Later, Pappy came out with a brawny necklace, which hung a golden triangular block and offered it to him. The locket was what gave the Felony Boys their identities and Bob was glad to have one.

As he thought about what happened last night, he stared at the deep wound the knife had made on his arm and wished he had not taken up the challenge. Bending over him with the towel in hand, Rasheed increased the pressure. Bob moaned a little as he thought about how Rasheed had been very nice and accommodating toward Eddy and him. He hadn't for once noticed any sign of anger in his conduct towards them in sharing of his room. The room, which comprised of a large wooden bed, two single armchairs, a sofa, a table carrying a radio cassette and a fan was fairly big and all right for three of them. On the blue walls of the room were posters of reputable film actors and actresses, some with nothing to wear. Although, the carpet needed changing, there was enough room to spread a mat on the floor to sleep.

"In about two weeks," Rasheed said as he straightened up, "you'll forget you had a fray," He went to the door and hung the towel on the handle.

"You've been very helpful," Bob, said, "I am really grateful."

"When Eddy arrives with the ointments, I will bandage it up," Rasheed said reassuringly.

Bob looked at the clock on the table. It was half past mid-night.

"He must be on his way back by now," he said.

Five minutes later. Eddy came in. He dropped the paper bag on his hand on the floor and threw himself on the bed. "How is your arm?" He said exhaustingly, looking at Bob as he fondled with the pillow.

"Getting fine," Bob said meekly. "Rasheed has just bathed it with hot water."

"That sounds fine," Eddy said. "Rasheed, you can make use of the medicine in the bag."

Rasheed picked up the paper bag on the floor, emptied its contents, took out large gauze, applied some antibiotic ointment and dressed up the wound on Bob's arm.

Five minutes later, the three men had a late night meal. Together they played a deck of cards and finally drifted into sleep.

Three weeks of gradual healing had dragged past. Bob had slowly and steadily recovered. The wound on his arm had finally given up to a long indelible scar.

Today was Monday, Bob thought as he startled up on the bed. He sat upright and stared at the empty darkness in the room. On the floor mat was Rasheed who rapped himself completely with the night cloth. On the couch was Eddy who was snoring heavily like a frog in a swamp. Bob stared blankly at him, his eyes unable focus on the heavy body that crumpled up on the couch. He removed his covering, got off the bed and found his way to the light switch. He flipped up the switch, but there was no light. As usual, Nigeria Electric Power Authority a.k.a. NEPA had struck. He cursed the corporation silently as he turned away from the wall. He went to the rack of clothes on the wall, found his trousers where he hung it before he slept, searched through the pockets and brought out a pack of matches. He brought out a stick, flicked it through the body of the matchbox, and walked to the table as the darkness disappeared. He rummaged through the repositories on the top drawer, found a candlestick and lit it. He turned the burning candle upside down, poured about three or four drops of wax on the table and stuck the base of the candle on the solidifying wax. The candle stood still, producing an artificial light that needed no electric or hydraulic power around a tiny thread that glowed brightly.

He pushed aside the ashtray on the table and looked at the table clock. It was exactly 6 A.M., reminding him of the exact time he woke to leave the prison about four weeks ago. Now, he said half aloud, it was time to track Charles down. Longing for something to incite his thought, he picked up the box of cigarette on the ashtray, slid back its flap and removed a stick. He lighted the cigarette from the candle on the table, went to one of the armchairs, and sat down. As he drew in a lungful of smoke from the cigarette, he noticed that sweats were beginning to form on his forehead. He thought it was due to the heat in the room, so he went to the window and opened it. As he was doing so, Rasheed turned to look at him for a second or two then fell back to sleep. Eddy was undisturbed; he seemed lost in sleep. Bob watched him as he changed sides and snored off again. Bastard! He thought. If he hadn't opened the window, the air coming out of Eddy's nostrils might be enough to raise the room temperature by one more degree. Only yesterday, Bob thought as he sat down, he had reminded Eddy about his plan while having lunch at the club. Eddy had agreed, but said it was too early for such an intricate job. After a lot of discussion on so many things he wanted to accomplish in life, Eddy thought he was right and said he could go ahead. Today therefore, he had decided to table his plan before Pappy and see how fast the Felony Boys act.

As Bob sat there, looking at the cigarette as it burned brightly between his fingers, he brooded and rehearsed what he had to tell Pappy. After a while, he was satisfied with what he had in mind. Nothing short of what he told Eddy before they left the prison, but this time; it needed a little exaggeration that would make it difficult for Charles to escape the Felony Boy's onslaught. Satisfied with himself, he stood up and took off his clothes. He entered the bathroom, pulled off his underwear and took a long bath as he prepared himself for the day ahead.

Around ten o'clock of the same morning, Pappy was in one of the rooms upstairs at the club sitting in a basket chair reserved exclusively for him. Pappy like to have his entire secret meeting with the rest of the Felony Boys at what they all called the strong room. Strangers are not allowed in the strong room.

Facing him on a long bench were Rasheed and Isiaka, the two men handling the affairs in the Cinema hall. Ever since Dona had told him about the problem Folly said he was having in collecting ticket sales from the boys, he had wanted to call and advice them that they should play their tricks in a way that would raise less suspicion from Folly. But busied with his own odd jobs, he had completely forgotten about the matter until it raised uproar again, last night between Folly and the boys. Folly had expected that with Bob's help, the collection of sales from the boys would be easier, but Bob thought he was unconcerned with whatever part of sales the boys kept back in as much as they accounted for the full amount of tickets they were given. That didn't satisfy Folly. He felt the club was being cheated whenever he compared the amount of money the boys delivered to the number of crowd that attended a popular show. Bob thought he couldn't help him on this, and as a matter of fact, none of the boys was prepared to help since this was where they realized what catered for a greater part of their daily expenses. Pappy normally took one-quarter of whatever the boys kept back on tickets' profit, while the rest went to the rest of the Felony Boys. They all thought if Folly was insisting they stay clear of the money that was not part of the club's legitimate profit, then he was finding a way of trampling on their feelings.

Pappy hated Folly. There were so many ways he could shelter money from the club but Folly was always around with curious eyes. He was always around every penny, pestering and inquiring about every transaction. He thought Folly was an Accountant from hell. He ignored his dislikes with unholy determination. For a man like Folly to be practically opposite in attitude to a group of boys whose criminal conduct baffled the people around them was a thing of surprise to Pappy. Although both men started as good friends, but later Pappy found Folly attitude too trustworthy. Folly would not support any act of deceit. Pappy withdrew his likings and discussed with Folly only on matters concerning the club.

Pappy's loathing for Folly was further accentuated by Bob's employment. As he viewed it, Bob was going well with the Felony Boys' perfidious activities. He appeared to be contented with the boys' ways of lives. This made him think that if Bob could master all aspects of Folly's work and do them effectively; he would do everything possible to get rid of Folly in the Casino. Pappy knew quite well that Dona couldn't afford to part with Folly. At the same time, he thought if an unexpected explosion that could just be framed as an accident happened to Folly, then Dona would be forced to part with Folly. He was thinking about all these before he called at the two men in front of him. As he thought about how troublesome Folly was becoming to the Felony Boys, he smiled subtly at the two men.

Isiaka was protesting bitterly that in as much as the full amount Folly gave them was provided for, Folly had no business interfering with whatever came as their gains. He admitted they got more than double the money they ought to deliver on tickets at times, but he argued that how could Folly be so stupid as to expect money greater than the number of tickets he gave them. Rasheed supported Isiaka idea and said that their gains had even being reduced with the insufficient number of tickets Folly was now giving them.

Pappy declared it was time they shut Folly's mouth. He said if Folly thought he could go on telling Dona all sorts of nonsense and doting around in their affairs, Folly would regret it. He was still expressing his bitterness about what Folly was doing when a knock came on the door. As one of them answered, Eddy opened the door, followed by Bob as he entered.

"Where have you two been since morning?" Rasheed asked as they came in, lighting his face with a wide grin.

"We've been nosing around the building to see if anything needs replacing," Bob answered, sitting beside the two men on the bench. Eddy walked past them to the window and leaned his back on the hedge, crossing his legs as he poised there.

"Did you find any?" Rasheed asked, looking at Bob's expressionless face.

"Sure, some of the seats in the film house have been ripped with blades. They need replacement."

"Eddy, aren't you going to the Warehouse today?" Pappy asked, forcing the other men to look at him.

"We are screening the film that was shown yesterday."

"Oh, I see."

"Pappy," Eddy suddenly said in a steady voice. "We are here for a crucial discussion with you. Do we stay here or go somewhere else."

"Do you want Isiaka and Rasheed out?"

"Yes. We want your opinion first," Eddy said.

Pappy excused the two men who were already getting to their feet.

"Some top secret?" Pappy asked as soon as the other two men left.

"More than confidential," Bob replied nimbly, staring at his reddish brown eyes.

Eddy went to the door, removed the key from the hole, and locked the door behind. He came back and sat down beside Bob.

Pappy stared at the two men for some time, saw the perturbing urgency of a soon to be exposed secret in their faces and said with an excitement, "let me weed my head before you fill it with your some misfortunes."

"I could do with some too." Eddy said, looking at Bob from the corners of his eyes.

"Care for some?" Pappy asked Bob as he began to roll the dried hemp on his hands in a clean-cut paper.

"No," Bob said, "it's too early for me."

"Are you saying it's too early for you to charge your brain?" Pappy asked persuasively. "Do you imagine I am going to listen to your tales of woe without seeing the smoke of weed coming out of your nostrils? That's impossible, brother."

"Well, give me some," Bob said unwillingly.

Eddy, who had already made his wrap, tossed the small tin containing the hemp to him and searched his pockets anxiously for a pack of matches.

As the three men began to smoke, there was a short undisturbed atmosphere of an individual desire to bite, drag, pull, and swallow the joints in their hands before Bobinson Okoye started his story.

CHAPTER 5

Among the row of beautiful commercial buildings along Broad Street in Lagos stood a large ten-story building that occupied several offices and department stores of various sizes. Many of the buildings had an unmistaken display of their titles and business location, allowing easy identification by most of the white collar employees. The whole street was flooded with people from all walks of life, milling about and indifference to each other's attention. The people; old and young, men and women, blacks and whites, busied their eyes with the various marketing activities going on in the street, with some pausing to stare at the goods displayed on shop windows and market stands. Traders looked in their eyes, hoping for the little they could purchase. The street traffic flowed evenly, but forced the motorists to stop for the teaming crowd to pass.

On this Saturday morning, among the few cars that sped in line with the traffic were Charles Aduwo's 504 Peugeot cars with its made in Nigeria label brightly displayed on the back windscreen. He was alone in the car with his belt tightly on. With his hands resting firmly on the steering wheel and with his foot on the break pedal, he stared at the traffic warden who had just stopped him to pass the vehicles on the other side. He wasn't in any hurry, so he waited patiently until the traffic cop turned to face him again. He moved off as soon as he was waved to pass, followed by other motorists who moved behind him in quick succession. As he approached the front of the large ten-story building, he slowed down and blew his horn for a taxi driver who was picking up a passenger in front of the building. As the cab driver exchanged gear and drove off, he swung his car over the curb in front of the building and parked behind other cars in line. He got out of the car and trotted up the steps to the entrance of his office building. Before swinging the door open, he paused to look at himself in the glass that reflected his image in front of the door. He winked satisfactorily to his clean-cut hair, his broad face, and the boldly knotted tie that was tucked on his three-piece coat. He entered into the reception and waved to the receptionist who smiled invitingly at him. Mid-way between the passages, he turned left, moved forward a few steps and then pressed the bottom on the wall. After a minute or so, the door of the lift swung open and he entered into its dimly lit room. The lift stopped on the third floor to pick two neatly dressed ladies, and then went unto the fifth floor to drop him. At the far end of the fifth floor, was a cubby with a sofa. Beside the cubby was Charles' office. Two gentlemen were sitting on the sofa when he arrived. They greeted him as he walked to the door of his office and knocked.

"Good morning, sir," his secretary said as she opened the door and stood aside for him to enter.

"Morning, Funmi. How are you doing? He replied, walking past her and moving into an inner office.

"Fine, sir," Funmi said, closing the door and then moving over to her table on which stood a telephone, a typewriter, a filing tray, and a stack of files arranged in a row on the table.

Unlike Charles who was now a few months to thirty-three years in age, Funmilayo Daramola was only nineteen. Slightly built with an average height, she was Charles's second secretary since he started his business and she had been with him now for almost two years. Soft spoken, ebony complexioned; with a small sensuous face she was beautiful without being told. Whenever Charles telephoned her he was coming to the office, she always looked forward to the time he would arrive.

"I was just thinking you must be on your way here when you arrived," she said, smiling at Charles as he opened the door of the inner office with a key he had just brought out of his pocket.

"You guessed right," he said as the door clicked open, moving in and stepping on the soft rug of his office.

Inside the small office, Charles's table stood against the window overlooking the main street. On it was small typewriter, a medium-sized calculator, a telephone, a desk diary, and two large manila wallet files containing his business documents. In front of the table were two movable armchairs and behind it was his freely movable cushion chair made of genuine Italian leather. A large cabinet with two long doors stood against one of the office walls, and slightly above it were the hanging pictures of the president, the state governor, and that of himself. On another wall was a battery clock, far below which stood a larger air-conditioner.

As soon as he entered into the office, he switched on the air-conditioner, went around the table and sat on the chair behind it. He remembered the last time he sat on the chair was about two weeks ago, so he opened the drawers, brought out a handkerchief and cleaned the table and the chair he was sitting on. Charles seldom came to his office. He was always there only when there was an important business in stock for him or whenever he felt like dusting off his molded appointments. He usually spent the major part of his time at Hotel de Executive, where he was keeping a suite to accommodate his smuggled trinkets and jewels. The rest of his time he spent at home with Shola, his wife, who had no knowledge of his suite at Hotel de Executive. The suite was also a secret to his secretary and his wife. To the two women, whenever Charles was gone for a week or two, he was either at the seaport or away overseas. None of them would know that Charles was staying at Hotel de Executive, negotiating and haggling on the price of smuggled trinkets and jewels with accredited merchants who always occupied his time with their crucial talks. Neither his secretary, nor his wife knew he was a notorious smuggler operating on both land and sea to earn his living. Working with him were five young men who always carried out his orders. One of them was a permanent driver on the job. Two of the men worked directly with him as bodyguards; they handled most of their stubborn customers and carried out most of the sea operations, and the last two men who worked as part time crew on ships.

About two weeks ago, Charles lost his permanent driver, James Igor, who died in a scuffle with a prostitute in one of the local pubs. Since then he had been looking for someone to take over James's job. About three days ago, he was at the Apapa wharf when he met a man who had been out of job for sometime. The man was helping some of the stevedores at the pier to offload their goods from the ship with little or no payment. He was using a forklift, and Charles was fascinated by the way he was handling the machine. He thought he could do a lot better with a car, so he approached him. The man was proud of showing his records. Charles noted the man had once served in the army, driving through difficult jungles in mortal tanks and last held a job as an ambulance driver. Charles gave him his office address and scheduled an interview with him today. This morning, he came to his office straight from home; expecting to meet the man at ten.

Now, as he looked at the time, he reckoned he still had about forty minutes to himself before the interview. He started to readjust the files on his table. As he was doing this, Funmi came in with a copy of the Times and the Punch newspapers.

"Let me have the progress report," he said as she put the newspapers on the table.

Funmi went out and came back with a brown flat folder. She opened it and placed it before him on the table.

"Thank you," he said, putting down the newspapers and drawing the folder towards him.

"You know I told you about James's death two weeks ago," he looked up and said as she turned to go.

"Yes, sir," Funmi said with a feeling of concern. "Has anything happened again?"

"No. I only want to tell you that a new man is coming to replace him today."

"How are the other guys doing?" Funmi said, asking about the men who worked with him.

"They are doing fine. We meet at the port everyday. The new man will soon be joining us. He'll be here by ten this morning, so show him in when he comes.

"Yes, sir," She said and left for her desk.

Charles began to look at the documents in the file. To his surprise, he found out his profits within the last six months had gone up tremendously. The payments to his men, his office and residential expenses, bribes to law enforcement agencies and other overhead spending amounted to an insignificant figure when compared with the profit on the balance sheet. He flicked through the pages again and stopped when he got to the one showing tax payments. The column of the total tax due to date recorded N31, 945.00 since the beginning of the year. That's plenty for the government, he thought. He opened through the pages again and stopped when he saw the list of his debtors. He examined those with over six months debt in thoroughness, and decided he would have to be rough in collecting his money from two of them whose debit balance was over $30, 000.00 each. Ali Joe and Co., a dealer in beads and jewels could be a liability if not pressured. Mama Gonza, another gang of gem seller, could also pose a problem if not dealt with in the right way. He decided he would put a call through to them first thing on Monday morning and ask them to pay in time. Next was the list of the new customers who were interested in his market, He always instructed his secretary to put forward adverts in the Times to invite those who might be interested in purchasing imported gems and precious stones. After running through the folder, he couldn't find the list. He closed the file and lifted the receiver of the phone.

"Funmi, let me have the file on our new customers," he said to his secretary. "You can bring the appointment sheet with it."

A minute later, Funmi came in with a brown folder containing the letters from those who had responded to the newspaper advertisement and handed it to him.

There were thirteen pages, half of them received within the last twenty-four hours. One by one, he began to check through each page. The first three were asking for the same information; they wanted to have a list of his jewels and a definite time to meet him. The forth-through sixth were asking if he could buy some imported trinkets. They didn't interest him, so he put a pen across them. The seventh sheet held his attention: its contents were written with a fine transparent ink, and the rich man who had written it was asking if he could get about half a dozen of sparkling diamonds to decorate his proposed fish pond that was to be commissioned in three month's time. Charles reckoned this would fetch him about N800, 000.00 if his men at the port could handle the new diamond consignment he was hoping to receive from a friend overseas in a month's time. He expected the job to be his biggest haul of the year if things went according to plan. He brought out a diary from the inner pocket of his coat, jotted down the man's address in a page and returned the diary to his pocket. Then he checked through the eight to the tenth pages without interest. He impatiently glanced through the eleventh and the twelfth, and just as he was about to dismiss the last sheet with a wave of hand and cover the file, a frightful diagram in the page held his eyes and hands back.

Written on top of the page beneath a diagram of a human skull was a company named 'Better than Pirate Associates.' Underneath the skull logo was a skeletal drawing of two crossed leg bones. Succinctly written in red, the letter stated: we required an ideal place to meet for a fundamentally important matter connected with your line of work. Your business will be ruined if you failed to show up. You must provide a special place to meet. No police and no spies. You must reply this letter within two weeks or else the information would reach the government, the law enforcement and the news media.

An impatient wave of hand ran through his hair as he read the letter again. He wondered who was behind it. He read the letter for the third time, this time more patiently, taking note of ever word and staring at the enigmatic design of signature it contained.

Despite the fact that Charles was a leader of a notorious business that was disobedient to government laws in every respect, he was still frightened of certain things. Things he knew must have been carefully planned and thoroughly rehearsed without his awareness and then suddenly shoved towards him. To him, it was like walking over a deep pit covered with a mat. For the past five and half years, he had been running his business without a hitch. Although some minor trouble did come into surface at times, but things were always promptly arrested by the chains of connections he had in both private and public sectors. Now, here was a letter, the writer of which he neither knew nor ever seen in life, proposing a meeting with him in committed terms. He wondered whether the letter had been written by someone acting under the tempo of a notorious gang that was interested in black mailing him. The tone of the letter sounded as if more than a single person wrote it, and the headline inferred a group of persons. Probably a group of guys who wanted some money or some rivals determined to stir out some trouble. He wondered whether this was a calculated attempt to hand him over to the law or a determined purpose to make his life miserable by a competitor. On the face of it all, the letter appeared threatening. Why the diagram of a skull? Was this writer's sign of showing he was dangerous, or was it put it there to indicate an imminent danger? The more he thought about it, the more perturbed he became.

Charles thought he had to do something; he couldn't sit there all day thinking of who had written the letter. He pulled out a drawer, brought out a staple removal and removed the staple on the sheets. With steady hands, he removed the letter, folded it, and put it on his breast pocket. He searched the drawer for a stapler. As he was stapling the remaining sheets together, a knock came on the door. He hesitated for a moment before answering it.

Segun Adio, an averagely built man with a face that carried one tribal mark on each side, bowed as he entered.

"You are fifteen minutes late," Charles said, looking at the battery clock on the wall.

"Traffic sir," Segun replied, "It was terrible on Iddo Bridge."

"Should that be a good excuse for your first appointment?"

"I couldn't help it, sir," Segun said pleadingly, "I trekked to this place from Idumata when I could no longer bear the hold-up."

"Alright, sit down," Charles said.

"Thank you, sir."

Charles quickly rubbed off the disturbed expression on his face as he pushed the file in front of him aside. Casually, he cleared the table to reabsorb himself, and then he conducted a short interview for the new man. Satisfied with what he heard, he fixed a salary for his new employee and then disclosed the skill required in the intricate job he was to be engaged. He gave him the details of all the necessary connections he ought to know and informed him about the risks involved in the business. Punctuality and time, he said, were so important that the time lag of a second could ruin a carefully prepared plan. He told him there were three operations to be carried out before the end of the month.

The first and second operations would come during the first and second weeks respectively. The last, which he expected to be one of the biggest operations of the year, would come at the end of the month. All the necessary arrangements for all the operations would be done in their suite at Hotel de Executive where he told him his men always met at the beginning of every week to plan for the week ahead. A meeting would be held there on Monday morning during which he would introduce him to others. After the interview, they agreed to meet on Monday at the hotel.

After Segun left, Charles resumed his thought about the strange letter. This time, the first thing that struck his mind was whether his secretary had read the letter. Obviously, there wasn't any correspondence that would be sent to him without passing through her hands. From time to time, he always instructed her to take care of every correspondence she received on his behalf. If any of them needed an immediate attention, she was to contact the operator on the ground floor, who knew where to get him. The operator, a big burly man with a terrible moustache, knew his tip for every message he passed to Charles. Whenever Funmi asked to know where her boss was speaking from, he would tell her it was from a local number beside the port. This particular letter, Charles thought, appeared not to have intrigued her, for if it did, she would have passed the message to him.

Funmi had not read the letter. When she understood her boss was coming to the office this morning, what she did was to gather the letters that came to the office this morning in a hurry, and arrange them for her master to see without going through. The letter Charles was worrying about was among the ones she received this morning and her hastiness didn't allow her to see the drawings on it, or read through it. Charles had almost picked up the phone receiver to ask if she had seen the letter when he cautioned himself. When the deal is completed, he concluded thoughtfully, she would be called and given the fitting explanation, The first thing he would do on Monday, he said half-aloud, was to show the letter to his men when they met at the hotel. His view and whatever they thought about it would probably help to solve the riddle. He was suddenly tired and wanted to call it quit for the day. He told himself he needed a rest and a sufficient time to device something. Slowly and steadily, he packed up the files and locked his drawer. As he was doing this, he remembered he had about twelve days to reply to the letter, but what he didn't know was the fact that his new driver, Segun Adio, was a regular customer of the Central Casino where the letter had come from.

CHAPTER 6

Today was Sunday, the day after Charles received the letter from the Central Casino. He was at home and he had planned to spend the day with Shola, his wife. He was in the living room, half burying himself in one of the three long sofas in the room. His legs crossed, rested on top of a footstool, revealing the thick skin that covered his bare feet. The Rolex watch on his wrist showed 11 A.M. as his bright and handsome face lit up the last page of the newspaper on his hands. He nodded in approval to the editorial comment on the President's visit to a neighboring country. Having scanned through the comment, he looked at the President's photograph next to it. He was clad all over in a white toga with a white cap that looked like a cone, and a pair of dark tinted glasses. As his eyes surveyed the last episode in the paper about a robber who was lynched in daylight by an irate mob, his eyelids began to close intermittently like a soldier on heavy duty. Without bothering to go through the last paragraph of the robber's misfortune, he unfolded his legs and tossed the paper on the sofa. He entered his feet into the slippers under the stool and stood up. His eyes traveled across the room to the bottle of J & B hundred percent whiskies on the dining table. He sauntered towards it, poured himself a half-glass, and carried it to the window. As he drew the blinds aside and leaned on the window hedge, the warmth breeze of the Lagos lagoon that stretched across the bridge around several homes in the area greeted his face. He sipped some gin from the drink on his hand and stared at the water. It was now a little over two years since he bought his house. He was formerly residing at Aguda where he was forced out as a result of the flood that menaced every rainy season. He liked his present location. The vantage view of the lagoon is spectacular. The building had a nice structure with easy view of the surrounding districts. Apart from his wife who shared the top floor with him, a young university graduate who preferred to remain alone for reasons best known to himself occupied the flat below. The university student always paid a year rent in advance. He came from a rich family and never caused any trouble. All the other buildings around were almost of similar erection, except the one in front that was near completion. The lagoon was never a threat to them.

Across the lagoon, a canoe steered aimlessly at the far side. The driver seemed to be having trouble with the paddle, looking as if the handle was too heavy for him as he dipped and steered wearily to the shore. Charles shifted his eyes away from the canoe man and descended them on a group of boys who were spiritedly playing the game of Cowboys and Indians near the lagoon. He watched them with burning inspiration; thinking that sometime in the past, he had been like them, rousing around in his youthful exuberance. But now, it was different with many responsibilities to be shouldered. Several problems had come and gone, and the means of survival had been pursued like a boat propelled with oars. The road to richness was rough. Few people, if at all there was any, waited for nature to provide them wealth. Envious and insidious enemies once acquired, would subject even the wealthiest to attacks.

Only yesterday, he received a strange letter from somebody wishing to tip him about something that could ruin his business if he didn't respond. He had thought about it all through yesterday night, but now, he wouldn't like to disturb his mind about it again. The only person he wished could come to him today was Bola Thompson, the only friend who had started with him from childhood, but who had gone on another line of business entirely different. Rather than being a smuggler, Bola was a stationary and goods supplier, rich in business and admired by his clients.

At first, Charles had started as a young stevedore, loading and off-loading goods in ships for three years at the dockside. During this time, he managed to qualify as an Efficient Deck Hand man. Another two years saw him with a Steering and Life Boat-man certificates. But already, he had decided he wasn't going to be a small time crew with ropes in hands. Instead, he wanted to occupy his time with how precious commodities could be towed home from foreign lands. Initially, he started by buying fine jewels from overseas at reduced prices and then selling then at home at high prices. But after sometime, he was frustrated by the amount of money he had to pay on customs duties before he could get his goods overboard. The money on duties was too much and he wasn't prepared to waste his profits on government laws. He decided to find a way of evading import duties, and found out that there was no satisfactory way of doing this except by smuggling his goods on board. He was prepared to risk life and with an inside help he found what he wanted.

He had met and parted with a lot of troubles. Sometime, it had to do with the police, and some other time it would be the customs men. In most cases, he had to bribe his way through. This satisfied him than complying with their corrupt infested formalities. However, there were times when he had to be crude and cruel, when he had to fight his way through before he could escape. He always commended himself for the untiring efforts he was putting on his job and he felt being rewarded with the amount of money he now had in hand. Lots of money ought to be expected from a lot of risks. But at times he would think that Bola, his friend, hadn't taken up to half the risk he had taken in life and yet his business was flourishing. Bola was far away from the harassment of the men in uniforms who threatened him for disobeying government rules and legislations. How many people could afford to keep such laws? He hadn't seen any since childbirth. In his day-to-day underhand dealings, he had seen so many highly placed public men inducing, aiding and abetting the bribes they often-publicly denounced. Should this be part of a progressing society? Or could it be referred to as a nation wide disease that cannot be entirely eliminated. He reminded himself that he once read somewhere that the society was nothing but individuals at large. If individual element of a society is corrupt then the society majority is bound to be corrupt. As far as he was concerned, he had been rough, unquiet and unpatriotic in order to be well placed in the society. He didn't see how he could lead a truthful life unless he wanted to lose his possessions. As these waves of thoughts radiated through his mind, he didn't know that he had finished the drink in his glass.

"Shoot!" He cried as he looked at the empty glass, straightened himself, and then went to the table to pour another half a cup. He took it in a swill, dropped the glass, and then reached for the phone. As his hand touched the receiver he remembered Bola couldn't be back from church. Bola had often told him that to attend church on Sundays was a practice he inherited from his father, so Sunday services were things he dared not miss. Charles couldn't remember the last time he had been to Church. Was it being when he was marrying Shola about two years ago? No, it wasn't. It was last December, when one of Shola's brothers was wedding at Yaba Methodist Church, and that was when he last prayed. Despite the fact that his father was an Evangelist, and his mother a supporter of the Apostolic Message, Charles didn't know how to pray. Now, he didn't want to think about prayers or his dead parents. All he wanted was how he could use his brain, skill, and talent to expand his business. He went back to the window, drew up the blinds, and then with short calculating steps, he walked to his wife's bedroom.

Shola was on the bed facing the wall when her husband came in. She turned when she heard the bedroom door clicked open and lit up her face with a bright smile when she saw Charles. Her dark eyeballs stared lovingly at him as he came to sit beside her. As he bent forward, she rolled closer to meet his demanding kiss, feeling the warmth effect of his damp lips on her tongue.

"Don't tell me you've been dreaming of how to kiss your husband," he said as he released her, grinning handsomely.

"Your guess is always right, dear," she said, showing the two light dimples on her high cheeks.

"You've slept since you had your breakfast," Charles said. "What have you been dreaming of besides kissing your husband?"

"I dreamt I was flying in the sky like the famous Iscariot. My wings were as high as those of the angles."

"Just how far did you go?"

"Darling, I went beyond the blue sky where the then Iscariot cannot even reach."

"Then you must be able to tell me what the Moon and the Stars look like, and how far they are above the ground."

"You see," she said, her eyes focusing on the white ceiling, "I observed that the Moon has a golden rim, a beautiful sphere of glowing light with a size twice as large as the world. The Stars, as I saw them, were shining like brilliant diamonds with rays that nearly blinded me as I flew past them. Then just when I was trying to see how far they are from the ground, my darling woke me up."

"Gee!" Charles exclaimed hysterically, "I should have slept with you; maybe I would have seen better then you did."

"If that had happened," Shola said, "we would have been swimming in the ocean of love."

Charles burst out laughing.

"Okay, when next I sleep," he said, "I'll remember to visit some important places in the outer space."

They looked at themselves for a few seconds, and then began to kiss and hug until they journeyed to an earthly paradise where a man and a woman fuse together.

An hour later, the telephone in the living room began to ring. Shola was in the kitchen busy preparing the lunch. She had left her husband in bed after their afternoon romance. She dropped the ball of tomato she was cutting and went out to answer the phone call.

"Hello?" A voice said from the other end.

"Yes, who is speaking?"

"Bola Thompson," the voice answered,

"Oh!" Shola cried excitedly. "Good afternoon, uncle."

"How are you my dear? How is everything over there?" Bola said.

"Fine, it's quite a long time since you came here. Is something wrong?" Shola asked.

"No dear. My job has been pretty tedious these days, so I scarcely have the time to see anybody when I leave the office. But things will soon return to normal and then I shall have time to see more of you and your husband again," Bola said.

"Well, you and your friend are really the same. It's always jobs in the office all the time. Anyway, how is Folake?" She asked about his wife.

"She's fine. We've just returned from church service. She is now in the kitchen. Is your husband in?"

"Yes. Should I call him for you?"

"That's what I want."

"Just a minute, sir," She said, and placed the receiver gently on the table.

A minute later, Charles was on the phone speaking to his friend. "How are you, son of Jesus?" Charles said into the receiver.

"Fine, friend of Judas, your wife said you are really enjoying life," Bola said.

"Correct, except for one thing I'll like to discuss with you." Charles said, looking over his shoulder to see if his wife was around.

"When and where?" Bola asked.

"Can yon come to our house this evening?" He asked expectantly, relaxing his grip on the receiver when he heard a clatter of plates in the kitchen.

"Okay, I will see you around six in the evening," Bola said, and then he added, "Do you want me in singular or plural?"

Charles hesitated for a moment, thinking if he came in singular, he would come alone, but if in plural, Folake was sure to come with him who in no doubt would keep Shola busy when he was discussing about the letter with her husband.

"Come in plural," he said his voice a little edgy. "But we'll separate when the time comes for us to talk."

"That's alright. Be expecting us at six."

"Thanks."

They chatted a little before Charles dropped the receiver. Then he went to the window and peered into the city below. Seeing nothing to amuse him, he strutted across the living room into the passage, and then turned to the kitchen door to see what his wife was cooking.

It was an oil-bean salad. He felt his mouth turned moist as the smelling of the food greeted him.

Hotel de Executive was situated at the end of a one-way street that ran like a crescent along Moiré's road in Lagos. The hotel consisted of a three one-story building joined together by an overhead hallway. It had all the modern things someone could find in a standard hotel including an extensive packing space, and models of a proposed swimming pool extension. The hotel was built by a joint venture between two chairmen of a large oil company in Lagos. It was directed and supervised by Mr. Gbade Aina, a man who had held various important assignments in many hotels in the city. Short and stumpy with a bridge of baldhead, Mr. Aina was around fifty-five and carried a round friendly face with a goatee. He had been running the hotel for the last five years without regrets. After all, his two children, a boy and a girl who had ever since grown past their teens, were now in the University, and his wife, the only woman he had grown to love, was always contended with whatever he gave her. Since the hotel started its operations at the time he began to manage it, he was satisfied that there had been no murder or burglar of any sort. The hotel had a good security system, and no commotion had ever been caused by the quite and rich people who came often to satisfy their inexhaustible appetites. He was glad of the people, listened to their complaints, examined the improvements they suggested, and satisfied their demands without compromise. On this Monday morning, he was discussing with one of the guards stationed in front of the hotel when he saw Charles arrived with three men in his Peugeot car. A smile of recognition lit his face as he waved to him. Charles waved back as he stopped behind the hotel van, parked, and came down with the three men. They walked to where Mr. Aina was standing and he shook hands with each of them. Mr. Aina recognized Fredrick Adekunle and John Osawe. He did not recognize the new man who came with them.

Charles quietly came forward and introduced the new man as Segun Adio.

Mr. Aina watched as Charles left for the hotel with the men, thinking of how lovely he looked in the tropical suit he was wearing, and approving of the quiet and sociable ways that always characterized his presence at the hotel. To him, Charles was debonair, altruistic, and formed part of the people who had been providing for the upkeep of the hotel. Ten minutes later, Wale Adebo and Olu Abiodum, the two crewmen who were the backbone of Charles's sea operations arrived in a taxi. They walked past the guard who was trying to clean the dirty spot on his beret cap when they passed, missing Mr. Aina who had just driven out in his car. Wale was wearing a blue sweater over a tight jean. He was a little above average in height with a broad inviting face. Olu was wearing a plain blue shirt over a black baggy trouser, and the shadow of his tall figure followed him as he mounted the steps and walked to the side entrance of the hotel.

The table was already set before the two men came inside, and as they joined the other four, they formed a circle of six as they sat around the large table. The suite they were in was at the upper floor of the hotel building. It consisted of two bedrooms, a living room where the six men were sitting, a bathroom with a toilet, and a kitchen. One of the bedrooms housed all sorts of smuggled gems and the other provided a sleeping nest for Charles whenever he's overworked.

The atmosphere in the living room seemed lively as the men exchanged greetings, broke and parted jokes, and chatted with the new face among them as if he had been with them for years. Two waiters came in, each with a tray of cups and drinks. They emptied the contents of the trays on the large table and left the room. Charles selected a cigarette from a pack of Benson and Hedges on the table, lit it and began to smoke. Each of the other men followed suit, and as they did, Charles assessed each of them in turn. He thought they looked good enough to handle a group of untrained rioters, some scamps, or a set of trouble-finding wastrels. After smoking for a while he touched off his cigarette on the ashtray, relaxed comfortably on the chair.

"Well, gentlemen, let get down to business," he said sarcastically.

The other men looked at him inquiringly, some letting out smoke from their mouths and nostrils, some sipping their drinks as they waited for him to break the silence that followed. Charles explored the pocket of his waistcoat and brought out his diary without delay. He opened it and removed the letter that was folded between the pages. With steady fingers, he unfolded and straightened the paper.

"This letter was posted to me last Friday, but I received it when I visited the office on Saturday," Charles said. He paused for a moment, and then continued, "How it got to the office so fast surprised me. Maybe someone just walked to the building and dropped it in the box, I don't know. Because of its importance, I've decided that it should be our center of discussion today. I'll ask some questions. Then later, we can all air our views about it."

He steadied the letter and read the contents, and then he passed the letter to each of the men to read.

"Here we are, and that's the news that came over the weekend," Charles sighed, satisfied that each person had read the letter. "My question is this: I want every one of you to examine your past or present associations and see if you know or once come across a business or an organization known as 'Better than Pirate Associates.' Try to recollect if you have ever seen the skeleton logo somewhere. It might be in a party, a club, a guest house, a hotel or any type of social gathering you've once attended. Probably when you were there, you talked too much or got carried away about the kind of things you do."

About one minute of silence elapsed after Charles had spoken.

"As far as I am concerned, the writer of this letter should not be taken seriously," Fred said a little upset. "It could have been written by some stupid and irresponsible fools who have nothing good to occupy their time, and who out of jealousy, are finding a way to distract our attention from our jobs. I don't think the letter is as serious as to allow it to waste the precious time we should have spent on other important issues. Anyone who has anything against our business should come here and tell us. Anything out of that is null and void. I don't think we should reply the letter."

"Excuse me, gentlemen," Wale said. "As of now, I believe we are still safe and protected. If we reply this letter that will bring us face to face with those we may not like to meet. Such people may use our reply as evidence against us. The letter is threatening, so I won't suggest we go out and meet people who have decided to make themselves known through this kind of gimmick. Such people might be nothing but killers. Assuming we didn't see the letter, it will still mean the same thing. So I share the same opinion with Fred that we shouldn't reply to the letter. We should be prepared to damn the consequences. Whoever is behind it should come out and talk to us if there is anything important to say."

"Apart from the six of us here, does anyone else know about this suite in the hotel?" Segun asked looking at Charles.

"Nobody else," Charles said, looking at him inquiringly.

"Could any of the hotel staff have passed out a word?"

"Passed word about what kind of stuff?" Charles asked interrogatively.

"About your business."

"Not a chance," Charles said. "All our goods are carefully stored in well locked safes, and besides there is a wire alarm that would upset the whole hotel if someone entered here illegally."

"So the possibility of obtaining any information about this place is ruled out," Segun said.

"I think that's why he sent the letter to the office."

"So if he goes to the police we can lock up this place and declare the office as our legitimate place of occupation."

"Sure. I have enough documents there to convince a jury about that."

"Then we don't need to bother our heads about the letter," Segun said.

"We can as well fold our hands and allow the writer to make the next move," John added.

"I support that idea," Wale said.

"So what you are all saying is that the letter should not be replied," Charles said, looking at the men.

"Is better we wait and see if the writer has the guts to go to the police," John said, "I am sure he'd end up behind the bars for giving false information if he did."

"Okay, let's wait and see," Charles said, relaxing back on his seat.

Although that was what he said aloud, he wasn't satisfied. As he sat on the sofa, he was thinking this business belonged to him. If it collapsed, all these men would go. But for him, he had nowhere to go. This was the business he had grown to know. To undermine anything that was likely to liquidate it was to stultify his life.

An unfortunate incident had happened two years ago when Charles lost his brother in the police force. His brother was gunned down while raiding the house of a sadist drug lord. He was shot twelve times without chance of survival. It was a tragic and terrible loss that took his family months to recover. Soon afterward he lost his parents to old age. Since the death of his brother, he had lost contact with most of his police friends. He wished he were alive now. He would have relegated the whole job to him without showing the letter to anyone. He wouldn't have spent a penny, and his brother would have solved the riddle without much relevant details. The few people he knew in the police force now were too corrupt to be confronted with this type of affair. In order to protect what he had spent years building he would have to reply the letter and propose a suitable place to meet the writer. He told himself he would choose one of his friends' local hotels and arrange for the meeting in the daylight. He would tackle the problem alone and informs nobody; not even Bola, his best friend. He would meet the writer and found what this is all about.

"Sir," Wale said, "We haven't got our fake papers for the Friday stuff.

Almost immediately, the words brought him back from his private thoughts to his field of notorious activities.

"That's ready," he said. "I got them when I was coming from the office on Saturday. They are here with me."

"John," Fred said, "where is the map of the area we sketched last week."

"It's here with me," John said, loosening a button on his jacket, and bringing out a folded sheet of paper on which about seven different routes to smuggle goods via the northern border of the city was sketched.

Fred got the map from him and spread it on the table.

The six men discussed and planned their schedule for the first land and sea operations of the month.

CHAPTER 7

The Night Garden hotel at Surulere was one of the few hotels Charles seldom visited. Like a few others, business had brought him there when the hotel manager, who was one of his best customers, had suggested his hotel as where they could meet to discuss the possibility of buying some of his merchandize. He had gone there, and liked what he saw. The hotel had well furnished rooms.

"In case you may need a room for anything private," the manager had said, "you are welcome here anytime."

Charles had acknowledged the gesture. He had visited the hotel about two or three times later and had a pleasant taste of the hotel services. Now that he had an unwelcome proposition he neither wanted to discuss in his house nor at the Hotel de executive, he was glad he knew the manager.

After his last meeting with his men at Hotel de Executive, he had dispatched the men to their various assignments, leaving them to go away with what they've agreed on. Later in the day, when he had decided on what to do, he had driven to the Night Garden hotel, met the manager, and booked a room in advance. On the day after, he replied the letter, proposed a time and a date and quoted the number of the room he booked at the hotel for the meeting.

As usual, the operation at the end of the week was successful. The effectiveness of his men on their jobs appeared to ease his tension and anxiety about the letter. Bola appeared to be satisfied with what he told him on the outcome of the meeting he had with the boys, but often, he would ask if there had been any other development about the letter whenever he telephoned him. He wished he shouldn't question him about the letter any more, and felt all would well as soon as he met the writer of the letter.

It was 10.00 o'clock Saturday morning. Charles took a taxi and went to the Night Garden hotel. He had avoided going in his own car, thinking it would be risky if the person, he was going to meet decided to follow him after the meeting. He thought that with the seemingly free flow of traffic that usually characterized weekends in the city, it would take him about 30 minutes from his home to reach the hotel. He had left his home an hour early, hoping to reach his destination 30 minutes earlier than his guest. Unfortunately, he was held up in a traffic jam that protracted his journey by 20 minutes.

At exactly ten minutes to eleven, Hercules spotted a man dressed in a black three-piece suit alighted from a taxi from his hiding. He immediately concluded that this was the man he was looking for. The large probing eyes, the pointed nose, the broad face and the stalwart figure matched the features Bob had given him. He had decided to spy on Charles after Bob said the man was always wearing expensive jewels. He was expecting to see Charles in a flying toga with gold roped round his neck, but the person he was looking was oppositely dressed. Maybe he preferred keeping his gold at home, he thought regrettably as he watched Charles heading towards the hotel's entrance door. Apart from his private obsession with gold, Hercules had been specially assigned for this job because he was regarded as the club's spy man. To observe someone from a distance and then tail unknowingly was a thing he considered his natural talent. He considered his selection to follow Charles a blessing and he was prepared to carry it out with utmost efficiency. Pappy had told him that it was essentially important to know where Charles was living. He said without that, they couldn't possibly hang on him. While the reply of the letter Bob had drafted to Charles was being awaited, Hercules had made two futile attempts to spot Charles at his office. During these periods, Charles didn't come to the office, and Hercules had reported back that he couldn't see anybody matching Charles's description in all the lengthy hours he had spent studying the people coming and going out of the building.

Pappy knew if Hercules couldn't spot Charles during those periods, and Bob insisted in keeping out of sight until they were able to track him down, then nobody would. He was glad when he saw Charles's reply to the letter they sent him and quickly assigned Hercules to take care of how his home was to be located on the day he proposed to meet them. The Felony Boys had no intention of having a face-to-face discussion with Charles. They wanted to do all their harm out of sight, as well as made him realize why he was being punished. They had vowed to do it, even if Charles was locked in a fortified military castle.

Today, Hercules was one-hour early. He had already sneaked through the Night Garden hotel entrance once unnoticed and had gone upstairs to make sure that the door of room 202, which Charles mentioned in his letter, was still locked. Looking at the hotel entrance door as it slid behind Charles, Hercules hesitated for a moment whether to follow him or not. He was peeping from a hole at the back of a disused old truck across the street. To his left, resting against the wall of a vacated shop was his motorcycle. Before crossing the road, he looked at it; saw nothing wrong the way it was packed then walked across the street to the hotel. He noted that there was a stairway after the entrance door that led quickly to the room. He reckoned Charles would take this; he walked past the stairway and headed down the passage that led to the bar. Except for a woman and two men who were drinking in one corner, the bar was empty.

Hercules walked past without looking at the people, passed through a row of pillars that supported the ceiling, and then turned to the corridor that separated the bar from the cleaning department. Facing the corridor was another stairway that led upstairs. Taking three stairs at a time, he ran up and entered the passage of the upper floor. As he stood doubting whether to walk down the length of the dimly lit passage, a door opened at the far end and a waiter came out with an empty tray. The waiter closed the door and headed towards him. The waiter was a young boy of about 18 years old, and as his eyes traveled down the passage, Hercules changed his position and took slow inquiring steps towards him.

"Morning," Hercules said to the boy as he came within reach.

"Good Morning, sir," the boy replied politely.

"I understand the manager is in one of the rooms here," he lied, "could you show me which?"

"The manager no dey stay in any of the rooms here," the boy replied in Pidgin English, "his office dey downstairs and he no dey come today."

"You want tell me say no be him room you comot now?" Hercules said, grinning slightly.

"You mean room 202, that one wey dey down there," the boy said, surprisingly pointing back.

"Yes. Abi no be there you just comot?" Hercules said, concealing his gladness as the boy mentioned the room number.

"No," the boy said, shaking his head, "not at all. Na one of our customers' dey there and our catering manager sey make I go serve him."

"You mean dat man wey wear black oyinbo coat, wey I see dey enter now."

"Yes, dat na the man. Na him dey there."

"I think say na him be your manager."

"No sir. No be him," the boy said, ready to leave. "You fit come back for evening time, may be he for don come by then."

"Thank you," Hercules said, as he followed the boy downstairs. He allowed the boy to walk ahead and watched, as he turned left to the kitchen. He took to his right, walked past the drinking bar, and went out to where he had parked his motorcycle.

After the boy who brought his drinks had gone, Charles settled himself on one of the two large velvet sofas in the room. He selected a bottle of bitter lemon and mixed a little of its contents with the whisky on the stool beside his seat. He drank a mouth full, sat back on the sofa, and glanced round the room. He acknowledged its luxury; it was fine and exquisitely furnished. The air conditioner in it was almost noiseless and he viewed the radio and television sets as perfect. None of his colleague knew of this strange meeting he was having today.

Not even Bola Thompson, Charles's closest friend, who was always ready to share any of his misfortunes, knew about the meeting. Since they started their friendship, nothing in the secret of his business was hidden from Bola apart from the existence of the suite he was keeping at Hotel de Executive. To his friend, Bola, where he always met his men was either his office or any of the cabins around the port.

Charles knew Bola was plain and open-minded. He knew he was friend to be relied upon at any time. That was why he not only knew most of his business secrets, but went as far as knowing everything worth knowing about his private affairs. All the steps he had taken to rectify the childlessness of his two years old marriage with Shola were as plain to Bola as the nose on his face. Why he had kept back this meeting from him was because he knew for certain that he would prevent him from coming. That, he didn't want. He was prepared for the consequences of this meeting he wanted to have today. He knew he would be blamed for his foolishness if what things turned sour but he was ready and prepared to accept the blame. At least, he told himself, he had the right to fight anything that was trying to root out his business.

The time was fifteen minutes past eleven when he looked at his watch. The person he was waiting for was now fifteen minutes late. He wondered what the problem was. Probably he was delayed by traffic-jam, or he was finding it difficult to locate the hotel. He stood up and went to the window, and looked out. Unfortunately for Charles, the window was not facing the main street. Possibly, he could have seen Hercules crouching near the abandoned lorry across the street, smoking a cigarette. Instead, the walls of a building beside the hotel disturbed his view. He stared blankly at the adjacent building then quickly shut the window as the stench that was coming up from the gutter below the building reached him.

He waited impatiently for another fifteen minutes. He glanced at his watch and reached for to the telephone on the table. He dialed a number from the directory sheet that was struck with an adhesive tape on the wall above the cradle. It was the number of the hotel's staff room and the phone rang for about 20 seconds before it was answered. He asked for the porter, who came up two minutes later. He wasn't as neat as the boy who brought him the drinks, but looked presentable enough to bear his message. Charles introduced himself and asked if anybody had left a message for him before he came in.

"No," the porter replied, scratching his head.

"Have you noticed any strange person in this hotel today?" Charles asked uncertainly.

"None, except you, sir," The man replied, looking doubtful.

During the first time Hercules had come up, the porter wasn't on his seat. He was at the back of the hotel teasing a girl who was selling oranges. But he was right on his seat when Charles came in, and he ought to have seen Hercules when he came in later. But because he had trained his eyes to recognize only expensively dressed persons, he didn't pay any attention to Hercules when he sneaked in and went out through the side exit.

"I presume you are taking your job very lightly," Charles said frankly. "What about the woman and the two men who went to the bar when I was coming in."

"They are regular customers," the porter said, grinning. "They aren't strangers here."

Charles sighed.

"Hasn't the manager arrived yet?"

"He wouldn't be here until evening. He went out of town for a meeting."

"Okay, okay," Charles said, suddenly tired of everything. "You can go. I will see you downstairs before I leave."

After the porter had gone, Charles began to pace up and down the room.

"This is extraordinary," he said aloud. The whole thing was beginning to look like a foolish idea to him. What must have precluded the man from coming? He asked himself poignantly. If the writer of the letter was really serious, the person ought to have been here by now. He had heard of many trivial anonymous letters; some are blessed messages, some portending danger, and some revealing hidden information to the business owners or the government. Maybe this letter he was so fussy about belonged to one of these categories. As one of his men had said, someone trying to distract his attention from his business could have written the letter. If this wasn't a lunatic proposal, why couldn't the writer produce himself? As he thought of all this and several other things that came to his mind, the time dragged to noontime.

After waiting for another thirty minutes, during which he almost finished the glass of whisky besides him, it dawned on him that the writer of the letter wasn't coming. He regretted coming and hated himself for honoring the letter. He stood up, retouched his coat and then rang the hotel's staff room to report he was leaving.

A moment later, the boy who brought his drink appeared. As he entered and closed the door behind him, he noticed the disturbed expression on Charles's face. But since he had been trained not to interfere in the private affairs of their customers, he only came in and acknowledged his call. Charles handed him the key and left a message of thanks for the manager.

"Here is the bill, sir," The boy said as Charles reached the door.

He stared at the bill in surprise.

"Why is the amount on the bill so small?"

"The manager said we shouldn't collect any amount for the room if you didn't spend the night here," the boy said. "He also allowed twenty-five percent discount for your drinks."

"That is very generous of him," Charles said, grinning. He opened his coat and took out two hundred naira notes from his pocket.

"Pay the cashier," he said, giving the money to the boy. "And keep the change"

"Thank you, sir," The boy said, bowing his head as he took the money.

"Tell your master I'll be here to say hello sometime later. And thank him a lot for his generosity."

"Yes sir."

Later, when Charles was talking with the porter downstairs, he realized the man was a wrong choice for his position. He was sleeping on the bench when Charles got downstairs, and now as he was talking with him, he continued to yawn like a restless captive. Charles realized it was needless asking if he had seen anybody looking for him. He wanted to give him his business card and part his hand with some money, but looking at him as he stretched and winced like a cat just out of sleep, he concluded that such a gesture might do him more harm than good. He left the porter's desk and came out of the hotel.

Hercules saw him as he came out. He didn't change his position until he had flagged down a taxi. He registered the number on the cab's plate as he walked furtively to where his motorcycle was parked. He was on it in time, and he never lost sight of the cab until it had taken Charles home.

Eight days after Hercules had followed Charles home from the Night Garden hotel, he was around again. Right across the road, he watched his flat with concentrated animation. He was behind the front wall of the uncompleted building in front of Charles's house, the same place he stood when he recorded his findings about a week ago. Now, he was certain there were only two families occupying the building; one on the lower floor and the other on the upper. He took note of this the first time he came there and he was sure the man he was after occupied the upper flat. Again, his eyes ran over the brick walls that enclosed the building in the front, noting the mass of broken bottles that decorated their tops. He looked at the gate. That wouldn't be a problem he thought; just a rectangular arrangement of pointed bars fitted to a height of about five feet. The gate looked as if it was locked, but to whoever bothered to have a closer look, it was only latched with a hanging padlock. He wondered why the occupants of the flats should lock their gates even when at home. Since he got to his position about thirty minutes ago, he hadn't recorded any movement. There wasn't any noise in the building. He couldn't hear any music or catch the whispering voice of a radio or television set. He was a little uneasy. He wasn't sure if Charles was in. Time was fast going and he knew he had to find something to report before his men grew out of patience. He would have been much calmer if he was the only Felony boy around. But at this moment, he wasn't.

The architects of the whole plan were down somewhere in the street, waiting for his signal. Down the street, in a taxi parked in front of a road side mechanic shop were Pappy, Bob, Eddy and Rasheed. The taxi was one of the two cabs that fetched Dona weekly revenue apart from the money being realized from the club. Whether Dona likes it or not, whenever the Felony Boys had an important operation, they always operated in either of the taxis, changing their number plates and replacing them after their operations. Yesterday evening, Godwin, the driver of the taxi they brought here this morning, gave the key to Pappy when he demanded it after returning from his daily routine. To Godwin, Pappy was the boss, so whenever he demanded anything, it meant it had to be given without complaint.

Today, Eddy was behind the wheel of the yellow cab with its belt of black stripes. Rasheed was in the front passenger seat while Pappy and Bob sat in the back seat. All the four men had a wild burning grass in their hands as the smoke from their hemp curled out of the slightly opened car windows before disappearing into the blue sky. The four men seemed unruffled as they sat silently in the cab, waiting for Hercules to signal them into action. They sat there waiting for two things and they were prepared to wait until the sun set. Hercules had told them there were only two families living in the building. They knew it was customary for families to go out and visit friends on Sundays in Lagos. They were either waiting for Charles to come out; hoping to follow him and track him down before he reached wherever he was going, or waiting in the hope that the family in the lower floor would leave on errand and then they would have the chance to move in and attacked him. If none of their first plan came as anticipated, then they were prepared to burgle the whole flat later at night and gave Charles a show down.

Pappy preferred the daylight operation. It always aroused him; providing him with some sort of personal enjoyment and satisfying his inexplicable sadistic appetite. He was more than confident on his thick hefty hands and his martial art skills. Pappy believed he could send a dozen of policemen with batons in hands to their graves. He had been told a dozen times that that he was brutal. He knew it and loved it that way. If brutality was the only way he could live and be successful, he was prepared to exercise it. He felt no guilt of conscience for the operation they were about to perform. To him, it was simply another job and it had to be carried out without failure. Charles, or whatever his name was, had simply crossed the path of the Felony Boys. Going by what Bob had told them, he had been merciless when he sent him to the prison and so they had to be merciless in dealing with him. He was confident Charles couldn't get away from the moment they started on him. He was now like a rat in a hole in the hands of the Felony Boys.

Pappy was calm and confident as he sat there smoking, considering each thought that came on his mind with shameless boldness. After a while, he sat bolt upright and looked at his watch. He noted without regret that they've spent an hour without any message from Hercules. That didn't worry him. He knew if he didn't talk, the other men in the cab wouldn't. Hercules was his second best and he never doubted his efficiency. He knew whenever he appeared; he would come with something worthwhile. Stretching his neck a little, he looked past the front windscreen into the open street. Hercules's motorcycle was just a few yards from them. He hadn't come with them in the taxi. Instead, he had allowed the men to follow him, tracing his way to the place and pointing to the building he was going as they got there. With the men around, he had casually parked his motorcycle on a nearby curb, knowing fully well that whoever attempted to tamper with it, would be burnt alive.

After surveying the road in front for a brief moment, Pappy turned his eyes to the motorcycle. Snatched with no certified documents and no genuine license number, Hercules had been using it for now for almost a year without trouble. He chuckled, as he looked at the faked faded number plate at its back and relaxed back on the seat to light another wrap of hemp.

At this particular moment, Hercules saw a man and a woman came out of the building he had been watching for the past hour. He recognized the man immediately. It was Charles, and the woman was clinging to him as if something would soon take him away from her. He guessed the woman must be his wife. The woman released him as he bent to open the car door in front of the building. Within that brief moment, Hercules slide out of his hiding and walked hurriedly to where the taxi was waiting. Rasheed was the first to spot him and brought the men in the taxi to attention.

"Do you have any news?" He asked as Hercules came and peered into the cab.

"He's coming out now with a lady," he said in a whispering voice. "So while you go after him, I'll stay here and rummage over his place as planned."

"All right, we'll see you back at the club," Bob said.

"I trust you," Pappy said flatly. "That's why I'm leaving you in charge of that place. So make sure you come back to the club with plenty of good stuff."

"At your services unlimited," Hercules said jokingly. Out of the corners of his eyes, he saw a car reversed out of the building up the street. The car steadied on the road, moved forward slowly, and then geared up towards them. "That's him coming," he said.

"Is he the man inside the Peugeot with the woman?" Eddy asked.

"Yes. I reckon that must be his wife."

"Wait till they pass us," Bob said, looking at the approaching car.

Charles was oblivious of what was being planned against him as he went past the men and shot the car down the road. None of the men in the taxi looked at his direction as he went past.

"LA 4529 KXE." Eddy said, quoting the Peugeot's registration number and following its movement through the driving mirror.

"Have a nice time. Hercules said, backing away from the cab.

"Let's swing into action!" Pappy retorted.

From the driving mirror, Eddy noted that the traffic indicator light of Charles's car was pointing intermittently to the left at the junction down the street. With a deft hand, he pressed the gear lever down, moved it to the right and then back to the rear. In one swift movement, he released the clutch, reversed and circled the car as he went after Charles with a harsh, piercing sound.

Two minutes after his men had gone; Hercules was back in front of Charles's house. After watching the building for about five minutes, he was satisfied he could enter unnoticed. He sighed as he felt the bulging edge of the knife handle in his jacket, and brought out a handkerchief containing a set of keys. He checked the handkerchief, making sure the keys were tightly stacked before dropping it back to his pocket. He took out a pair of black leather gloves from another pocket on the jacket and slid them on his hands. He buttoned up his back pocket, moved out of where he was hiding, looked up and down the length of the deserted street and walked quickly across to the building's gate. He was up the gate within five seconds and jumped to the opposite side like a professional burglar. He landed on his toes noiselessly and moved hurriedly into the blind alley at the side of the building. There were two doors at the side of the building. He went past the first one, thinking the second should be meant for the people upstairs as he went to it. He pressed the door's handle, and to his surprise, the door clicked open. He closed the door silently behind him and climbed the flight of stairs facing him in two at a time.

The front door to the room upstairs was locked. Hercules brought out the handkerchief containing the set of keys from his pocket, untied it and began a preliminary test of each key on the lock. The third trial opened the door. Cautiously, he stepped into a carpeted passage with white walls. His eyes registered the rooms on each side of the walls as he came in. A door stood at the end of the hallway. He reckoned it must be the door to the living room as he advanced forward. He caught sight of the kitchen and paused to look at the fine collection of genuine hardware it contained. He went past the kitchen to the door of the living room. He successfully opened the door after the forth trial of his keys. He nearly fell on the rug that sank his boots as he entered. He closed the door, and then ran his eyes over the widely extended room. The room was expensively furnished, neat and finely decorated. He was so impressed by all the fine collection of artwork on the walls that he didn't know where to start. However, he reminded himself he was here only for expensive jewels and brilliant diamonds. Somewhere in this house must be those materials. He had to be fast and check every corner to make sure he got what he wanted. He unbuttoned his jacket and brought out a medium sized handbag from an inner pocket. He began to walk around.

On a table in one corner of the room was a small golden carve of an elephant. It was typical of those found in the museum. He went to the table, picked it up, and dropped it in the bag. He looked around again. This time his eyes caught a rope of gold wrapped around a hanging photograph of Charles on the wall. He climbed the sofa below the photograph, removed the gold chain and tossed it into the bag on his hands. On a pile of records on top of the stereo set in the room was an envelope. Hercules went to the set, picked up the unsealed envelope and looked inside. Two shining diamond finger rings reflected on his eyes as he stared inside. He smiled as he dropped the envelope into the leather case, and then looked up again. Facing him as he did was a large mirror. Hercules stared at the mirror, and was taken back by the blue transparent curtain that reflected behind his own his image. He turned back quickly and stared at the curtain. Its color was completely blended with the paint on the walls with a length that screened the door behind it. Whoever didn't look well wouldn't know the door was there. Hercules went to the curtain and drew it aside. He pressed the door's handle, but the door was intact. He tested all the keys he had with him on the lock; but none of them could open it. He bent down and peeped into the keyhole. A sudden idea came to his head. He checked his pockets and found a scarf-pin. He brought it out, straightens it, and inserted it into the keyhole. He screwed it to the left, back to the right, and then brought it out. He looked at the new shape, and then pushed it back into the keyhole. The door opened as soon as he flicked the pin. Facing him as he entered the room was an enormous bed with high posts. Beside the bed was a wardrobe. He opened it and rummaged through the stack of clothes inside. Finding nothing important, he went over to the cabinet and tried the handles. The two handles were firm and stiff. He thought of what to do. He had come across this type of cabinet somewhere in the past, but couldn't' remember where. He knew the cabinet could only be opened with special unduplicated keys and he had no such keys with him. He was certain the cabinet contained something important. Probably this was where Charles was keeping his diamonds and jewels. If he could open it, he told himself, he could make a fortune. He couldn't stand there all day staring at the cabinet without doing something.

He pulled up his jacket and reached for the knife on his trousers. He produced a short wooden knife and flicked the blade into view. He bent down and placed the tip of the knife on the screw below the cabinet handle. Within 60 seconds, he had loosened all the four screws on the handles. He pressed the handles without luck; it was as if he had done nothing. After a short hesitation, he went out of the room into the kitchen and came back with a short pestle and a cutlass. He was glad the kitchen provided the instruments he needed, and he grinned ruefully as he bent down again. He placed the cutlass on the base of one of the cabinet handles and then began to strike with the pestle. The cabinet handle he was striking did not move. He couldn't bear the noise from the hammering. He thought the noise could start something, and he knew if he had to break the handle, he had to strike harder. He was so annoyed he wanted to hammer the pestle with all his strength. After a second thought, he ran back to the kitchen, found a small towel, came back and wrapped it around the same cabinet's handle. He began to hammer on the cutlass with the pestle, striking a little harder when necessary. After a short while, the handle began to give way but with a tiny opening. If he had to try two handles, he guessed it could take him the whole day to break. He had already spent about ten minutes in the house, and he didn't want to stay any longer. Any more time would be damn too risky, he thought. He knew the Felony Boys were quick in liquidating their victims. By now, they might have done all they wanted with Charles and his wife, and if the police were quick to find out what had happened, they would be in the house any moment from now. What he had gathered in the house wasn't much, he thought, and he was sure the cabinet would fetch him all he needed. He suddenly wanted to damn it all. So he began to beat fiercely on the cutlass as he placed it on the handle of the cabinet, carrying the noise across the room into the whole building as he did.

Bassey Okogie woke up with a startle. He was the only occupant of the flat below. Fresh from London, he had just rented all the rooms on the ground floor, hoping to bring back his wife who was soon to finish her studies in United States of America. As far as he was concerned, the couple upstairs was far from the kind of noise that was now ringing bell in his ears. He had to cover his ears with his palms by the time he got out of bed. Wearing his pajamas, and dragging his legs into light feathery slippers, he came out of his flat, walked around to the door of the upper flat and mounted the stairs.

"Who is there?" He shouted as he reached the entrance door.

The beating stopped, but nobody answered. He entered into the passage, walked to the living room and shouted again but nobody answered. This time, he was sure somebody had unlawfully entered into the house. He heard a short, scraping sound of something dropping on the floor in a room adjacent to where he was standing. He looked at the direction, but instead of staying where he was, his curiosity overcame his reasoning. He stepped into the living room and gaped at all the tools on the floor.

Hercules saw a man coming and he quickly stepped behind the door. He peeped from the door's hinge and was in time to see the man stepping into the room. Without allowing the surprise that overtook Bassey's face to disappear, he smashed the door on his face with all his strength. Bassey crashed against the door and then went down senselessly. The building seemed to turn upside down on his face as he landed on the floor. Hercules came out from the back of the door and rammed the boots on his forehead. The boots made a deep cut on Bassey's brow, rushing blood to his face as he gave a faint horrifying sound. Hercules bent over his unconscious body and then dragged it aside. He looked wildly around for a cloth to clean the blood on the floor.

He was pulling off a shirt from Charles's wardrobe when he heard the noise of a car stopping in front of the building. The driver blew his horn three times before switching off the engine. He darted out and went to one of the windows in the living room to peep through the glasses. He was just in time to see a man removing the padlock and opened the gates. He went to another window and peeped at the alley below. The man was coming to the door of the flat upstairs. With a quick lightening movement, he went back to the room, picked up his knife, tied the handkerchief containing the keys, dropped them both into the bag and rushed out of the room into the passage. Mid-way between the hallways, he heard the sound of a short light movement on the stairs. He knew if he didn't walk fast and disappear in time, he would meet the man coming. That was what he wanted to avoid at all cost. He didn't want the police to find two bodies in the house. He ran to the door at the entrance of the stairs and hid himself behind it.

Charles' best friend, Bola Thompson, was whistling softly as he came in, lightening up his day with an imitation of the record he heard before switching off the radio in his car. He went past where Hercules was hiding unsuspicious and headed straight to the living room. He was still whistling when Hercules came out and bolted through the door. His paused lips and twisted tongue suddenly relaxed when he noticed the unusual silence in the room. Whenever he came in to his friend's house and saw the doors opened and the curtains flying, it was either the stereo was playing, or the Television was making some noise. None of these was happening. He wondered whether Charles and his wife were staging an afternoon romance.

"Hello friends!" He shouted, hoping to attract their attention as he entered the living room.

Nobody answered him.

He knew where to find Charles, so without caring to know whoever was with him, he went to the door behind the blue curtain and knocked. There was no answer. He drew the curtain aside and looked in. He almost collapsed when he saw the body on the ground. Panic stricken, and confused about what to do, he ran out of the building, crying for help as he darted out into the open street.

Chapter 8

Sediment of sweet African palm wine settled in a small circle at the bottom of the white glass on the table. The white liquid bubbled under the cardboard that covered it. Beside the glass of palm wine was a pile of record player albums. The photographs of the artists on the albums stood in clear imitation of what they had recorded. A turntable, a radio cassette, and a table fan, stood in that order beside the albums. Near the table was a large standing mirror. As Bisi Ajoye entered the room, the mirror reflected on the towel that ran over her breast into her armpit. She closed the door and then locked it from behind. She moved hurriedly to the long curtain that screened her bed from the remaining part of the room, drew it aside, entered into the small space behind the bed, put off her slippers, and closed the curtain as she came out. She untied the towel on her body and threw it over the curtain. Her nakedness unfolded the tight underwear on her buttocks and then went up to show the tip of the full breasts that stood straight on her flat chest. The breasts danced, sagged, and echoed the chorus of her movement as she walked to the table. She looked at the covered glass of palm wine and shivered. Somehow, she had not been able to defecate for the past three days. She had taken all the drugs she bought from the chemist without success. Only yesterday, a friend told her to drink two days old palm wine to rid her of the constipation.

Today, Bisi bought a bottle from a local bar and here on the table was a glass of palm wine from the bottle. A shrill of nervousness ran through her spine as she carried the glass and removed the cover. She closed her eyes and then drank the palm wine in a swill. She opened her eyes, sighed, and then dropped the glass on the table. She switched on the radio on the table and then turned the volume to pick the frequency of Radio Nigeria 2. The DJ's voice drifted out of the radio. He was spinning a record of Diana Ross, and she imitated the tone as she bent down to study her straight legs, fiddling with the nails on her toes with her long fingers. She looked at her ebony complexion as she stood up, marveling at the smoothness of her own beautiful body.

Everyman she had met said she was beautiful. That was what Fredrick Akintunde had said when he first met her. Without being told, she herself knew she was a mistress of beauty. All her friends confirmed it, and that was why Fred loved her, catered, and provided for her. If there was any man she loved, it was Fred. She felt him everywhere and right now, he was on her mind. Today was her birthday and she had planned to celebrate it with him. In less than 30 minutes from now, she expected to see him. She expected him to come in and give her his warm embrace. She had prepared everything they would take to the beach where they hoped to enjoy the day in company of Fred's boss and his wife. She liked the couple for their unpretending courteousness. Charles, she thought, was non-flamboyant, and Shola, his wife, was moderately competent in manners. They were a very likable couple. They minded their own business and never intruded in other people's affairs. They never allowed outsiders to interfere in their matrimonial disagreements and that was probably why they've been living very happily. As she paddled her neatly done hair with her hands, she prayed silently that she too would have a happy married life with Fred as his boss did with his wife.

Under the standing mirror beside the table was her box of cosmetics. She bent down and opened the box. For the next ten minutes she attended to her face with the make up and finished with her face neatly powdered, her brows faintly lined with a dark pencil, her lids covered with eye-shadow and her lips reddened with thick rouge. To give her lips a convenient set, she smacked them together in front of the mirror and smiled quietly to herself. She looked at her hair. It was still freshly dressed, as the hairdresser had done it yesterday; thickly flicked, clipped and shaved into fantastic patterns. Feeling contended, she turned away from the mirror and moved to the wardrobe in one corner of the room. From the stock of clothes inside, she selected a blouse and a pleated skirt with belt. She entered into the two clothes and fastened the belt. It fitted into her body well, and revealed the shape of her hips, as Fred always wanted it. From a small bowl in one corner of the wardrobe, she brought out a necklace, two diamond earrings, a pair of tennis bracelet and a 14k gold engagement ring. She entered her neck into the locket; put on all her jewelries, put on her shoes, and removed her handbag from the hook inside the wardrobe. She carried the handbag to the table, opened it, and took out a tiny comb and a cylinder of perfume. She trimmed the edge of her hair with the comb, dropped it back into the bag, and reached for the perfume. As she began to spray her body with the perfume, a tap came on the door. It was gentle and unmistakable, the tap of her fiancé. She dropped the perfume, moved with short quick steps to the door and unlocked it.

"Just in time, honey," she said as Fred confronted her with a wide smile.

"Some perfume," he said, winking an eye at her as he came in. "It smells good."

"It's all for you," she said, closing the door. She turned to look at his blue expensive coat.

"Some outfit," she remarked. That is a nice dress for this occasion?"

Fred didn't answer. He kept looking at her as she swayed past him; shaking her body as she went to the table.

"Good legs, high hips and a great body," he said.

"Do you mind telling me where you inherited those features?"

"For heaven's sake, will you stop that? Bisi cried, standing at akimbo as she turned to face him.

"Baby, I love you," Fred said, staring at her. "That's why I keep expressing my feelings about you."

"Honestly, you are sick in the head," she said and turned to face the mirror. She saw Fred's reflection as he came silently behind her, placed his hands on her shoulders and held tightly. Their eyes met in the mirror, and at that moment, they knew they both loved each other. They remained like that for about 30 seconds or so, and then Bisi turned to face him.

"It's time to go," she said slowly.

He resisted the temptation to kiss her.

"Are you fully prepared?" He asked, parting her shoulders,

"I am ready. Did you bring the swimming suit you promised?"

"Yes. It's in the car," Fred said. "We'll get the food and drinks we need at the beach hotel. We'll have a short get-together at the hotel with my boss and his wife, and then later, we shall go to the beach, rent a tent, and do some sight seeing."

"That's alright," Bisi said, picking up her handbag. "Our guests must be on their way by now."

"Sure," Fred said, looking at his wristwatch. "We have less than an hour to meet them. Let's go."

Fiddling with the bunch of keys on his hand, he held her hand as he started for the door.

At a junction along the highway that ran to the Lagos Bar beach was a traffic box. A tall and lean policeman stood inside the traffic box, waving his gloved hands with imperious audacity, and frowning his long aggressive face occasionally at those stubborn motorists who like to beat the lines when ordered to stop. He hated the traffic behind him because the line of vehicles there seemed to be flowing endlessly. But since it was incumbent on him to do his job without being petulant, he could only conceal his grudge by waving them along in growing hastiness. As the traffic in front of him slowed down, he turned to face the one behind. Before his hands could travel up in a movement of upright lethargy, the first few cars in front were already in motion. It was at this time that Charles joined the queue. Almost immediately, a taxi drew up two cars behind him, following the suit as the other cars moved along. The four men in the taxi grinned happily and exchanged some meaningful glances as Charles and his wife passed the traffic cop and took to the beach.

Charles was least suspicious as the taxi slowed down and allowed him to find a parking spot. Twice on his way coming, this same taxi had gone past him in quick succession, and had dropped back after a while to keep track of his movement. Bisi's conversation during the drive had kept him unsuspicious, and besides, several cabs had fired past in unrefined recklessness as he kept half-driving, half-listening to his wife.

On the second turn along the road that ran to the beach was the signpost of the beach hotel. Charles drove past the signpost and turned slowly towards the hotel's entrance. The parking lot was already overcrowded. He looked wearily at the line of cars in front, hesitated for some seconds, and then maneuvered his car an inch away from the sidewalk until he found a suitable parking spot. The taxi that had been following him sped past and stopped some few feet up the road. It dropped some of its occupants and then drove rapidly away.

Charles's face lit up in a smug of smile as he spotted Fred's Volkswagen among the cars in the parking lot. He held his wife's hand, and led her towards the hotel. Several people were coming and passing as they moved along, some neatly dressed and some caring less about what they wear. He was unaware that they were being watched as they mounted the steps at the entrance of the hotel. Eventually, he got to the entrance door, pushed it open, stood aside for his wife to enter, and left the door to slide behind them. About a dozen or more couples stared lovingly at them as they came in and embraced Fred and his fiancée.

While Charles and his wife were meeting with their friends, Eddy arrived where his men were standing; having parked the car, making sure it's within easy reach of getaway.

"Have they gone in?" He asked, coming to stand beside Bob.

"We can't keep on standing here," Pappy said his face a little impious. "Get organized."

The side of the snack depot where the four men were standing provided a good view of the hotel's entrance. The depot stood across the road facing the hotel building, and right now, several people were lounging on the fine sand that surrounded it, cooling their raving appetite with sandwiches, peppered snails, smoked bush meat and canned beef. Although there were few benches around, most of the people preferred to sit on the soft sand, some gulping their beers to quench the thirst from the sun that came out early.

To avoid suspicion, Pappy and his men bought a can of beer each and then moved away from the people surrounding the depot. They sat on the ground a little away from a couple that was flipping sand at themselves. Pappy was wearing a T-shirt that revealed his muscular arms over jean trousers, Bob a purple flannel shirt over brown trousers, Eddy a sports shirt on a faded jeans, and Rasheed a safari suit in blue print. All except Bob revealed their neck chains.

"You are not taking your beer now," Pappy said, looking at Rasheed, "you are going inside that hotel to see what that man is doing with his wife. I want to know if he's alone or meeting some people. I don't see why this place should be flooded with so many cars.

"I've been thinking about that myself," Bob said.

"It's as if a conference is going on inside the hotel."

"Okay, Rasheed," Pappy said, "Go inside and see what's happening."

Rasheed stood up, dusted off his cloth and started for the hotel. He crossed the road, found his way between the parked cars, and trotted up the steps to the front door. Ten minutes later, he came back.

"Our man and his wife are having merriment with another couple," Rasheed said, sitting on the sand to face the three men. "I heard them saying something about going to the beach after leaving the hotel."

"How is the other couple like?" Bob asked.

"Not tough looking, but gorgeous as our man and his wife."

"Did you say you heard them saying something about going to the beach?" Pappy asked.

"Sure. That's what I picked before I left them."

"I think our problem is half-solved," Pappy said, throwing off the empty can on his hand.

"Eddy, this is where your assignment starts. I think one of the reasons why the front of the hotel is full of many cars is because some people prefer leaving their cars there and trekking to the beach. I've seen about four or five couples doing that just before Rasheed came back. And that's what I think our man is going to do if he's leaving for the beach. So, Eddy, what you are going to do is to stay here and take his car to the club as soon as he left. I don't want him to leave here in that car," he paused and brought out a set of master keys from his pocket. He tossed it to Eddy who stopped the clattering noise with a quick catch. "The first three keys on that bunch can open any brand of Peugeot car. It's important the car gets to the club. So as soon as he came out and left for the beach we'll follow him and leave you to take care of the car.

"Assuming the other couple follows them," Eddy said, looking at Pappy. "How are you going to take care of them?"

"You forget about that," Pappy said raucously. "Just take the car to the club and keep it safe."

"Alright, so long you come to the club with good news," Eddy said.

They sat for twenty long minutes, waiting for Charles and his wife to come out, but they didn't appear. Then Pappy decided he was going inside the hotel to see things for himself.

About two or three couples inside the hotel restaurant raised their heads to look at him as he stumped in. He headed straight to where the bartender was standing and leaned on the counter.

"Small bottle of stout," he said sharply.

The bartender shot a quick look at him and then disappeared behind the counter. Pappy inadvertently looked down the length of the restaurant and spotted Charles and his wife laughing in front of a man and a woman on the same table. Charles was sitting in a chair with his back turned to him. He wondered what he was saying that was so funny at that moment that kept making the people sitting with him laughing uncontrollably. He looked steadily at the man in his front and studied his handsome features with contempt. He couldn't see anything offensive in Fred's long face that carried a pointed nose, small sharp eyes and light flexible lips that, barely moved when he talked. The lady beside him was a beauty he would stop at nothing from snatching if he had the chance. He had stolen a good look at Charles's wife all the time they were running after them when they were coming, and as he looked at her now beside her husband, he thought she looked like an adored queen. He was still contemplating on how to get near them without compromising himself when the bartender touched his arm with the cold bottle of beer he ordered.

"You never see them before?" The man asked.

"See who!" He answered angrily. "Are lice crawling on your head?"

The man was so started by his reaction that he quickly apologized and backed away. He dropped the money for the beer he bought on the counter, hesitated for a moment and then moved inadvertently to where Charles and his friends were sitting.

A pillar stood next to Charles table. Pappy got to a vacant table next to the pillar, behind Charles. He drew back a chair stealthily, sat down, and opened the bottle of beer on his hands with his teeth.

"When are we leaving for the beach?" He heard Charles asking the man in front of him.

"Any moment from now," the man replied.

"Where are you going when you leave the beach?" Charles asked.

"I am taking Bisi to the National Theatre."

"What's on the screen today?" Shola asked.

"Black Shampoo," Bisi answered.

"We could as well go together. Couldn't we?" Shola asked Charles expectantly.

"You can go with them if you like," Charles said. "I am still going to see Bola and his wife tonight."

"I'll rather go with you. I'll like to see them myself," Shola said.

"That leaves room to hold my Bisi tight," Fred said.

The other burst out laughing.

"We'd better leave now," Charles said, emptying the remaining drink on his glass.

Hearing this, Pappy drank up his beer. Before Charles and those with him could settle their bills, he was out and darted across the road to where his gang was sitting.

"They are coming out any moment from now," Pappy said to his men. "And they are heading straight to the beach. Eddy, take care of the car. We are going after them."

"What about the other couple?" Eddy asked, a little irritable. "Are they going with them?"

"Hold your tongue!" Pappy bawled." Did I ever tell you I'm going to do something and fail? You better be careful, or else I'll leave the whole thing for you to handle."

"Forget about it. I don't mean to upset you," Eddy said as he tossed the cab key to Rasheed.

Pappy took a deep breath.

"He's not leaving here alive," he said coldly. "We've taken all the trouble to follow him here, and where he's now going is the best place we can lay our hands on him. So consider him dead."

Bob knew Pappy meant what he had just said. He knew now there was nothing Charles could do to escape from Pappy's brutal hands. The firm and positive look on Pappy's face this morning had now changed into a weird, frigid determination to attack and kill.

Inwardly, Bob was suddenly frenzied. He was delighted at the way Pappy was handling the operation. He wanted Charles dead as soon as possible. The two times he had caught his glimpse on their way coming had aggravated his desire to get his hands on his throat, and all he wanted now was to make him realize the harms he had done to him. Before Pappy killed him, he would like to bend over him and tell him why he was dying. Nothing except that would satisfy him.

But there was something Bob couldn't understand. Why had Pappy masterminded this job as if he was the one Charles had made to taste the scourge of prison humiliation. He had prefigured death or a return to prison if he was to do the job alone. He was prepared for whatever would have been the consequence. But now under the shield of the Felonys Boys, with Pappy craving as the leader, he thought there was nothing preventing him from running away if the job turned sour. From what he had gathered from the other boys, it was rare before Pappy took part in outside jobs. He preferred doing the planning and instructing the boys on how to carry it out. But whenever he took part, he always acted beyond pardon and carried out his part with natural cruelties. Bob couldn't purport what his full attention to this particular job meant. He was thinking this when Pappy was inside the hotel, listening to what Charles and his company were planning to do. And now that he was here before them, controlling what he was saying with determination, he suddenly felt they would get away with what they were about to do without risk of detection.

"Just one more thing," Pappy said to Eddy as he took a step away from them. "Don't speed too much on your way back, and make sure no cop is following you."

"No problem," Eddy said, looking at him. "You can always trust me to my jobs."

At that moment, the entrance door of the hotel opened and Charles came out with the other three. The four men stood motionless, looking at them as they found their ways between the cars in the parking lot. For a moment Pappy thought they were going away in their cars, but when Fred opened the front lid of the Volkswagen and brought out a rucksack, he was relieved when he handed it over to the woman with him. He watched Charles as he brought out a suitcase from his car checked the doors, and locked them.

Leaving Eddy to stare after them, the three men moved past a number of men and women sitting lazily around, and then joined those heading for the beach. They kept behind Charles and his company, walking unevenly among the people as they went, and thinking of the pandemonium that might break loose if they made any move at them.

Soon, the group arrived at the beach and took to different directions. Walking to the opposite side, the Felony Boys watched as Charles and the other three trudged to a tent, talked to the tent's attendant and then entered.

Five minutes or so after the Felony Boys have been waiting; Pappy pointed his forefinger toward the tent as he led the way.

While Pappy and his men were coming, Bisi was in the tent changing from her clothes to a swimming gown. Fred was already in his swimming shorts, looking at Charles and his wife as they lounged in one corner of the tent. The floor of the tent was covered with finely knitted mats and the space inside could occupy about five or six people at a time. Of the four pillows that lay on top of the mats, two rested against the upright pole that supported the tent in the center, and the other two lay scattered around. Unprepared for a swimming show, and ready for something else, Charles grabbed his wife, hitched her up and said, "Let's stroll around. We could buy some fish home from here."

"That's a good suggestion," Shola said, retouching her down to heels maxi dress worn over a green trouser.

"Aren't you swimming?" Fred asked, coming around.

"Maybe when we come back," Charles said.

"Don't mind him," Shola said. "He's afraid of water."

"That's a lie," Charles said. "You know for fact that none of you here can swim as I do."

"It's true. I'll take seventh where he comes first," Fred said, obviously remembering how his boss used to swim across the river with sheathed contrabands when his business was just growing.

"Okay Mr. Swimmer, I rest my case," Shola said.

"Hope you won't be long," Bisi said, covering her head with a tight fitting cap.

"We'll be back soon," Charles said, bowing out of the tent.

"Keep fit, my dear," Shola said, following her husband out.

If Charles had looked to his left, he would probably have been suspicious of the three powerfully built men who were walking toward the tent but suddenly stopped as he stepped out. Instead, he was looking directly at the three swimmers who were been cheered on by the spectators as they approach the shore with fierce, powerful strokes.

"Let's see who wins," he said, holding his wife on the arm and dragging her toward the sloping edge of the beach sand to the midst of the clapping crowd. A number of men in the crowd had pulled off their shoes and were holding them in their hands. They folded their trousers to the knees and allowed the surf to flee past their legs. The women and young girls clutched their dresses to the hips, grinning happily at the three men in the water. The man who was in the second position had suddenly overtaken the first and was swimming ahead with incredible speed. He disappeared as the billow embraced him, surfaced again, shot forward and came out of the water to the rowing crowd. A man held out his hand and gave him a warm handshake.

"That man is good," Shola remarked as she found her way out of the dispersing crowd, following Charles who took to the left and shuffled forward with his hands in the pockets. Chatting as they went, and glancing occasionally at the group of young children who were running to meet the waves, they were completely unaware of the danger that surrounded them. They walked towards the bollards of the fishermen at the far side.

Bob was no longer with his men. He had walked a few meters away from them when Charles and his wife came out of the tent. Although he had changed a lot in appearance since he had his quarrel with Charles, he still feared an immediate recognition should he spot him. Now, he was sitting beside a group of small children who were scooping holes on the sand, and he was glad when he saw Charles walking away to the opposite direction with his wife. He understood Rasheed's intention as he followed them immediately and stood up when he saw Pappy coming towards him.

"You hang around here and keep an eye on those two inside," Pappy said. "I am going after them. If anything happens, I'll let you know."

"Pappy," Bob said roughly, "I want to see him dying."

"As soon as I get the chance to strike him," Pappy said, grinning ruefully, "Rasheed will get in touch with you before he dies."

"Okay," Bob said, nodding his head.

Pappy took a few steps back, turned, and then walked hurriedly away from him. He paused to look at the entrance of the tent where Charles and his wife had come out. He couldn't make out anything as he glanced quickly at it and then walked past the remaining row of tents, wondering what the other couple was doing inside. He touched the sheath of the small dagger in his pocket, frisked at its sharp edge for a few seconds and then quickened his steps. A pretty but insipid young lady was paddling in the surf as he moved on. The girl winked at him, but he frowned back, forcing the girl to roll off her eyes.

About hundred yards or so from the hotel, some fishermen had just pulled up to the shore with their canoe. Charles and his wife were just getting there. Pappy stood watching, and then chuckled as Rasheed joined the group of customers, standing next to Charles as he began to peer at the contents of the canoe. At that moment, some of the fishermen were pushing back the women who surrounded the canoe. Most of the women clogged baskets to their arms, waiting anxiously for the deal to take off. Two of the oarsmen dragged out the net between the thwarts and exposed the fishes on the ground. One of them regarded Charles and his wife.

"Madam," the man said, beckoning to Shola. "Come take ya own."

A young girl with a dozen of nylon bags thrust one at her as she moved forward. She gave her a 50K coin, got the bag and then pointed at three big fishes lying at the feet of the man who called her.

"Bring twenty naira, madam," The man said.

As Shola opened her purse, thinking it was damn too cheap to haggle down, a girl in a nylon blouse tucked inside a cream trousers pushed past some of the people standing, and went to the fisherman. Almost everybody in the place turned to look at the girl. She was wearing an expensive diamond necklace that glittered as the sun reflected on it. The locket was so brilliant that one of the fishermen standing beside her pretentiously touched her neck. Charles too saw the necklace, and then the event that was to change his life began. The necklace at the girl's neck was an exact simile of the one he wanted to present to Bisi for her twenty-first birthday. He wanted to give her right here at the beach, for he had planned to leave earlier than expected. But it wasn't in the suitcase he brought here. It was right there at the back of his car in a small gift case, and he felt his mouth turned dry as he thought of the distance he had to walk before getting the necklace from the car.

After Charles and Shola left, Bisi and Fred hadn't left the tent. Bob was still outside, strutting around alongside the roaring sea and glancing occasionally at the entrance of the tent. Inside, Fred and Bisi sat together, hand in hand, and mouth to mouth. They had been like that for over five minutes. Bisi had loosened the buttons on her shoulders, allowing the swimming gown to expose her cupped breasts, and rubbing them gently against Fred's chest as she looked up at him.

"What do you think of me?" She asked as he released her lips.

"Without you," he said plainly," I am certain I can't live on this earth."

"Sure?" She asked, her eyes glowing.

"Honestly," he said, touching her soft cheeks.

"For me," she said, "you are my life and sunshine. Without you, I am spiritless."

He looked at her with unbridled admiration. "Honey," he said, "I think you are undoubtedly sensational."

"I Love you," she said. "Please take me in your arms."

He looked at her for a few seconds. She was sexually annoying. She drove him crazy. Caring not to hurt her, he gently lifted her up with half his strength. Taking a few steps forward, he carried her to one corner of the tent and lowered her gently on the mat. As he took hold of her breasts and pinched her nipples forcing her to give a soft moan, Shola bowed in with the bag of fish in hand.

CHAPTER 9

Pappy couldn't explain what was happening when he saw Charles heading to the hotel and his wife going back to the tent. He wondered whether he had been charmed and bewitched to enter their trap. He was concealing his view with another canoe that just came ashore, pretending to be looking out at the sea, but tensed and waiting anxiously as Rasheed came over.

"What's the matter?" Pappy asked.

"It seems he forgets something in the car and he's going back to take it," Rasheed said.

"Okay. Run fast and tell Bob what's happening. Tell him to get fast into the cab and wait there until I call him out. Then, you come back and keep close behind me."

Pappy stood there for some seconds, watching Rasheed as he walked hurriedly past Shola and ran with short quick steps towards Bob. He walked away cautiously from where he was standing and headed after Charles who was still shuffling on the sand as he moved toward the main road. After a minute or so, he saw him staring at the sand, bent down to pick up something, and then continued to move again. He increased his steps and after another minute, he saw Bob running across the street to where the taxi was parked. The cab was at the entrance of a dirt road about twenty yards from the hotel not too far from the highway entrance. He saw Bob slid behind the driving wheel. He looked to his left and saw Rasheed walking slowly and cunningly towards him.

By now, Charles was on the main road. From where he was, the parking lot of the hotel was visible and more visible was the sidewalk. The exact spot he had parked his car was empty. He stopped abruptly and stared again. Had his car been stolen or towed away by a patrol team? He asked himself, somewhat bewildered. The former seemed to be likely, when he remembered the alarming rate of car theft currently going on in the city. Then he turned his head and looked back to see if the car was somewhere around before he proceeded to the hotel. For a few second, he nearly stopped breathing. He stood still and remained horrified as he stared at the man coming towards him. The man was almost within reach and concealed on the puff of his jeans shirt was a short dagger. The man looked at him callously for some seconds, and then like a lightening movement, the blade of the dagger on his hand suddenly came into view.

Charles immediate reaction was to turn back, break into a run and shout for help. But a quick thought told him the man he was staring at was a professional killer. The man's three quick strides would throw him off the ground and the knife would enter his body in seconds. Charles knew the man had come for him and the only way to get away was to rely on his own wits. The terror that had paralyzed Charles was suddenly thrown into a desire to defend and save his own life.

Almost immediately, Pappy registered Charles intention. He grinned ruefully, showing the hostile expression he reserved for dangerous moments as he moved cautiously towards Charles.

Charles suddenly remembered the pebble stone he picked up from the ground on his way coming. The stone was still there, squashed between his clenched fist. Realizing the advantage of using it, he suddenly flung it with all his strength, aiming it at Pappy's head.

As if expecting it, Pappy ducked. The stone went past him with a terrible speed and struck Rasheed on the head.

Rasheed was coming back to join Pappy and was getting behind Pappy when he got hit. He went down screaming, clutching his head as he did.

Pappy didn't give a damn to what was happening behind him. He ran toward Charles, aiming the knife at his belly. Charles jumped aside and attempted to grasp Pappy's wrist. It was a bad jump. Pappy stopped his movement by flashing up his powerful arms. The dagger caught Charles below the left wrist and ripped his skin open. He felt the pain, but he was able to grab Pappy's wrists as he came towards him again with the knife. Pappy didn't realize Charles strength as he held his arms and forced the dagger to nose downward. He looked at him for a second as they struggle, then with his teeth clenched and all his neck muscles tightened, he used all his power, forced the knife to reverse direction and wrenched his hands free. Charles was startled, and before he could register his surprise, Pappy threw him a vicious kick that brought him to the ground. Then he stamped down a foot on his chest with uncontrolled fury as he lay with his back on the ground. Pappy stood still with the knife in hand, breathing heavily and glaring down at him. "You've come to the end of your road," he said and spat on his face.

"Let me go!" Charles cried, squirming on the ground.

"Go where! Shut up or I'll empty your bowel with this knife."

"You are crazy! What have I done to you?" Charles shouted, trying to throw off his leg.

"Make a noise again and I will bring out the bone in your forehead," Pappy said, bringing the knife down. He yelled at Bob to come over.

At this moment, Bob was helping Rasheed who has just regained his consciousness into the cab. He pushed him behind the wheel. "You better stay awake and keep your eye on the road." he said as he slammed the door and then ran over to where Pappy was standing over Charles with long strides.

"Did you say this man was responsible for your imprisonment?" Pappy asked, looking at Charles.

"Sure. He was the jinx," Bob said and moved closer. Then he raised his boot and kicked Charles viciously on the face. "You are a rotten idiot. You made me a jailer, didn't you? You remember me. Didn't you?" He kicked him again. "Five years ago, you did your worst. I was a victim of you and your brother's punishment. In your own capacity, and recklessness, you threw aside the law and did justice with your own hands. You cared less if I died, and nearly killed me in a show of power. You've forgotten I would come out of the prison, and fulfill my desire to revenge what you've done to me. Now, here you are, dying as I wish. The police will soon pick up your lifeless body and then we'll see how fast your brother will come and help you out."

As rapidly as he was speaking, Charles wasn't listening. As soon as Pappy had shouted Bob's name, he became fully aware that he was under the bondage of Better than pirates Associates. So he was still being haunted by that lunatic writer! He had thought the letter was a fake, but now he realized he was still being followed and shadowed by the nasty gang. How had they managed to follow him here? And how the hell had he been so foolishly unaware? He was still thinking about all this when Bob came and rammed his boot on his face. As his first few words echoed, the memories of his menacing speech before he was thrown into the prison returned. So it was Bobinson Okoye! The clever thief had merged with a brutal gang to avenge the punishment of his misdeeds. He remembered fully now how he had vowed that he would live to regret what he had done to him as he was being led away in handcuffs to the waiting police car. He shifted his eyes to the man beside him. He was brutal, vicious and repulsive. He knew the knife on his hand would soon sink to his body if he didn't act fast. He had started to feel the burning effect of the knife that had cut through his hand. Then all of a sudden, the distance noise of a police siren came into his ears. He saw Bob looked frightfully behind him, and Pappy turning his attention to the blaring noise.

"Pappy! Stick him now!" Bob shouted.

Within that few seconds, Charles pushed off Pappy's feet and kicked him violently with the tip of his shoe. Pappy staggered back and swore silently. As he regained balance, he rushed at Charles, aiming to pin him down with the knife. Charles rolled off the target as Pappy stabbed the floor with the sharp edge of the knife. The weight of the knife couldn't hold him and he fell forward to the ground, skipping the knife by an inch. Within seconds, the knife was on his hands again as he stood up to face Charles who was already on his feet.

Bob was so disturbed by the noise of the police siren that he didn't know what to do. He could hear the blaring siren of the police car that was speeding towards them. He looked across the street car as Rasheed blew the horn and swerved the car to a getaway standstill.

"Get fast into the car and leave!" Pappy suddenly barked. "I can't leave this man here! As long as he's alive, we are not safe!" Even as he was speaking, he didn't keep his eyes off Charles.

Bob darted across the road as Rasheed slammed the car into a sudden break. The noise off the tires was so much it startled both Pappy and Charles. For a moment Pappy thought the car had knocked off Bob, but when he saw him standing up from where he had flung himself across the road and then broke into a run towards the cab, he sighed. Before Pappy could compose himself, Charles took off, shouting and yelling for help as he ran frantically towards the hotel. Without caring for the consequence, Pappy started after him, jumping and striding with the dagger in hand like a loosed lunatic.

The pandemonium in front of the beach hotel was a little hectic. The people there were still cursing the driver of the car that had just sped past when a load of cops appeared in a police jeep with a flashing headlamp. The cops were a special squad of anti-riot policemen attached to Obalende police station. They were on a patrol routine when they ran into a car consisting of three bandits who were holding people at ransom at a nearby gas station. The men fled when they saw the police vehicle and since then it had been a ding-dong affair between them and the cops. As the three men in the car took dangerously to the road in front of the beach hotel, the driver of the police vehicle eased the gas pedal to a desired limit, swung to the road and headed after them. The people around the hotel took to different directions, thinking the cops had come to whisk off the undesirables. On the police vehicle, two tough looking policemen were leaning on the driver cabin with rifles in hands. Another four with rough and determined faces hung on the side rail. They all carried rifles and horsewhips, except the sergeant sitting beside the driver in front seat who was holding a double-barreled pistol.

As soon as the police driver moved up the road a little, the sergeant saw two men running towards them on the sidewalk. One of the men was holding a nasty looking knife as he was running after the other whose face was twitched in fear. He ordered the driver to stop, and before the vehicle could screech to a halt, the six policemen at the back were already on the ground. The sergeant jerked the door open, came down, ran forward a little and covered the two men coming with the gun.

"Get going and get those bastards," The sergeant barked, instructing his men to go after the bandits. "You and you," he said, pointing to two of the cops. "Stay behind."

The other four vaulted back into the jeep as the driver exchanged jeer, leaving the sergeant and two of them behind.

Charles was breathing heavily, looking at the policemen. Pappy stood still, looking stubbornly at the gun on the sergeant's hand. The two cops ran to where he was standing and one of them jerked off the knife on his hand. He looked past the sergeant into the perplexed faces of the people around as the two cops held him, then like a broken pendulum he swiveled around, wrenched his hands free, grabbed the two cops on the necks and smashed their heads together. The cops spun blindly around and crashed against the sergeant. As the sergeant staggered back, Pappy jumped forward, gave him a furious back hand blow and pushed him down. He ran past him and headed towards the hotel front door. The sergeant wobbled up and took two aimless shots at him. The bullets sped past his ears and splashed on the entrance door. Pappy swung himself at the door and roiled into the temporary safety of the deserted bar. He stood up quickly, leveled his back against the door post and waited anxiously for the sergeant to appear. The sergeant spun in with the gun in hand, but before he could know what was happening, a blow landed on his wrist and brought down the gun on his hand. Then Pappy held the officer's hands and threw him violently against some of the tables in the bar. The sergeant crashed on a set of chairs and tables and scattered the dishes on them. He watched helplessly as Pappy took his gun, ran down the length of the bar and disappeared in a corner. As he stood up awkwardly, the two cops outside darted in with sweats on their faces.

"Down there!" He snarled, pointing down the bar. "You're got to be careful. He has got my gun!" He looked at his swollen wrist with disbelief and then followed his men as they walked cautiously down the bar with their guns at alert.

In the dressing room beside the hotel's kitchen, Pappy looked at the gun on his hands. He studied it with stern admiration, his eyes taking note of the safety catch, the butt, the trigger, and the barrels. If he had been with this type of weapon, he thought, it wouldn't have taken him this kind of trouble to nail Charles. He suddenly realized the advantage of using the gun. All he had to do was just squeezed the trigger and the bullets would keep coming out, nailing his enemy the way he wanted. His thought was stopped short by a faint sound from one of the rooms in the passage. He had already bolted the door and he knew the men outside would be breaking in as soon as they realized the door was locked. He shoved the gun into his hip pocket and went silently to the window. With a deft of professional hand, he removed the first four panes above the window-sill, peered outside and noted excitedly that the ground below was an alley behind the hotel. He climbed out and lowered himself gently into the alley. He looked wearily at the low height of unprotected walls that guarded the alley. He heaved himself up, climb over, and jump to the safety of the other side. The policemen inside were still running in and out of the rooms in the hotel as he escaped from the hotel.

In front of the hotel, Charles was trembling like a leaf, holding his bleeding arm in a relentless clutch. A crowd of people gathered around him, peering at his wound with weary curiosity.

One of the hotel's male staff came out with a first-aid box. Five minutes of careful attention to Charles's wound saw the bleeding stopped and the arm bandaged with a sling around his neck. Charles sent the hotel staff to get his wife. He delivered his message just as Shola was beginning to wonder about what was keeping her husband away for so long. As Fred and Bisi ran into the tent to park their bags, she broke into a run and ran frantically to the hotel. Her shrilling noise as she shouted her husband's name turned the crowd to her direction. She stopped short in front of him, staring incredibly at his sight. "Oh good Lord," she cried. "What happened?"

"A devil of a man attacked me," Charles said, looking at her. "But thank god, the police came in time. I am alright now, darling."

She sighed. "Did he stab you?"

"Yes. He almost killed me before the police came. He ran into the hotel and they are in there looking for him."

She looked at the hotel and caught her breath at the sight of the battered entrance door.

"Did they shoot at him?"

"Yes. But he escaped from the shots and ran in."

"And they haven't got him out?"

"We are still waiting for them. I can't even find my car."

At that moment, Fred and Bisi ran to where they were standing breathlessly.

"What's the matter?" Fred asked, gaping at Charles.

"A guy who taught I had some money in my pockets attacked me," he lied, fearing of what might come over his wife if he told him the exact story.

"Why?" Fred asked a little disturbed. "He must be crazy."

"Yes, you need to see him. You'll know he's more than crazy," Charles said.

At that instant, the two young cops who had gone in with the sergeant came out and ran to the back of the hotel. The crowd dispersed again, and Charles moved nearer to the hotel with his people.

A moment later, the sergeant appeared with a disappointed face. Although defeated, he walked briskly to where Charles stood with the other three. Charles was expecting a half-dead Pappy in a blood-soaked cloth to be dragged out. But looking at the sergeant without his gun in hand as he approached them with an obvious look of disappointment, he felt the whole world was turning upside down.

"Excuse me, mister," the sergeant said, beckoning to Charles.

Charles moved away from the other three. "Where is he?" He asked the sergeant.

"I am afraid," the sergeant said unreservedly," he had long escaped before we discovered his outlet, but my men are still looking around to see if they can find him."

"And why did you come to me?" Charles said annoyingly.

"Can't you see I am helpless without my gun?"

"He took your gun?" Charles asked in disbelief. "Officer, are you telling me he snatched away your gun?"

"I am lucky he didn't break my neck."

"The entire police force won't forgive you for this," Charles said, steaming in annoyance.

Fred could no longer stand with the women. He came to join them." Is this where you are going to stay until he gets to where you can't find him. "He asked the sergeant peevishly.

"Look gentlemen," the sergeant said, a little disappointed, "we didn't anticipate all this. We were after those rogues in the car when you suddenly came on our way. I thought it was my duty to protect you when I saw that man running after you with that kind of knife. His attack was so fast and unexpected that my resolve to track him don cost me my gun. I admit he's tough, but that didn't mean he couldn't be caught. What I need now is some useful statement from you and then we shall embark on how to track him down.

Charles looked for some time at the face of man in front of him. Through utter carelessness, he thought, he allowed himself to be defeated and lost his gun. He now wanted a statement. He knew he would soon be facing his superiors and then he would have to explain how he was so reckless as to allow his gun to be snatched away by a rogue. This was something that could earn him his job and he had to find a way of talking himself out of it. Somehow, he thought, if the officer was willing to cooperate, he could give him a statement that would lessen his trouble.

Charles knew he was hard up against a sadistic killer who now has a gun. A nemesis that floored three policemen and escaped unhurt. Who knew where he was now hiding? Maybe he was somewhere around, aiming the gun at his head. He suddenly felt unsafe. He looked over his shoulder. Bisi and his wife were still standing behind them, clutching their hands on their chest. At the same time, the two cops who had run to the back of the hotel reappeared, hanging their guns loosely as they trudged towards them. It now dawn on him that Pappy had escaped. Suddenly, he felt deflated, tired and exhausted.

For the first time, he noted the burning effect of the wound on his hand. Then, leaving the two women to stare after them he went with Fred and the sergeant into the hotel. There on the chairs and tables of the deserted bar, he began a lengthy story of how it all started about five years ago.

The Obalende police station was only a fifteen minutes drive from the beach. It stood on the short route that forked left into Sand gross Market; depicting a clear view of the Criminal Bureau's building.

At the realm of duty this afternoon was Assistant Superintendent of police Idowu Abimbola. His grim inquiring face was staring at the page of the detective magazine on his hands when a knock came on the door of his office. Without shifting his eyes off the magazine, he answered the knock and then lowered the paper when Sergeant Adekunie Taiwo came in. His vast years of police work told him instantly that something was wrong as he looked at the sergeant.

As the sergeant was giving a half-salute, the telephone on the table began to ring. He scooped up the receiver, clamped it on his ear and listened.

"Good afternoon, Officer," A voice said in his ear.

"Yes, good afternoon. ASP Abimbola, speaking."

"This is Doctor Oladele Olawuyi, Lagos State General Hospital emergency unit."

"Yes, Doctor. Is there anything I can do for you?"

"Yes. I have a case here for you."

"Okay, speak on."

"I was on duty this afternoon when a man who identified himself as Mr Bola Thompson brought in an unconscious man in company of another colleague. He made a statement here that he had gone out to visit his friend when he saw the body of the patient on the floor of his friend's bedroom. His friend whom he called Charles Aduwo had gone out with his wife before he arrived there. He said he was left with no other alternative than to rush the patient here with the help of a neighbor. We've tried our possible best to rescue his critical condition which I must say is still about fifty percent chance of success. We've arranged for a specialist to come and examine his shrunken forehead and our final report will depend on what he finds out. The patient is not in any condition to be questioned at present, but if we are to go by what Mr. Thompson said, he must have been attacked by a burglar. We haven't seen Mr. Thompson since he went out an hour ago to search for his friend.

The other man who came with him is still here. His name is Mr. Clinton Udoh, an occupant of the house nest to where the incident occurred."

The ASP looked at the names of the people he had quickly jotted down during the course of the doctor's report. He observed that the name of the patient was not there.

"Doctor," he said into the phone, "what's the patient's name."

"Mr. Bassey Okogie."

"You said he was found on Charles Aduwo's house."

"That's right Inspector."

"Ex … cuse me, sir." the sergeant stammered out.

"What's it!" The ASP barked, covering the mouth piece with his thick hand.

"The name of the man you've just mentioned is the name of the person that waiting outside with his friends."

"Is that right?" The ASP asked a little surprise.

"Yes, sir."

The ASP removed his hand from the mouth-piece and said, "Doctor, I am sorry for the little delay. One of my men is just informing me that Mr Charles Aduwo is here."

"You mean the owner of the room where Mr. Bassey was found?"

"Yes."

"That's fantastic."

"Thanks for the report, Doctor. I wish Mr. Bassey a speedy recovery. We'll start investigation right away. Some of my men will be in your place any moment from now. Goodbye," he said and hung up.

Before the sergeant could begin his explanation, he ordered that Charles be brought in immediately. He was surprised to see his bandaged arm and dirty clothes as he came in with the sergeant.

"What's the meaning of all this?" He asked standing up to offer him a seat.

Charles sat down, looking crushed and spiritless.

Without allowing Charles to drain himself again with the full account of what had happened, the sergeant restated everything he told him at the beach hotel and then topped it with their encounter with Pappy. He had already told Charles he was prepared to take whatever was coming to him regarding the loss of his gun and defeat. So without holding anything back, he stated everything as it had happened.

The ASP listened to what the sergeant had said without interruption. He was furious at the way he handled the events at the beach hotel, and declared that unless the culprits were found and punished accordingly, he would be demoted to a constable for his utter carelessness. Then he unfolded what he had just received from the hospital to the two men. Charles was stupefied. He could only gape and yawn as he listened to the Inspector.

Put together, the ASP concluded, the whole event was a dramatic demonstration of cruelties by a group of criminal syndicate employed by Bob. He expressed his disagreement over the way Charles had handled the letter without informing the police and blamed him for destroying the letter rather than keeping it. Charles had put in his statement that he had destroyed the letter without any serious consideration. He didn't tell them he went to the Night Garden hotel to meet the writer of the letter and didn't tell them the letter mentioned anything unscrupulous about his business. He simply convinced the two men he was an importer and exporter of precious gems and after his short explanation of what he was doing for a living, the two men knew something good would be coming to them if they could help him out of his present difficulty. Whatever was coming, the ASP was determined not to show it. In a bid to arrest the exalting situation, he quickly arranged for a police Landover and three cops to carry Charles and his wife to the hospital, leaving Fred and his girlfriend to follow them in their Volkswagen car.

Having obtained Pappy's and Bob's descriptions, and the particulars of the stolen car, the ASP instructed a police rider to notify ail checking points. He obtained Charles's home address, gave it to the sergeant and sent him together with two other cops to his apartment.

Back in the police vehicle and faced with the threats of demotion, the sergeant began a systematic campaign of how to track down the Felony Boys.

Charles arrived at the state General Hospital in a doubtful state of mind. From what the ASP had told him, Bassey's fate now lay in the hands of the brain surgeon. To him, Bassey was such a kind hearted man that he wouldn't hurt a fly. How he had fallen into the burglar's hands surprised him. He staggered to a standstill as he entered the observation ward with one of the cops. A young attractive female nurse came to their aid and directed them to a row of plastic chairs arranged neatly in one corner of the ward.

Mr. Clinton Udoh, Charles' other neighbor, sat in one of the chairs, burying his head behind the newspaper on his hands. He waved the paper aside, looked up at the men coming towards him and recognized Charles. For a moment, he was unable to say anything as he stared at his bandaged arm and soiled clothes. Charles waved to him to keep off his surprise and then came to seat beside him. Mr. Udoh was still explaining how Bola had discovered Bassey in his room when two men in surgical gowns appeared from an inner room marked 'Treatment Room'. One of the men was short, bald and carried a round fleshy face. He was wearing a plain prescription glasses that made him looked like one of those cats on Christmas cards. The other man was fairly tall, slimly built with bushy hair. Charles watched the two men nodding approvingly to a point, and then the tall one turned and headed towards them.

A constable stood guard at the entrance to the treatment room. He stopped Charles and asked, "Are you from the Inspector's office?"

"If you mean officer Abimbola, yes, sir."

"Is that Mr. Charles?" The doctor asked, walking past the cop to where Charles was sitting. Charles stood up and shook hands with the doctor.

"How is he?" He asked expectantly.

"He's doing fine," the doctor said. "The Neurosurgeon says there is nothing to worry about. He'll live and be able to tell the story, but right now, he needs a little rest. I'll suggest you come and see him tomorrow."

"Thanks for your effort to save his life, Doctor," Charles said. "I am very grateful."

"You are welcome," the doctor said, grinning confidently. "The ASP told me just before you arrived over the phone about what happened to you and some of his men. He said all the incidents must have been carried out by the same group of men. Today must have been a terrible day for you."

"It is an Intolerable day indeed," Charles confirmed regretfully.

"How about your arm, I am sure you need a better treatment."

"I will like you to take a look at it, Doctor."

"Okay, let's see what we can do for you," the doctor called one of the nurses. Charles was still receiving treatment when Bola Thompson walked in, carrying a quiet and serious expression on his face as he joined the people in the observation ward.

CHAPTER 10

Around 2 A.M. on Monday morning, all the Felony Boys gathered in the strong room for an emergency meeting. Sitting on the basket chair below the window was Pappy. To his left on a plywood bench sat Bob, Eddy, Hercules and Sharafa, while Rasheed, Dele, Bello and Isiaka sat to his right on another bench. In that position, the nine men almost formed a straight line except for Pappy's chair that separated them. This quick meeting was necessitated as a result of the misfortunes that marred almost all their outings on Sunday. Before Pappy reappeared at the club around 7 P. M. on Sunday, almost every member of the Felony Boys thought he was already in the hands of the police.

Bob had informed the Felony Boys of the sudden appearance of the cops. He was utterly disturbed by the time he got to the club. Twice while coming, he nearly ran over two pedestrians as he drove in waves of ceaseless frustrations and anxiety. He wondered what would happen to him if Charles escaped from Pappy and what would happen to the Felony Boys if Pappy was caught by the police. He couldn't bring himself to any possible conclusion as he hated to think of the consequences. He arrived at the club with the factual instinct that Pappy was in terrible situation. As soon as he informed Eddy and Hercules of what was happening at the beach, Hercules brought out his motorcycle and Eddy climbed to the back as they drove rapidly to the beach. Two hours later, the two men had come back without Pappy.

There was confusion among the Felony Boys as the news spread that Pappy had been arrested. As if the whole of them were to be overtaken by the rumors, none of them thought of how to organize a search for him. They were only disturbed and wondering about what to do. The atmosphere was so charged that neither Hercules nor Eddy remembered to brief the rest about the outcome of their assignment. They were still wondering about their next line of action when they heard the shouts of Pappy's name outside the club. The hailing of his name by some of the boys lounging around brought out all the Felony Boys out immediately.

Later, Pappy told the gang how he got away from the cops, but he didn't tell them he now had the gun he got from the sergeant. He also listened to how Eddy and Hercules carried out their parts, but noted with dismay that only Eddy had been successful. He had carefully removed Charles car from the beach hotel, drove it to the club and hid it at the back of the club. Hercules's report had been marred by his encounter with the man who interrupted him in Charles's house. Pappy knew Hercules could be malicious when dealing with his assailant. He probably might have killed the man in his attempt to make him unconscious. Then there was Bob. His indecent language when Charles was lying there on the ground at the beach was the only motive so far the police could use in finding them. If there was anything the police were good in finding, it was an ex-convict. By now, Bob's photograph might probably have been with the press, and then they would be subjected to those probing and inquisitive stare that hung in the face of every cop in the street. Pappy knew they had to do something fast, and that was why he had called for this meeting.

The Felony Boys never played with any of their difficult moments. Though perpetrated by a group of hardened criminals, the gang believed that any mistake in operation committed by anyone of them must be collectively rectified. They believed that any mistake not properly taken care of could ruin their background. What seriously called for attention on their part was how to tackle an offense that could expose and raze their unbridled criminality. No matter the enormity of a mistake committed by any member, in as much as such a member was not caught during the operation, the mistake would be disregarded and a quick way evolved to forestall any arrest. In doing that, the Felony Boys had on several times fought openly with the police. Their local rivals, notably the local butchers, the district bus thugs, and other daring gangs always ended up with casualties of several wounded and many dead whenever they fought openly. Student riots, workers strike and a clash between the army and the civilians were never to be missed chances to ransack and terrorize the local inhabitants by the Felony Boys and other local common criminals. These flagrant and astonishing violations of the rule of peace, done and carried out with relative impunity, had turned them into a feared and dreaded gang. They are regarded as a group of people who enjoy in causing confusion without caring for the consequences. This was what they had become and what made the people and the police in the area feared them.

Sitting together in their so called strong room with a common view to deliver them from the danger that now seemed to envelope them, the whole men looked frigid and mean. They sat there with their hungry and hard-bitten faces, each of them with a roll of dried hemp in hand. The hemps hung loosely between their fingers, burning and nesting in the gloomy effrontery of the dimly-lit room. They called it 'kukuye'. Pappy had just lit his own. He dragged deeply, feeling a tickling beat in the muscle of his neck and allowing the smoke to cram the funnel of his breathing pipe, pushing down his rib cage, his stomach and the contents of his bowel as far as they could go. He felt his guts rise as he released his twisted jaw, gripped the burning grass again with his stained teeth and sucked hard at it. He breathed in as the smoke drift into him and swallowed his saliva. He looked at the burning stick as the ash burned closely to his fingers, looked up, swallowed the smoke, swallowed it again and sighed. Two glittering eyeballs flicked out as his eyes came into focus. He stared emptily for some seconds and then with a foot stamp, he killed the stump of the weed on the floor.

The rest of the men were still smoking their joints. As soon as Pappy had finished, they all took a quick long drags, breathed in short hasty inhalations and extinguished their sticks. None of them noticed the bulging edge of the gun concealed in Pappy's trousers. As each of the men looked up and gave him an expressionless stare, Pappy suddenly leaned back on his seat and drew out the double-barreled gun.

"Don't move," he shouted, pointing the gun at the rest.

All the men stared at the sight of the gun woodenly. It appeared as if none of them had ever been thrown into such bewilderment at the sight of such a dangerous looking gun. Pappy took a stock of their perplexity, and then he dropped the gun and burst into a reckless laughter. "So none of you guys want to die," he said, still laughing mockingly.

"Suppose you tell us where you got it," Hercules said, looking at him.

Pappy was still laughing, but realizing he was undermining their present situation, he suddenly frown his face and said raucously, "I snatched it from a careless police sergeant."

"How and where?" Eddy cut in.

"At the beach, but don't ask me how I did it," Pappy said, sitting back on the chair. "Eddy, suppose you bring out what you found in the car."

The men turned to look at Eddy, but Rasheed didn't. He wasn't in a good mood because of his aching head. His forehead was stuck with a plaster at the exact point the stone had hit him. He was edgy and irritable and all he wanted not was a soft bed where he could relax and sleep till the dawn came.

Eddy took up a swollen paper bag from his lap and emptied its contents on the desk. An identity card, a business card, a toy dog, a briefcase, and a folded paper tucked in a blue envelope were orderly arranged on the bench with his short and thick fingers. Pappy looked at what lay on the bench without interest.

"Why did you bring that thing here?" He said, pointing to the toy dog that was jerking its head on the desk.

"Because it's one of those little things that can give us away if left in the car," Pappy nodded.

"What's in that case?" He asked feebly.

"I haven't opened it yet," Eddy lied,

"Then open it and let's see."

Eddy had already opened the case when he saw it at the back of the car. He had been greatly impressed when he saw the diamond necklace in it, but he didn't want to show how happy he was until the men saw it. He opened the case and brought out the necklace. The men chuckled as Pappy got it from him and examined it closely. The collar had several diamond dots that sparkled when shaken.

"Did you find anything like this?" Pappy asked Hercules, dangling the diamond chain in his hand.

Hercules opened the leather case on his hands, and brought what he stole from Charles's house. He arranged the small golden carved elephant, the gold necklace, and the pair of diamond finger-rings evenly on the desk.

All the men continued to smile as they examined the jewelry in turn.

"Dele," Pappy said, looking at the necklaces, "How much do you think all these will give us."

Dele, the D. J. for the club, was also the salesman for all snatched and stolen articles. He was an expert in underhand dealings and he knew the worth of every jewel in the black market. He brushed his hair to the back with his palm in a moment of hesitation and said, "The diamond finger-rings will fetch us around N350, 000.00, the necklace around N600, 000.00 and the elephant decoration about N50, 000.00. That gold is about three quarter of a foot. I am sure it will earn us about N150, 000.00."

"That means we should expect around N1.15million," Bob said.

"That's good," Hercules said. "We did go out for something."

Pappy picked up the jewels and tossed them one at a time to Dele. "That settles there," he said. "What about those cards and the envelope."

"These two cards are not important to us," Eddy said, picking up the identity card and the business card. "But I am sure the letter in the envelope will certainly interest us."

The identity card contained Charles's photograph and it bore the same name and address as that on the business card.

"Leave the letter alone for the meantime," Pappy said flatly. He sat upright in the chair, then after a moment silent, he said, "I presume we are all now aware that the Lagos State Police is out for us," he paused, not looking at the men. "Those cops I attacked at the beach now know what I look like, and without doubt, Charles would have told them who Bob is. We must now assume that they will connect both of us with what happened at Charles's house and also match us with his stolen car. All these will tell them a gang is operating, and that will increase their search for us. So far, the only lead they have now is the fact that Bob is out of prison, and he's desperately looking for Charles. They don't know he's here, but they'll keep looking for him. So, sooner or later, we are bound to see some strange faces in this club, looking for information about us. So our first assignment is to be on our guards and be battle ready. We'll stay alert to police approach. While the rest of you are out preventing any form of interrogation in this joint, Bob and myself will have to stay under cover, doing most of our jobs up here. That didn't mean I am calling off this operation, but under the present condition, Charles will be given some breathing space. It will take a little time before we get him. No matter the amount of protection he now has, we must get him. But right now, the most important thing is our next move. We must be very careful about it. This is an operation we mustn't rush. It is important Charles is dead, and it is important we succeed. How we are going to succeed is why I need a little time. Meanwhile, if any of you have any suggestion to offer, this is the right time to table it because once I've made up my mind nobody is changing it."

Eddy moved to the edge of the bench and said, "Our gang is noted around here for brutal dealings. I am positive the police can't just break in here like a smuggling store and say they are looking for some guys we didn't know. Those of them around here knew what they realized from the director, so they would be careful about the way they come here. We've dealt with inquisitive cops before and we still know how to deal with them. If they suddenly become dangerous and come here like a dog without owner, we'll show them who we are. All I know is that we mustn't leave Charles entirely alone because as long as he's alive, we are not safe."

As long as he's alive, we are not safe! These same words Eddy had just uttered, Pappy was thinking, were the same words he uttered when he was fighting Charles at the beach. The words suddenly echoed and rebounded in his ears, drifting in with fierce urgency.

"That son of a bitch had been too lucky?" Pappy suddenly shouted, ramming the desk with a clenched fist. "He mustn't be given a second chance. He was lucky that those bastards arrived in time. Now I want him before the end of this week. He mustn't be allowed to live longer than that. When I mean I want him, the Felony Boys want him, the coffin wants him, and the grave wants him. I must get my hands at him even if the whole policemen in the city are now guarding him."

They all knew him better than to talk whenever he was at the vertex of his fury. He stood up and began to pace up and down the room, speaking to himself as he did. He soon stopped, and as he was coming back, his eyes caught the envelope on the desk. He tore it open, took out the letter and threw it to Eddy.

"Let's hear the contents," he said, sitting down.

Eddy unfolded the letter and handed it to Bob.

"You read it," he said without looking at him, "I have a bitter pronunciation."

Bob spread out the letter, peered at the content and read out the following:

'Sir: All arrangements about the diamond consignment have been completed. Mr. Akim really did a perfect job in getting the gem on board. As usual, we'll expect you to meet us around five o'clock of Friday afternoon at the kroon's junction. We expect a first class handling of this precious jewel as this is likely going to be our biggest take of the year.

Regards,
Wale and Olu.'

They all remained silent for a while, and then Pappy said, "When was it dated?"

Bob looked at the letter again.

"Addressed to Charles and dated last Saturday," he said.

"You mean three days ago."

"Yes," Bob said. He picked up the envelope on the table and looked at it.

"It must have been delivered to him by hand. This envelope has no stamp on it."

"That's good," Pappy said. "It means the operation will be carried out this Friday."

"Yes. That's what it means," Bob replied.

"Let's hear the contents again," Bob read the letter again.

"Looks tike sea smuggling stuff," Hercules said.

"The letter says 5 P.M. at the kroon's junction," Bob said. "Anyone guess what that means?"

"Kroon's junction!" Pappy suddenly shouted, jumping up from the chair.

"Don't tell us you don't know the place," Eddy said.

"Have I been dreaming?" Pappy said surprisingly. "Crazy, Judas. I know the place as I know the in and out of this club. That's where my father died some years ago."

"Tell us about it then." Hercules said, painting his face with a curious expression.

Some years back, Pappy's father had been a hard and reckless smuggler, feeding the Lagos market with lots of contrabands from both inland and sea. He was so versatile in his nefarious activities that all through the period of his smuggling life, he was neither caught nor arrested until he met his fate. His craving ways of walking past the police and customs nets were as surreptitious as the movement of a rattlesnake through the crowded leaves of a bamboo tree. He had a nasty ruthlessness that he concealed well in good manners. Before he died, he had adored and cared for his son. His death to Pappy had been a terrible loss. From the moment he died, Pappy had been struck with the solemn determination, of never to be moved by anybody's death.

Pappy had inherited his father's ruthlessness to perfection. In addition, local environmental factors made Pappy grew up without any civilized manner. He grew up with a bunch of local antisocial adolescents. Most of his life he had been indifferent to public ridicule and, at any slightest chance, openly and shamelessly exposed his vulgarity.

On the night Pappy's father was to meet his fate, they had parted as if nature had forewarned them.

"Angus," his father had said, for that was his darling name for him. "Take care of the house. I may not be coming back tonight. So sleep well and keep fit until I see you tomorrow."

"Where are you going, father?" He had asked.

"One of my friends is arriving from Britain tonight," he lied. "He will be coming by ship and I'll wait for him at the port until he arrives. If he comes in time, I'll be back tonight, but if he doesn't, you'll see me tomorrow."

"But, Daddy," He had said with concern, "I'll be happy if you come back tonight. I hate to sleep without you."

"No, my son," his father had said. "The security at the port is very tight. The area is guarded by tough police. If I leave there late at night, they'll think I'm a thief and they'll shoot me. Would you like your father to be shot?"

Pappy had shaken his head and said no. After adoring his son as he usually did, his father had left but never returned. Pappy spent the second day in loneliness. Then on the morning of the third day, he went to his mother who had deserted his father out of his unwillingness to give up the dirty job he was doing. Together with her, they had gone to the port in search of his father; and it was there they saw his body floating aimlessly on the surface of the lagoon. Later, he was informed that his father had died when trying to escape with a canoe full of contraband goods. He had been cornered at the Kroon's junction by the anti-smuggling men who fired at him as he took a dive to the water.

Then year in year out, on the exact date of his father's death, he would go to the port, hire a canoe, row to the kroon's junction and pay a tribute to his father. He had noted shrewdly that the kroon's junction was right in the middle of Lagos Island lagoon where a flag was installed to direct the movement of every cargo coming and going to the port. During the first three times he had gone there, he had at each time noted that a large ship would stop at the junction for some few minutes before proceeding to wherever it was going. He had been stern and unruffled at the sight and largeness of the ships. But as he was preparing to visit the place on the forth time, his mother died and something he couldn't understand prevented him from going back to the Kroon's junction.

The death of his parents had struck him like the loss of a loved one to a ghastly accident. By then, he was seventeen and he was in class two of an unapproved secondary school he had been forced to attend by his mother. He expelled himself from the school and joined the society of wild and rebellious teenagers. It was a fast life he couldn't stop as he dined and wined among several species of moral imbecility. He roamed from one place to another in the city before his path eventually led him to Dona's casino. At first, he was a little thing, unknown and unrewarded among the group of hogs who always stormed the club with their rough and awkward behavior. But after a while, he grew strong and rough.

Then there was a day Pappy was involved in a fight with one of the club's die-hards. He slashed and floored the man in utter shamelessness. Dona himself came to intervene, but the way he did it annoyed Pappy, and he slapped him with uncared boldness. It was a rash encroachment that filled Dona with delight, and he quickly made him the leader of all the boys working at the club. This authority was what turned him to a feared and dreaded criminal.

Now that he was suddenly animated by a proposition that reminded him of his father's death, his mind flashed back to the time he used to row a hired canoe on the lagoon to where his father had been shot. He knew this wasn't the time to think of his father's misfortunes. This was a time for action. A time to clear the cloud of uncertainty that now hung over them.

"The kroon's junction," he said, staring inadvertently at the men, "its right in the middle of Lagos lagoon at the outskirt of Lagos Island. I used to visit the place when my father died. It's a sort of place ships have to wait for some few minutes before proceeding to the port. Why they have to do this is what I don't know. I will say the only thing I used to recognize the place is the yellow flag on top of a pole in the middle of the lagoon. That's all to it."

"How did you know all this?" Hercules asked.

"I've just said my father died there some years ago," he said coldly. "I used to go there and pay him a tribute every year, but I stopped that when my mother died."

"How did you normally get there, Boss?" Bello asked, speaking for the first time.

"I used to hire a canoe from some of the fishermen at the shore, go there, and do what I wanted."

"We don't know if that's how Charles and his men do it," Dele said.

Pappy's brain worked swiftly. "The idea is this," he said, tapping the desk in front with a forefinger, "I think our dear Charles operates with a group of men who might be tough or not, depending on the type of men he came across. Those who signed this letter must surely be among his men. It sounded as if they would be in the ship that was to bring the stuff. That man mentioned in the letter, Mr. Akim, must have obtained the diamond and took all the risk to put it on board. It's my bet Charles and the rest of his men are going to meet them at the time mentioned in the letter. I'll bet my life that only death could prevent Charles from carrying out this operation. This is something he can't do without and this is our chance to knock him off. We could have given out a lot of money to obtain this kind of information, but here it is, dropping freely on our laps. We all know how the smugglers operate. They'd be somewhere around on the date mentioned in the letter, waiting for the ship to come before they get the stuff and disappear. But this time, it's not going to be easy for them. The Felony Boys are going to be there too. We are going there not only to destroy Charles and his men, but also to take the diamond consignment and bolt away. May be this is where we are going to become rich."

For the first time in the room, the nine men laughed contentedly.

"There is one important thing," Pappy said abruptly, "how do we get guns?"

"Why do we need guns?" Dele asked surprisingly.

"What a silly question!" Pappy snarled. "If not because of how important this meeting is, I would have thrown you out of the window."

"Why?" Hercules said. "We are not staging a gun competition?"

"What we are going to do at the Kroon's junction is more than a gun competition," Pappy cried heatedly. "The port is full of anti-smuggling forces. What do you think will prevent them from attacking us as soon as they spot us?"

"I didn't think about that," Hercules said regretfully.

"Who will supply us the stuff then?" Eddy asked a little exited.

"I know of someone who can help," Hercules said.

"Who do you have in mind?" Pappy asked fretfully.

"Ginny."

"Well! I'll be damned," Pappy cried, "If we couldn't get as man guns as we want from Ginny, then we wouldn't get them from anywhere."

In the faculty of underworld dealings, Ginny, real name Ganiyu Akanda, was a man to be reckoned with. He was third to Pappy in the underworld, but his problem was he paraded himself with a lot of boys who couldn't do without landing themselves in constant trouble at every hour of the day. Despite the compromising attitude of his boys, every man in the underworld respects Ginny because he has brain with his brutality. He was someone who could defeat what power couldn't defeat with his shrewdness. On several occasions, Ginny had wangled his way out of the most solitary confinement people could ever imagine. The men in the underworld knew if all the vagabonds in the district were rounded up, Ginny would probably be the first to escape. Apart from being one of the leading arms dealer in the district, a job which only a few in the underworld knew he was doing, he was the leader of another set of brutal gang who enjoyed causing trouble. But in all their stubbornness, Ginny and his boys always bowed whenever they came across the Felony Boys. Ginny had a high regard for Pappy and his men. He knew if they couldn't get away with something, then none of the other groups of the underworld men around could do so. It was therefore with a mixed feeling of concern and respect that he always listened to them whenever they approached him.

As soon as Hercules had mentioned Ginny's name, Pappy knew their problem was not how to get guns, but how perfectly well they could use them. He had on two occasions cornered Ginny with boxes of guns and ammunitions during their night raids. On both occasions, he had met him loading the boxes into a pick-up van on the route that usually served as their savior whenever they ran into the police. On the first time, he had watched him and went past without saying a word. But on the second occasion, he stepped out of the taxi they were using for their operation and went to where Ginny was lifting the boxes into the van with the help of another man. Ginny didn't protest as soon as he came and demanded to know what was inside the boxes. He truthfully told him what was inside, and as he made a move to open one of them, Pappy stopped him. He told him he wasn't interested in guns, that he had only come to know how good in stock his raids were. Ginny wanted to give him the short pistol in his pocket, but he refused, telling him he wasn't good in keeping guns. He had been surprised at how he could lay his hands on such volume of arms in the boxes, but up till today, he hadn't bothered to ask him.

"Ginny will provide us with everything we need," Hercules said, looking at Pappy.

"Only heaven will help him if he didn't," Pappy said.

"How do we get the stuff here?" Bob said.

"I'll give you a note to him," Pappy said to Hercules. "You'll go with Eddy and bring the stuff here. The security of how they get here is your business."

"That's no problem," Hercules said. "As long as he can release the stuff they'll get here safe."

"How about what to give him," Dele said. "Wouldn't he ask for something?"

"You don't imagine he will part with all those guns without getting something?" Pappy said. "But I'll see to that side when we meet."

Later, they discussed further on how to take care of new faces that would be coming to the club, and then went further to lay out a comprehensive plan of how to attack Charles and his men at kroon's junction.

CHAPTER 11

Sergeant Adekunle Taiwo sat behind the empty desk in front of him with a fine incline bow of his head. His service cap was resting limply on the bridge of his broad nose, shading his brown aggressive eyes as he inspected the newspaper on his hands curiously. He knew quite well that the paper was printed about a week ago, but that didn't worry him. He needed something to occupy his time before others arrived. He inadvertently read through the first few pages.

This morning, the sergeant had woken up from his house earlier than usual. He had dressed up hurriedly and rushed to the office in the hope of gaining some information from some of his friends on morning duty about the Felony Boys. Almost all his trustees had gone home before he arrived, except two constables who were too fresh in the department to know anything about the underworld. About ten minutes later, the two young officers left, forcing him to stay in the office until those who were to resume duty for the day would arrive.

As he sat there, he began to brood over the events of the last few days. He wasn't sure of how to get Pappy and his men. What Charles had told him when he went for a routine check of his house yesterday was only smattering information compared with the mass of details he wanted about the gang? Charles had even said he wasn't sure about what he was saying because he was only telling him what he heard from one of his staff. Though as slim as the information was, he had immediately inferred that he would need a batch of well armed policemen to burst into a hideous underworld inhabited by a group of sadistic rogues. Unless an order came from a superior police officer, he had no hope of gaining such a company. Besides, every policeman on duty was always busy with one case or the other in this city where the number of policemen available was so small compared with the rising crimes. Pappy's get away had been caused by his own carelessness. He knew from experience that to grab such a man who could floor three policemen with guns in hands wouldn't be easy. Worst, Pappy now had his gun, and Charles had been scared to hell because of this.

Taiwo had a terrible time persuading Charles to stay home yesterday.

Charles had said in as much as Pappy could escape from the policemen at the beach, there was nothing preventing Pappy from coming back to kill him in his own residence. Taiwo had two police constables stationed outside Charles house. Despite Taiwo's persuasions, Charles was unimpressed.

"Relax," Taiwo had said. "Its part of what happens sometimes in police force. We couldn't go on shooting at him with the crowd there. If I hadn't been careful with the two shots I took at him, I would have had about two or more corpses at the scene."

"I am not interested in your feeble excuse," Charles had snarled. "Look at the way he slashed your men, slashed you and got away with it. Imagine he had killed me, he would have got away, and nobody would be around to give you a reliable statement. No matter the amount of your men guarding this house, I am not staying here until you've found him and that rogue."

"Are you telling me you are leaving your belongings behind and running away?" Taiwo had asked.

"Of cause yes. I am more concerned about my life than any property. I have a place l can stay until you find them."

"What makes you think we are going to find them?" Taiwo replied, not meaning what he said.

"You just said that you stand a risk of loosing your stripes if you didn't. You wouldn't want that. Would you?"

Taiwo had scratched his head wearily and shrugged. He had considered what Charles had said, and had thought convincingly that he had to find Pappy and Bob by all means. He had no other way to live except through this police job. He had been making a good progress right from the time he started the work. He had been fast and up to where those who had started at the same time with him hadn't been up to. He had struggled relentlessly to obtain his present rank, and he wouldn't like to lose it in a flurry of carelessness.

Right now, he had about four kids and a wife to cater for. Age was fast falling on his mother who too depended on him for her up-keep. If his stripes were suddenly stripped off, he wouldn't be able to keep up with his family. He had no one else to supplement or salvage for him. If he had to keep his job and get higher in the ladder of police worthiness, he must not only get at Pappy to avenge his unjust attack, but he also had to get at his gang and raze their underworld trench.

Taiwo couldn't blame Charles for his decision. He had watched him parked few of his belongings in disbelieve and then moved out with his wife in fear of being attacked by Bob and his aides. He had said he was moving to one Hotel de Executive in the town, and had given him his address and telephone number. For fear of suspicion, he had turned him back half-way to the hotel as he escorted him and his wife in the police Land rover that followed the taxi they boarded. He had driven back to his house, instructed the cops there to stay guard, and then rushed home for two or three hours rest. This morning, he had rushed to the office and thought he would call Charles as soon as he had his way with the Assistant Superintendent of Police.

As Taiwo sat behind the front desk staring aimlessly at the pages of the old newspaper on his hands, waiting anxiously for the ASP to arrive, a sudden insipid thought ran through his mind. He looked up fretfully, hesitated for a few seconds whether to carry out what he had just thought, decided nothing would happen if he did it, dropped the newspaper and stood up. He turned around and moved hurriedly to the door facing him. He eased the door open, closed it softly behind him, and entered into the small unfurnished office. He walked past a desk and a table, moved further to another door, turned the handle to the right, opened it, and entered into another inner office. A large safe with a chest of four drawers stood facing him as he came in. He walked over to the safe, which was almost of same height with him, peered wearily at its top and noted with disappointment that its key was not there. To his right was the ASP table. He walked past the large table, tested the pair of side drawers under it without success, searched hurriedly through the piles of papers and frisked the pile of magazines on top with a shrug of despair. As he was about to give up searching for the safe's key, his eyes caught the large diary on the table. He hesitated for a second or two before picking it up, leafed through the sheets without interest, and then as he was about to replace it, his hand pushed off a box of paper clips on the table. The scraping noise that clinked with the movement of the clips brought him to a sudden attention.

He lifted the paper clip box, opened it and saw the key inside. He removed the key, moved over to the safe and operated the lock. A dozen or so automatic pistols reflected on his eyes as he opened the first drawer. He picked up one of the guns, checked it and found out it wasn't loaded. He closed the first drawer, opened the second and stared intently at the load of the live ammunition in it. He took out some bullets from one of the boxes and loaded the gun. He took out a dozen more bullets and shoved them in his pockets. As he made a move to open the third drawer in the safe, the familiar sound of a police siren drifted into the office and rang blaringly in his ears. He bent down, rolled up his trouser and shoved the gun inside his boot. Like a rat that was about to be caught in a hole he hurriedly arranged everything as they were, and ran back to his desk.

About four or five cops came in and started signing in hurriedly. He knew instantly something was wrong, the siren outside the station, and everyone rushing to clock in. Either the commissioner is here or there is some shooting nearby.

The ASP came in, acknowledged the men and walked to Taiwo desk.

"They are just coming in, sir," he said to the ASP.

"Let me have the report on your findings on Mr. Charles's house. You may be having two assignments in your hands now," the ASP said.

Taiwo didn't say anything. He watched the commissioner as he barged in, saw the deluge of salutes going on around and stood frigidly in spot in a salute posture.

"What's going on around here?" The commissioner suddenly barked as he turned around.

Some of the cops exchanged unnerve glances and remained silent with hidden presentiment.

"Idowu I expect some action!" The commissioner exploded. "You mean none of your men is aware of what has happened."

"The telephone was out of order yesterday night and as such all calls from other units couldn't reach us," The ASP said.

"And what have you done about it since then."

"It would be repaired this morning, sir."

"I want all these men out!" The commissioner said irritably.

"Get all of them armed. Get them dispatched to all underworld hideouts in the city. We can't afford to loss three of our best men overnight without getting the culprits. You hear me? Get them out. Tell them not to come back until they've found those bastards!"

The ASP himself was startled. Since he had been working with the commissioner he had never known him to be in such an irritable mood. He had been very surprised when he had driven to his house this morning with his two police escorts. It was so early he was still straining himself on the bed when he heard his usual horn signal. He had hurriedly through his usual morning routine as the commissioner bitterly told him that three of their highly rated men who were staying guard at the Federal Minting Establishment in the outskirt of the city were shot dead by some robbers who raided the company overnight. He knew the entire police force in the state wouldn't rest until the robbers have been found. One thing he was certain of was the fact that the press boys would be around as soon as they heard the news, crowding them with their dangerous pens and asking them some unimaginable questions. If there was anything the commissioner hated, he knew it was the publication of this type of incident that would throw the entire police force in the state to public ridicule and reproach. If other units had already deployed their men into action, then what the crap was he waiting for? It was this sudden event that completely thrown out Charles episode from his mind until he saw Taiwo again this morning.

Right now as the commissioner was barking out his orders, the ASP had nobody to lead this poignant job except Sergeant Taiwo. He knew Taiwo could be reckless at times, but in this type of job, he knew no other man in his unit was as reliable as the sergeant. So it was with a feeling that Charles job was in danger, and a fear of being thrown into an incompetence unit that he had to call on Taiwo to abandon Charles's case for the meantime and take over the new job.

"Get two Land rovers and a couple of armed men ready within ten minutes," The ASP said to Taiwo, watching the commissioner as he paced up and down."

"Yes sir," Taiwo said and left hurriedly.

CHAPTER 12

Charles had been in pain over the last few days except today. He lay on the couch with a pillow supporting his bandaged arm. A bottle of beer stood on the stool beside him.

It's been five days since he had been in this averagely furnished suite with his wife, and yet he hadn't informed her he was keeping another suite in the same hotel. Ever since he was here, Shola had been inspiringly good and had almost redeemed his crushed and spiritless mind. Whenever he can, he would sneak out to the other suite whenever she wasn't around; giving him an inexplicable uneasiness that made him wonder at times whether she knew the type of business he was doing and pretended not to know or she really didn't know anything about it at all. From the time they had started together as a boyfriend and a girlfriend, until now that marriage had joined them he had been disguising as a manager of importing and exporting company which she never bothered to inquire about. Whenever he brought an expensive gold or a precious jewel home, he would either inform her that the pearl was a gift from some foreign client, or that it was part of the goods he consigned home from abroad. She only knew he had an office in Lagos where she visited occasionally whenever she went out shopping. She knew too he had a lady secretary in his office, a good friend named Bola Thompson and a host of others who visited them at home as business clients. But what cleverly evaded her knowledge were her husband's nefarious activities. She neither knew he was a hard sea smuggler, nor knew he had another suite at the hotel they were now staying. She first knew about Hotel de Executive when she came there with her husband five days ago. Though there as her temporary residence, she hoped everything would soon return to normal for her husband so that they'd have the chance to return to their rightful home.

In her usual softness, she had left for work this morning, parting her husband with a passionate kiss, and promising him she would return before her normal closing time to give him the motherly care he needed at this time. Charles had thanked her and told her his arm had almost healed and that what he needed now was time to rest before getting back to his business. And when she had left, he had settled down for a nice breakfast, smoked about half a dozen cigarettes and fell into a heavy sleep. Two hours later, he had woken up, cleared his face and ordered a bottle of beer. There now, self and lonely in this newly accommodated suite in the lower stair of the hotel's first building, a radiating thought of what had happened within the past four days came on his mind. It was a haunting memory of flagrant events that kept sweeping through his brain.

First, there were Bob and Pappy. He was extremely upset about their disappearance and the inability of the police to find them. If there were any of the two men he dreaded most, it was Pappy. Without him, he was sure Bob couldn't operate. He feared him as a child feared a monster. Every time he remembered him, he would have in mind a clear picture of his brutally drawn face while he was fighting him at the beach. His insensate rage as he attacked the two policemen who were holding him and then escaped from their shots still staggered his imagination. On the other hand, he couldn't stop thinking about Bob. He must have suffered greatly in the prison; which could explain why he was still mad about him. He must be aware now that he now knew about his intention, and unless he wanted to spend the rest of his life in jail, he must stop craving around for revenge of his punishment in the prison. Only yesterday, the ASP telephoned him that Bob didn't leave the address of the place he was going when he left the prison. Though the police officer said their search for him was still in progress, but he wondered if they would be able to find him.

His mind shifted to Sergeant Adekunie Taiwo. He thought of the trouble he had taken to safe his life. He had come to the hotel on Tuesday and gave him a gun. He had said he should handle the gun and protect himself with it until Pappy and his men were found. He had accepted the gun and thanked him for his unbelievable courtesy, but he was discontented that another job had been relegated to him. He was sure the sergeant would not be released until he had completed his assignment. Who knew how many days the job was going to take him? It could be weeks, and then Pappy and his men would have the chance to either get away or narrow their chance to find him. His thought stopped momentarily as he reached for the glass of beer on the stool. He raised his head, gulped down the beer and refilled the glass to the brim. He leaned back and rested his head on the arm of the chair again.

This time, his mind shifted to Bassey Okoye's mishap. Although the man was fast recovering, but the doctor said he would still spend more than a week in the hospital before he could be finally discharged. Shola had visited Bassey at the hospital yesterday. After she came back, she recounted what Bassey had said about the burglar who attacked him in the house. It was after listening to her story that Charles believed that all the incidents that happened on Sunday were carried out by the same set of people as the ASP had said. It was as soon as they left for the beach on Sunday that Bassey heard the noise upstairs. The burglar must have been waiting for them to leave and so he had come up. Bassey had gone up to check who it was when he was attacked. He didn't even see his assailant. Later, some people in the neighborhood said they saw a man leaving hurriedly in a motorcycle when the incident occurred, but hadn't said a thing to the police for fear of reprisal. He was thankful that Bassey hadn't been killed. With luck and time, he told himself, Pappy and his gang might be found. He didn't know how this would be done, but Taiwo had told him he would do it.

Slowly and steadily, Charles's mind reflected back to his business. Fred and the rest of his men were doing well. Since he sustained his injury, they had almost collected all the money owed by their customers. They had also made some useful arrangements for the jobs they were soon to undertake. But whether he was well or not, there was one important job he couldn't afford to miss. And that was the job tomorrow around 5 P.M. He had been thinking of the trouble his arm could give if it didn't heal well before they undertook the operation, but he waved off that idea when the wound started to absorb shocks without much pain today. He had convinced himself that given about twelve more hours, his arm would be good enough to support the effort of others in paddling a canoe. Tomorrow's job was a job that required a good supervision. It needed a thorough and efficient handling. He thought he just had to make himself available so that everything would go well. Although he wasn't expecting any trouble, he had to be careful with his men. With the gun Taiwo had given him and with the alerting mind that now awaken him to all suspicious movements, he felt self protected and cared less about anti smuggling's men activity.

He suddenly thought about his wife. He knew she would ask where he was going when he was prepared to leave. But as usual, there were those convincing words, 'Business Connections.' But this time he knew he would really have to convince her before they could part. Then he remembered his car. The police hadn't found it yet and he needed something to move around as soon as he was well enough to start his business in full. He had thought about this during the past few days, and had finally concluded he would have to buy another car. The only other vehicle meant for his business was a Mazda Van at the port, and he couldn't afford to go there and get it today. If Fred could help with his Volkswagen car, then with it, then he could use the Mazda van in transporting the diamond consignment here tomorrow. As he shifted his weight aside and stretched out his hand at the glass of beer on the stool, a tap came on the door. He frowned his face as he sat upright, thinking of who might be standing there knocking. Shola still has about three hours more before she could return from work, and Sergeant Taiwo didn't tell him he was coming today, he thought. Maybe one of his men, he said without spoken; standing up. He went to the table facing him, picked up the key and tip-toed silently to the door. As he bent down and peeped through the key-hole, the knock came again. He could just make out a shining steel of belt buckle in front of black trousers.

"Who is it?" Charles asked hoarsely.

"It's Fred, sir."

He recognized the voice and sighed. He stood straight, inserted the key into the hole, and opened the door.

"You nearly scared me off my wits," he said, standing aside for Fred to come in. Then he closed the door and locked it.

"You mean you haven't got over your fear about those vagabonds" Fred said, strutting over to a chair and sitting down.

"I've got to be on the alert until they are rounded up," Charles said.

"I can't afford to take chances."

"If the police failed to find them," Fred said seriously, "we'll get them ourselves."

Charles didn't answer. Instead, he went over to the telephone on the table, dialed a number, spoke softly into the receiver and replaced it.

"I was thinking you had a visitor," Fred said, looking at him as he came to sit down.

"No. I wasn't expecting you so early. I thought you'd be here later in the evening to tell me about your movement tomorrow."

"There's nothing else to my movement except to come here and get you."

Charles wanted to say something, but he was stopped by the knock that came on the door. At the same time, the telephone on the table began to ring.

"That must be the waiter I've just called to bring you a bottle of beer." He said as he stood up. "Go and open the door for him. I'll get the phone."

Two minutes later, he came back to his seat.

"Who rang?" Fred said softly.

"Shola. She phoned from the office and asked how I was feeling."

"She's really a lovely woman," Fred said, pouring himself a drink. He looked up and saw the way Charles was stretching his arm carelessly around his waist. "You think your arm is ripe enough for that kind of exercise," he asked surprisingly.

"Do you imagine I will follow you tomorrow if it isn't?"

Fred chuckled and shrugged.

"Since when has it been treated?"

"I just have it checked by the hotel's doctor on Tuesday. I don't think I need any treatment for it again."

"Sure?"

"Yes. Can you do me a favor?"

"Yes. What is it?"

"I want you to unwind the bandage on it."

"Why, sure, if that's what you want, I'll do it."

A minute later, Charles smiled satisfactorily at the sight of the flabby scar on his lower arm.

"See what I mean," he said, showing Fred the scar. "The wound is completely covered by new skin."

"Not yet," Fred said, "It will take some time for those fleshy dots on the surface to disappear."

"As long as it's not that painful, that's no problem." He said and then began to flex and extend his arm.

"Do you think we'll have problem handling the stuff tomorrow? Fred asked.

"Not any I can think of," he said, not looking at him. "We'll do everything as we've been doing before. As long as we can arrive there in time, I'm sure everything will go well."

"Oh, that reminds me," Fred said, "Are you still with that letter Wale sent to you. The one you were showing me last Saturday."

"I don't think I have it here," Charles said. "Why bothering yourself about the letter. I suppose we know the right thing to do."

"Sure," Fred said. "I am just thinking that letter must not be left where somebody could easily pick it up."

"No. That can never happen," Charles said. "Although it's not here in the hotel with me, I am sure I kept it safe before I left the house."

"That's right then," Fred said, drinking from the glass of beer in his hand. "I wish everything goes well with us from now on. If we should expect trouble, it should be from our business, and not from some bastards who enjoy spending all their lives in jail."

"I am certain there wouldn't be any more trouble either from our business or anybody," Charles said. "As soon as we are through with what is coming up tomorrow, I'll get in touch with a number of people who know how to take care of some jobless idiots. There and then, any other problem coming up will be dealt with accordingly."

Though Charles thought he was confident about what he had just said, but if he had been aware of what the Felony Boys had planned for him and his men, he would have known that it was not only a problem that lay ahead of them, but that there were so many things they would have to contend with.

Almost all the newspapers carried the news of all the suspects arrested in connection with the robbery which took place over the weekend at the Federal Minting Establishment in Lagos. About eight men were rounded up with glaring evidence of conviction, and it appeared the entire state police were geared to the arrest. One interesting piece of the news was sergeant Taiwo's display of cleverness which allowed the policemen, from his unit to gain control over the robber's hideout. His full length photograph was splashed on the front pages of some of the newspapers, and it nearly overshadowed that of the commissioner, who as usual, looked stern and determine as if the remaining robbers in the city would soon be given their overdue punishment.

Bob was frisking through the roll of tickets on his hands when Folly came in with two newspapers. He looked up sharply at him as he dropped them on the table and went past to the window without a word. He was expecting him to say his usual 'good morning, Bob' when he came for the first time today, but doing as he did now, he immediately inferred that he was still annoyed of the way Pappy had treated him yesterday.

Pappy had stormed into the office around nine o'clock last night and went straight for Folly. He had grabbed the neck of Folly's shirt, hauled him up from his chair, and shook him violently for some seconds. "Listen!" He had shouted. "And listen for the last time! Stop poking your nose into our gains! If you want peace in this club, you better leave us alone. I repeat. Leave me and leave the boys alone. Concern your guts only with your rightful profit. When next I hear any noise about our cut-backs, you'll rue it. Understand?"

Folly hadn't answered. During the few seconds that followed, Pappy and Folly had looked at each other with the kind of hatred that told Bob that the aversion between the two men could never end. And when Folly came in this morning without saying a word to him, Bob wondered whether he had grouped him among his enemies in the club. Out of the corners of his eyes, he looked at Folly again. He was throwing the dirty curtain on the window over the cord, and covering his eyes from the rays of sun that reflected past his body into the office. He shifted his eyes off as Folly moved away from the window, walked past him, and out into the passage.

Bob waited patiently for Folly's short silent steps to die down. Satisfied he had gone; he stood up, went to the door, opened it and looked stealthily up and down the passage. He closed the door silently and went back into the office. He cursed himself silently as he hit his thigh against the bulging edge of the table that seemed to occupy most of the space in the office. He went over to the load of small boxes that stood over one another in one corner of the office, lifted the first three, rummaged through the used receipts in the forth and removed the roll of N100 notes he had been hiding there since he came to the club. He replaced the boxes, folded the notes and walked hurriedly to the window. As he was shoving the money into the pockets at the back of his trousers, he heard the movement of someone coming to the door. He turned swiftly and moved away from the window. He was still making sure his shirt covered his swollen pockets well when the door opened and Pappy barged in with a face too difficult to judge.

"If that stupid wastrel who doesn't know he's old enough to go and die and thinks he can be pushing everybody around as he likes in this club, then he's in for a show."

"You mean you haven't forgotten about what happened yesterday," Bob asked in a stiff interrogating tone.

"Why Should I?" Pappy said, moving over to the chair in front of the table and sitting down. "Anybody who tries to block my means of survival is my greatest enemy. Folly is trying that, and I therefore consider him my greatest enemy on earth."

"You have to forget what he has done. I am sure he won't try anything again after the way you spoke to him yesterday. We have many important things to do than wasting our time with him."

"I am not going to forgive Folly even if I forget what he has done to us. He had been given such a chance that he now thinks he can open his mouth to any length. And I swear by my father that I will shut that mouth for him."

"That won't lead you anywhere," Bob said impatiently. "Suppose you harm him, are you going to get the tickets from him and sell it yourself?"

"Listen!" Pappy exclaimed wildly, almost deafening Bob's ears. "Are you now with him? Or what's the meaning of this entire foolish defense you are giving him. I'll do whatever I want with him. Not even Dona himself can stop me from dealing with whoever crosses my way."

Bob didn't say anything. He was looking directly at Pappy's bulging eyes with contempt. Certainly, he thought, he couldn't continue to endure this type it of barking from Pappy. If he wished to have his ways in whatever was happening in the club, then both of them couldn't live in the same place or else there would be blood shed.

"Look!" Pappy snarled, cutting off his thoughts. "I am here to discuss something important with you. I have no time to waste at this moment, so you better listen and let it stick on your throat for good."

Bob wanted to stand up and give him a dirty slap, but realizing if he did, their whole plan for the afternoon would be automatically stultified, he checked himself and said, "Look, Pappy. I don't like the way you are shouting at me. We can't afford to quarrel at this moment, so if you have anything important to say let's find a better place."

Pappy stared at him for a few seconds with obtuse eyes. Then thinking of how sensible of what he had just said was, and thinking of how important of what he had in mind for him, he shifted his eyes away from him to the top of the table. He saw the folded newspapers, reached for them, unfolded them and looked at the front page.

"Bastards!" He suddenly exploded and stood up so violently he nearly fell off the chair.

"What's it." Bob demanded anxiously.

"They've caught Ginny!" Pappy yelled, pointing at a man among the suspects pictured in front of the paper. "Those bastards are too fast for him this time."

Bob snatched the paper from him and stared unbelievably at Ginny's photograph. A pair of hand cuffs chained his hands, and so were the hands of those caught with him. He didn't make any attempts to hide his strong face from the camera. The half-sized photograph clearly showed his hard muscular body and it appeared ironically as if he was smiling.

"That's unfortunate." Bob said. "How are we going to get more guns?"

"Ginny is damn too good to be caught!" Pappy cried again. "No. I can't believe this." He bawled, damping his lower lip with the full length of his frontal teeth.

"Do you think he could mention anything about us?" Bob said, shifting his eyes to the picture of the commissioner, and then unto that of Sergeant Taiwo.

"Not a chance." Pappy said bitterly staring thoughtfully on the ground.

Bob read the bravo words under the sergeant's picture, and then he gave the newspaper to Pappy.

"Look at the cop who did the evil job. He's got the backing of the pen boys."

Pappy looked at the picture. He suddenly flicked up his eye-lids and widened his eyes to have a clear focus at the cop. He wearily exchanged the paper for the other, and stared again at the same picture on the front page.

"Impossible!" Pappy exclaimed in a stupefied tone.

"What?" Bob asked surprisingly, staring curiously at the newspaper on his hands.

"This is the same bastard who crossed us at the beach! Damn it!"

"You must be kidding," Bob fumed, standing up and crowding Taiwo's picture with his eyes as he came to stand near Pappy.

"What a surprise," Pappy said, grinning ruefully. "Look at yesterday's coward turning to an overnight hero today."

"Maybe this is the job that has been keeping him out of our track till now," Bob said, a little apprehensive, "he might be willing to turn the heat on us now that he's through with this job."

"Why?" Pappy said irritably. "He's not the only cop in the police force. And if he tries that on us, in or out of this joint, I'll make sure I put an end to his carrier."

"How will you do that?" Bob asked.

"You wouldn't ask a married woman where she got her pregnancy. Would you?"

"Of course, not, but I might be tempted if her husband is impotent."

"Good. That is if the legality of the pregnancy is in doubt."

"I still don't understand," Bob grinned.

"Right, you'll understand when I kill a cop who is looking for public recognition and departmental promotion by trailing us around."

Bob stared at Pappy for a brief seconds, looking curiously at his deeply set face. He wondered whether he feared death or not as he swiftly thought of his display of brutality. He approached everything without conscience. If Pappy was calm and unnerve in the face of threatening danger, then why couldn't he do the same. Only just now before he came in, he had grabbed all the money he had in the club. He had decided today would be his last day in the club if what they've planned for late afternoon went wrong. Not that the money was such an amount that could last long, but he thought the N10,000.00 in his pocket could help until he found his way out of the country. He hadn't decided yet on where to go, but Ghana or Liberia was his priority. He thought he had a certain presentiment for the job they were going to pull today. He couldn't understand why. But he just had that inward feeling that things weren't going to be alright as they had figured it. The whole plan was built up on how to attack Charles and his men as well as ward off police intervention if there was any at the kroon's junction. The protection they thought of giving themselves by having those guns was right in the normal circumstances. They had enough bullets that could last half an hour shootings. But all of these not withstanding, things could still go wrong. One thing that puzzled him was how Ginny had managed to supply them all those weapons they needed. His perplexity had been lessened when Ginny called at the club about three days ago. He had told them that most of the weapons were obtained through the help of his friends working in the immigration office. His other supplies were ex-armed forces officers who were responsible to a dealer he couldn't mention. He was simply introduced to Bob as 'Ginny Kill,' and truly to him, his appearance did confirm that he was one of those few ruthless killers remained in the underworld.

Unlike Pappy, Ginny was short and bald. Although he carried a slight protruding belly, he always wears a tight sport shirt and like to show off the bands of muscles all over his body that made him looked like a Michelin tire advertisement cartoon. He had cold alerting eyes that appeared to predict uneasiness all the time, and his quiet way of assessing situation told Bob that although Pappy could be more popular and dangerous, Ginny had an inward core of knowledge that could blot out Pappy's external cruelties.

Somehow, Bob didn't know how Pappy had talked Ginny into agreeing that half the money they would pay for renting the guns would be paid before the operation, and the other half paid afterwards. It was on record that Ginny never parted with his guns and ammunitions except the full amount covering the rent and loss had been paid. But with the Felony Boys, he only got half down, and the half didn't even cover the loss. Another thing had happened; Ginny wanted to take part in the operation, and the Felonys had agreed. He had said if the operation was successful, they needn't bother to pay the remaining half of the money covering the guns they rented. They also agreed that nothing would tamper with his share of whatever they made away with.

Pappy hadn't disagreed with Ginny. He viewed his decision as another convenient way of strengthening his gang, and besides, he too had helped Ginny at one time or the other, most especially when their association had required a merciless opposition against their rivals.

The whole Felony Boys had endorsed Ginny's participation, and Bob saw it as a more convenient way of getting out of their onslaught against Charles if the operation proved abortive. Bob thought that things are now different. Ginny had fallen into the hands of police and that meant a reduction in their criminal strength. Could this be a prelude to their failure? Probably not, he thought reassuringly. At least if Ginny hadn't opted to join them, they'd still do what they had planned without him. Besides, Charles just had to die. If he was to be freed from perpetual fear of police arrest, he must be killed today, even if they couldn't touch the diamond consignments they were hoping to grab.

Bob controlled his eyes, blinking them into focus from their aimless stare, and looked up at Pappy who seemed to be digesting the contents of the newspapers as he turned page after page for references about the big catch.

"We could as well say we've lost a good company," Bob said as Pappy looked up to meet his probing eyes.

"Not yet," Pappy said sharply.

"What do you mean?" Bob asked.

"I know Ginny," Pappy said seriously, biting at every word. "He's damn too tricky in prison cells, most especially when he's in this type of jam with a job in mind. I wouldn't be surprised if he knocked off the guards and walked right into this place as we speak. It's a thing he has done before, and any slightest chance won't prevent him from doing it again. Ginny is a specialized criminal, he could do anything."

"Even if he gets away," Bob said, "he wouldn't feel free again. To kill a cop and get caught is a bad thing. If you killed a cop and got away with it, you are as lucky as a man who wins a million naira in a lottery game."

Pappy knew Bob was right. He knew killing a cop was an encroachment in crime that could ostracize a robber for life. "Well," he said, "Let's wait and see. His absence didn't mean much, and it wouldn't prevent us from carrying out our plan. Suppose he didn't turn up if he wasn't caught. It would still mean the same thing. So, man wake up, it only means this job is strictly for the Felony Boys.

"Sure," Bob said, envying Pappy's courage.

"We've done what is greater than this before," Pappy said indifferently, dropping the papers on the table. "We'll surprise Charles and his men this afternoon. They'll die so fast it will appear as if they aren't human beings."

"Shall we call the boys and tell them of what had happened to Ginny."

"Not now," Pappy said flatly. "Let's finish our discussion first."

Bob nodded.

"Where shall we go?" He asked.

"Let's go to the back of the club."

Bob packed the tickets together, opened the top drawer, and put them inside. He locked the drawers and followed Pappy out of the office.

Folly had just crammed his belly with two plates of 'Amala' in a roadside canteen at the side of the club. He found it difficult to regulate his breathing which seemed to be coming in beats faster than normal. He had consumed the dish covetously and now as he jumped over the gutter at the back of the canteen, the plopping sound of the water he had drank over the excessive food came in short distinctive sound in his ears. He walked unevenly for about six or seven meters, turned to a cleared path that was lined by withered grass and moved further for another six or seven meters. He reached a small alley squared off by a fenced wall that was packed full of logs and woods, where an old man who died some years back left his unwanted belongings. He barely fit into the small gap between the old fences that was hiding a dilapidated old building.

The building had housed a car for almost a week. If you weren't a member of the Felony Boys or their close acquaintance, you wouldn't have access to the back alley behind the club. That means there was no way you could see the car. Folly was used to taking the back alley whenever he was going for his breakfast at the roadside canteen, and he had seen the rear view of the car for up to about three times now, but he hadn't thought of given it any serious attention. Not that this was his first time of seeing a car hidden in the old building. Several cars had been brought there before, but most of them were either brought in the evening and taken away overnight, or kept there for a day at most. This particular car he was now willing to check had been there longer than usual. He wondered why. He knew quite well that the car was hidden there by the Felony Boys. The old building was their base for stolen cars. It was there they had their meetings with their local supporters, smoked their joints to dizziness, and entertain their acquaintances.

The Felony Boys, Folly thought, were becoming too powerful for him. They had suddenly become hostile simply because he was doing his job. They wanted their individual gains at all costs. Not that he was fighting against that; what he was saying was that they mustn't overdo it. "Just look at Pappy," he said aloud, talking to himself, "that crazy boy wants a gain of 75kobo for every N1 ticket! And I mustn't talk! I must keep mute and allow everything to flop. Bastard! We've just started. I've been dump up till now, but right from today, I'll show them they'll all leave the club without my cooperation." Folly continued talking to himself as he advanced towards the outdated building. He suddenly stopped speaking and smiled as he thought of what he was about to do. He wanted to look at the car and then call the police to come and take it. Sure, he thought, nodding to himself, that'd be the first way of touching off their secrets. They should be expecting more, for this was just the beginning. He had nearly reached the building when he stopped abruptly. He bent down and looked at the deep tread of tires that came out of the building. The lines told his curious eyes that a car had just been driven out of the place. To confirm his suspicion, he ran to the building and stopped short at the level ground that ran to the garage. The empty garage where the car had been before confirmed his suspicion. It was as if they knew he was coming, he thought, looking at the dirty building. He suddenly wanted to see what was in some of the rooms. He went in silently, peeping through some of the first few rooms. Most of them were full of hollows and ridges. He moved cautiously around, walking as if stepping on glass. He had a feeling someone could be hiding in one of the rooms watching him. He suddenly wanted to turn back and run away. A voice from someone shouting in one of the rooms at the far end corner held his legs still. He had lived with Pappy for years and so he couldn't mistake his voice. He heard him saying, "He must die! Not tomorrow, but today!" He couldn't recognize the other voice which seemed to be answering him in fear. He wanted to know who must die so soon. He edged forward, moving silently until he reached the nearest window. He listened attentively to the voices that were coming out of the room.

"We are going through with our operation at the kroon's junction," his ears registered Pappy's words.

"He dies as soon as we come back"

"But Dona wouldn't be pleased," he heard Bob saying, "from the way I look at things in that club, he values his job most."

"I've already taken charge of that," Pappy said. "I know how to deal with Dona. Folly's death wouldn't mean a thing to him as soon as I told him what I have in mind."

Folly noted few seconds lapsed before Bob answered.

"Well, if Dona didn't suspect anything that will be alright."

"Don't get the idea you can agree with me now and disagree later. I am tough with this kind of thing, so be very careful with yourself. So far, we are the only people who know about this plan, and I want you to keep it that way. Your business is to take over his job and do it so well Dona will forget about him in weeks. I'll do the killing myself and the way I am going to take care of it is my business. So do what you are told to do, and everything will be fine."

"I am only thinking of the circumstances that will surround the whole thing if he suddenly dies."

"Who the hell will be looking for any evidence if a rascal like Folly dies?" Pappy said. "Come to think it. You don't imagine I will be crazy about killing

Charles without something you can do for us. This is the only place you can help the Felony Boys. If you know you can't, we better pack it up."

"But why are you talking like this," Bob said nervously. "I am saying I will take over his job and do it well. You've been nice to me, and besides I have no other choice at this time of my life. I'll cooperate and act without suspicion. I will live up to expectation."

On the other hand Bob was thinking, well, it was only today. If everything went wrong, he had all his things ready. He would disappear and none of them would see him again.

"Remember," Pappy said as if reading his thoughts. "You are now a fully fledged Felony Boy. Every Felony Boy stays with each other in times of need and trouble. Don't ever think you can run away from the Felony Boys. If you did, you'd know that Pappy has a spirit that kills everywhere. You've taken your decision, so stick with it and never slide. That's how every Felony Boy does, and you must do the same.

"Once I've said I'll do something, I will definitely do it," Bob said, trying to sound confident. "Folly death is nothing to me. He is not important than those who are helping me, and I can't desert my friends because he has suddenly ceased to exist. Keep to your promise that his murder will be full proof, and then you'll see how good I can play my part."

Folly was drenched in sweats. His heart was beating fast, and his head had become so heavy he wanted to collapse. He couldn't believe his ears. So he was just an inch away from death, he thought, shaking like a leaf. An instinct told him to find his way out without delay. With wobbly legs and weak arms; he walked back silently and found his way out of the building. As soon as he came out, the first thing that came to his mind was how to get to the police station as fast as possible.

CHAPTER 13

Around two o'clock of Friday afternoon, Sergeant Taiwo got the order he had been expecting from the ASP. Somehow, the sergeant thought, the ASP had been so occupied all morning that only once did he cast a glimpse of his sweating face among the rank of officers who flared around him in the conference room at the back of the station. He had no idea of what gathered the officers there, and whatever it was, all he was now concerned with was to arrest Pappy and his gang. He was very glad when at last a constable handed him a sheet from the ASP. He looked curiously at the instructions in the sheet, nodded, and smiled to the names of the ten cops assigned to follow him. With an air of authority, he handed the sheet to his assistant. "Get those men together in ten minutes, "he said and left for the inner office in a flurry of excitement.

Fifteen minutes later, two Land rovers full of armed policemen were on their way to the Central Casino. Taiwo sat in front of the leading vehicle with the director of the club in mind. Sitting beside him, next to the driver, was Corporal Yemi Benson. The corporal was averagely built with a kind of shape that fitted him into any kind of selection. He had two thick brows, a pair of big brown eyes and an edge of nose that pointed to the sky. Taiwo had requested that he should be in the list because he was viable and utterly dependable in this type of outing. The name of the driver beside him was Matti Daniel. He had just joined the force and this was his first outing. His black beret cap was slightly shading his forehead, giving his youthful look a hard and griming face of an intrusive cop. At the back of the Land rover sat about three young cops with rifles on their thighs. They looked fit and battle ready.

Unlike the vehicle in front, the Land rover following it was uncovered. One of the three cops at the back rested his gun on top of the driver cabin. The other two sat at the edge of the trunk in combat ready-position. Sergeant Bolaji Lawal sat with the driver in front. The butt of his .38 police special felt hard on his hands as he lifted it from his laps and examined it with expert eyes. Around five feet ten in height, he was gifted with a crumpled face that seemed to be full of contempt whenever he remained silent. But in contrast to this facial appearance, he was light hearted, straightforward, and debonair. Israel Onojeta, the driver beside him, was a rough and awkward cop who spoke with his fists. His face was as rough as his manners, and as he sat behind the wheel, looking at the red light from the tail of the vehicle in front, he deliberately stamped his foot on the break pedal, released his other foot from the clutch, and pressed the accelerator flat with his hard boot.

"What's the matter with you?" Sergeant Bolaji cried sharply.

"She's crying for more, Officer," Israel muttered.

"You better be careful. Don't kill us before the battle starts."

"Not a chance, sir."

In the front of the leading vehicle, Sergeant Taiwo saw that the traffic warden in the junction they were about to pass had purposely kept on waving to avoid them of any undue delay. He watched as the drivers swept past the warden and raced to the connecting road in quick succession.

As Taiwo sat there looking at the road in front, he thought about what had been happening to him so far. For the past three or four days, he had been engaged in a devastating assignment that had finally ended with a fierce battle. A battle that had taken away two of his best friends who dared not retreat in the face of the hard and nasty guns of armed robbers. Professional probity, he told himself, was what the police job required. It is a meticulous occupation that required an ample devotion in the presence of several intolerable odds. Few people, if at all there were any, could withstand the severally moral and strict discipline the job needed. His experience in the police work had taught him that if you had two demanding jobs to be carried out under the supervision of a superior officer, you always attended first to the more serious one. That was why he had answered first to the general call that demanded a first class attention, and then came to bother with the one he was now going to do. By virtue of luck, he thought he wouldn't call it bravery; he had fought through his last assignment and earned himself an excellent public praise. Praises and encouragements are what inspired men for better performance. That was why he was back on this job. During the past few days he had spent on the last assignment, he had gathered a lot about the Felony Boys. The crusade had detailed him with their criminal reputation. He had met a few friends working at the police station entrusted to their area, and they had detailed him with their unrivalled criminality. He had concluded that the Felony Boys were too cruel to live in a civilized society. He wondered whether their devilish act was being endorsed by certain members of the force. Why should such a vulgar act of wickedness against fellow citizens continued without arrest. Sooner or later, if such unabridged acts of violence remained unrestricted, the state police would be thrown into an irredeemable mediocre of government arm.

He was so dejected about the attitude of the Felony Boys that he had to call the ASP this morning and told him about it. The ASP too was surprised that such a bundle of uncouth men whose sources of living were derived from terrorism, insane vices, wanton destruction of lives and properties, robbery, illegal raids and undue molestation were still allowed to exist in the state. Their alarming rate of criminality was one of the things he mentioned this morning when all the district officers gathered in his station. All the officers had unanimously agreed that it was good to dispatch a unit that was practically unknown to the Felony Boys to arrest them. This order was given to Taiwo and his aides had been instructed to shoot if they resisted arrest.

Taiwo knew the task ahead of him wasn't going to be easy. He had been told that all the Felony Boys were like rough passengers who enjoyed being driven by rough drivers. They didn't care if their rowdiness in the bus landed them in a deep valley. They had an awesome reputation for violence and the people around them respected them as soldiers respect dynamites. They didn't fear the police, no matter which arm they came from. Taiwo knew they were hard nuts, but somehow, he thought, they had to be cracked.

"Should I turn or continue straight, sir?" the driver asked as he approached the junction that led to the club.

Taiwo sighed, and then stared ahead. "Straight. No more turnings." He realized he had spent about a minute or two thinking, and noted that within the next two or three minutes, they'd get to the club. He straightened himself on the seat and put his head out of the window to look at the Land rover behind them. Sergeant Bolaji winked to him. He nodded, brought in his head in again, and looked through the windshield to the road in front.

About a hundred meters or so ahead, a car was parked next to a bus stop curb. Taiwo saw the abandoned car as soon as the vehicle had crossed the junction. He fixed his eyes on it, noting it was totally covered with dust. All the external lights and the registration plate have been removed. The driver had almost gone past the Peugeot car before Taiwo could get a good look at the color.

"Stop!" Taiwo cried. "That must be Mr. Charles's car."

He was already on the ground before the driver could gain control of the break and ran back to the car. The second Land rover also screeched to a halt, and a few seconds later, the corporal and the other sergeant joined him.

"It's the car alright," Taiwo said, pointing to the registration number that was engraved on one of the side mirror. "They even left the key on the wheel, Bastards."

"Things are beginning to turn the right way," Sergeant Bolaji said. "We've found Mr. Charles's car in a place not too far from his assailant's hideout. Sooner or later, we'll catch the culprits themselves,"

"Now, what do we do about it?" Corporal Yemi said,

"We'll tell one of the boys to get it down to headquarters," Taiwo said, looking at the crowd that had quickly gathered at the bus stop. As Taiwo turned to call one of the boys at the back of the second Land rover, a traffic warden in a yellow and black uniform appeared, coming to where they were standing.

"This guy could take care of the car for us," one of the cops said, looking at the warden as he came over.

Sergeant Bolaji turned to look at the warden.

"Hi, Morgan," he said recognizably.

"Fine, sir," the warden replied, giving a half-salute.

"Do you know him?" Taiwo asked,

"Yes, he's a nice boy."

"Where are you stationed?" Taiwo asked.

"Surulere G Eleven, sir."

"Okay, be a good cop," Taiwo said. "Take this car to the HQ. I will give you a note to an officer there. Report to him as soon as you get there, then, tomorrow morning, report at Obalende police station for a recommendation to your officer. Understand?"

"Yes, sir," Morgan said, standing at alert.

Taiwo jotted something down on a note he took from his breast pocket. He gave it to Morgan who folded it and tucked it in his pocket. As the warden made a move to take control of the Peugeot car, the policemen turned and ran to the waiting Land rovers.

A minute later, the two Landover were again on their way to the Central Casino. But what the cops in them didn't observe was the fact that while they were busy looking over Charles's car, the Felony Boys had passed through the opposite lane in a taxi and were heading fast to the kroon's junction.

Folly pulled the window blind to the side. The light from the blazing sun was just in time to reflect on his blue jacket as he withdrew himself from the window. He was in a barber shop across the road in front of the Casino and he had been there now for almost thirty-minutes, watching the entrance of the club, and waiting anxiously for Pappy and his men to leave. Just now, he saw him and four of the boys leaving in one of Dona's taxis, and for the first time since he knew about the plot to kill him, he heaved a sigh of relief.

On a bench opposite the window he had just left, the barber was snoring like a frog in a deserted swamp and breathing too heavy for his tiny chest. Folly walked over to him and shook the bench.

"Hum ... what?" the barber pestered out.

"Hey man, wake up, I dey go." Folly said, staring at his shinning skull. He felt like touching it, but he checked himself.

"Okay, good bye," The barber said, then turned to his other side and continued sleeping.

Certainly, Folly thought, looking at him, sleep has an unbridgeable power over nature. He wondered why the spirit should be taken away and the body left completely free to echo the sound of life in sleep. He turned to the door and purposely shifted his eyes away from the image that imitated him in the mirror behind the door. Hands in pockets, he came out of the shop with what to do about Pappy's plot in mind. He had already dismissed the idea of going to the police. Several people had been to the police entrusted to their district with blood oozing out of their necks to complain about the Felony Boys, but nothing had been done to them. Besides, he had no clear evidence, to support his allegation if he went to the police and reported Pappy and his men. However, something kept bordering his mind. Why did Pappy and Bob hold their discussion in private? The Felony Boys never did anything in secret. Could it be they had discussed the plot already and Pappy was making sure Bob was well with plan, or was it just two of them planning to kill him? Whichever way they were going about it, all he knew now was the fact that Pappy could never change his mind. Pappy could do anything. He could even kill his mother if she got in his way. Now was the time to find his way out of the club, or else he would be dead by tomorrow morning.

First, Folly thought regretfully, he had to go inside the club and packed the few things he had there. Then second, he had to see Dona at his house and tell him why he was leaving. He knew how disappointed the man would be, but he had already decided that no amount of persuasion from Dona would make him return to the club.

He thought of where to go after leaving the Casino. He had an uncle in the army living at mile 20 barrack. They liked each other, and he had no doubt that his uncle would gladly accept him now that he was in danger of being murdered.

Folly had almost reached the steps of the club's pavement before he stopped thinking. As he mounted the steps, Dele came out with two colorful posters and pinned them on the boards outside. He stared at the posters without interest, and as Dele stood upright, they looked at each other. Folly noted the depressive look on the boy's face. He suddenly thought of asking him some inquisitive questions.

"Why do you look so sad?" He said, looking at Dele. "What's the matter with you?"

"Even if I answer you, you can't solve my problem," Dele said.

"Are you sad because you've not been going out with your friends these days?" Folly said.

Dele stared at him for a few seconds, wondering how on earth he knew what was on his mind.

"I think Pappy is crazy," Dele said. "Since that guy called Bob came to this club, he hadn't given me a single chance to follow them out."

"On special jobs," Folly asked, willing he should say more.

"Sure," Dele said his face grim and hard. "Today's job is as important as my mother's wedding but Pappy wants me to take care of the club as if the whole thing here is running away. How I hate what he does these days."

Folly reasoned quickly. He thought with the way Dele was now speaking, Pappy and Bob have not spoken to the remaining Felony Boys about their plan to kill him.

"Well," he said, his tension a little eased. "I saw five of them going out just now. Is it for the job you are having in mind?"

Dele suddenly frowned.

"What job did I tell you I have in mind?"

Folly thought it was time he struck the point.

"Pappy told me he had a Job at kroon's junction," he lied, saying what he heard when he was listening to Pappy's and Bob's conversation at the back of the club. "Isn't that where you are longing to be?"

"For the first time on earth," Dele said, concealing his surprise at Folly's mention of kroon's junction, "you speak a strange thing. I am sure you heard what you've just said from somebody else. Don't kid me. You are not in good terms with Pappy, so he couldn't have told you that."

I must be very careful now. Folly thought, or else I would give myself away.

"We settled our quarrel before he went away this afternoon," he said," He even told me the job is going to be big. And that they are after one man called Charles."

Dele couldn't believe what Folly was saying.

"What the hell are you talking about," he bawled, thinking what Folly said had some meaning. "Pappy will never tell you that. I may be mad at him, but he will never tell you that."

"Don't feel so surprised about what I'm saying. What I'm telling you is true. I know if I want happiness in this club, I have to play it right with you guys. I've spoken to Pappy this morning and I promised him I will give you guys my utmost cooperation. He felt so good he didn't hide what they were to do today from me."

Dele stared at him, not believing what he was saying. Folly had never talked like this to any of them. His sudden friendliness surprised him.

"Where is Rasheed?" Folly asked cutting his thoughts, and anxious to change the subject. He knew there was nothing he could say again to convince the boy.

"Are you going to tell him this?" Dele said, still staring at him incredulously.

"No. I want to see him for something else."

"He has just gone for lunch."

"He didn't follow them?"

"No."

"How many of you are left behind to take care of the club?" Folly asked, not knowing why he was asking such question.

"Bello and Isiaka have gone to the board's office to collect the films. We have an important show tonight, and I think we are going to have a big time with our Racketeers this evening. That's why Pappy wants us to stay behind. Why all these questions. Are you not aware of what is going on in the club again?"

"No. Not that," Folly said. "I just want to see if I can tell some boys to help you."

"We've already arranged for that," Dele said. "You don't imagine I believe what you've just said you heard from Pappy. Do you?"

"You'll believe when Pappy comes," Folly said, grinning at him.

Could it be what Folly was saying was true? Dele thought. Could it be he had settled his quarrel with Pappy and had agreed to cooperate with them? If not, then how did he hear something about kroon's junction? How did he even hear they were after Charles? Did he overhear all this from Pappy or had he thoughtlessly mentioned it in his presence? He was still pondering over this when two police Land rovers arrived at the club and slammed their breaks so hard everybody around startled.

"Don't move!" A voice barked as Dele took two steps back and ducked behind the pillar at his back.

Folly stood motionless, his mouth hung open, his body trembling. Then the unexpected happened. Dele had another pillar to reach before reaching the side entrance of the club. He had so many things to hide before the cops began their search. He knew if he could get to the entrance, they would succeed in pinning nothing on them. Then he took the risk. Keeping himself low, he took a wild dive at the other pillar. The distance was too long for such a risk. The cop leaning on the driver's cabin didn't hesitate. He turned the rifle to his direction as if he had been expecting him to move and released the trigger in two quick successions. The bullets came out with a lightning speed and threw Dele up. He crashed against the wall of the building and rolled to face up with two holes on his chest. Everything happened so fast it looked like a nightmare to Folly's horrifying eyes. He was still staring at the body on the ground when the butt of a gun crashed on his head.

"Where are the rest?" A voice yelled at him as he struggled to regain balance. "Speak! Or you'll feel the bullet in your tummy."

Even as Folly stood there gaping at the cop who was shouting at him, he was grateful that the voice speaking to him was not that of Pappy. Even if he didn't know where to start, he thought, feeling the pain on his head, he at least knew that Pappy and some of his men had gone to the kroon's junction.

For some seconds, Ginny stared contemptuously at the impenetrable darkness of walls that surrounded him. It was a hell of a cell, so rigidly confined that he could only sit and sit alone. The darkness surrounding him was so awful that if he should remain there for about a week more, it would take him nothing less than two weeks to regain his sight properly. He knew there was nothing he could do in this lugubrious cell. He was trapped like a fly in a sealed palm wine keg. In the pitch of the darkness, he carried up his short powerful arms and tried his eyes on the strong chains that married them. He couldn't make out a thing. The handcuffs were completely blended with the gloomy cell.

As bad and lonesome as the room was, Ginny was not a bit disturbed. He had only one aim. His brain was running all the scenario of how to escape at all costs. He knew the offence that brought him to this dreadful solitary was the one that carried a death sentence by firing squad. He had robbed with violent, and he had done it with the six other men who were sharing the same fate with him in the surrounding cells. They had been too bold, rash, indifferent and irreverent. Those three policemen wouldn't have died if they had done as they have been told. Ginny and his men had broken through their stronghold unaware, surrounded the cops so quickly they have them all in a command and surrender mode. But suddenly three of cops had mistakenly gone smart, and Ginny had eliminated the three of them single handedly. More would have gone if they had done the same because he was determined to stop at nothing from grabbing the money in the printing office as soon as they had the chance to enter.

Ginny and his men had made away with N5 million, the largest amount of money they had ever seen in their lives. Everything could have gone well, but as it happened later, one of them was not satisfied with what he parted with. The disgruntled man had gone out and tipped the police about their where about. They had a lot of men guiding their hideout, but most of them were wiped out in the clash that ensured with the police. They had all fought until they had no more ammunitions, and it was then the police came and surrendered the rest of them. Without being told, they knew they couldn't escape the jury verdict on death penalty by firing squad.

Not that Ginny lacked the courage to watch his body being riddled with bullets. But to be conveyed in that awful Black Maria vehicle to the bar beach, and staked in front of those drums that were stacked full of sand, and then executed before the mocking eyes of Lagos crowd was a thing he abhorred. He had vowed within the underworld circle that such a death would come over his dead body. Although he was aware that some of his colleagues regarded this as an empty boast, to him, it wasn't empty; it was a boast he had to carry out against all odds. To die in an attempt to escape and respect his resolution contended him than to die by firing squad.

If it was possible, as Ginny had been thinking for some hours now, he wanted to avoid that dying aspect in his bid to escape. This was necessitated by his willingness to join the Felony Boys in that operation scheduled for today. He was in good terms with the Felony Boys. They were his favorites and he enjoyed working with them. If he could escape and take part in the big job slated for this afternoon, he would not only be saved from the police, but the death penalty looming over him could disappear.

Although all the armed robbers had all been brought to a smaller jail before their court arrangement, the security there was tight and secured.

Right now, Ginny had no idea of what the time was. All he knew was the day was dying fast, judging from the long uninteresting hours he had spent sitting since the dawn came. Only once had the food been brought to him. And that was within the early hours of the morning, when a badly peppered porridge was pushed in through what he wouldn't call a door, but a cage that should be meant to trap animals. The guards know they are heavily handcuffed so they so they allowed the door to open just enough to push the food in. He didn't know when the server would come again, but each time he approached, he would be followed by a fierce looking police dog and an all armed mobile policeman. He was brought in on Wednesday night, and today was his second day in the cell. Yesterday, the food was brought in two times by the servicing warder; one in the morning, the last towards sunset. The servicing warder is usually accompanied by the gun carrying guard. Today, he had kept the food that was brought in the morning until he took it about an hour ago, the consumption of which he purposely belated to strengthen him for what he had planned to do when the time for his other meal came.

He had to do something before his court day tomorrow. He knew he would be sent to a bigger prison with unrivalled security once the judge is through with them.

Ginny had no idea of how many policemen were now guarding them. But at the time they were brought in, he was quick to spot about six guards, some with dogs and each with short automatic rifles. Within the short time they had spent leading them to the cells; he had quickly marked out some delicate differences. He had noted the height of the surrounding walls that isolated the jail from the city. No one, he had concluded instantly, could jump over such walls especially with the top decorated fierce looking barbed wire. On the other hand, he thought, if he could just find one thing, he might be able to make the impossible possible. He knew he wouldn't pass through those guards and dogs without being turned to shreds. His only chance of escape, he had thought grimly, would have to be through the high surrounding walls.

It wasn't until others were being pushed into their individual cells, and Ginny was standing there waiting for his turn, that he saw what he had been hoping to see. It was a long horizontal piece of a flexible water pipe that ran from where he was standing to the jail's lavatory. It ran the length of the cells about 200 yards or so and was high up on the wall near the ceiling. He knew instantly that to blow off the required length he would need, he had to lay his hands on one of those guns held by the guards. When and how to do this had been his mathematical obsession since he was shut in his cell. Before being shoved into the cell, the guards had removed their leg chains but allowed the handcuffs to remain in place with enough length to allow feeding.

After so many hours of racking his brain, Ginny thought he knew what to do. Inside the cell, he sat there waiting for his time. About fifteen minutes to 4 P.M. his alert ears suddenly picked up the noise of fast approaching footsteps. He crept up and sat on his heels. He heard the coming steps stopped, and then a key operated on the cell beside him. He listened to some noise, and then the approaching steps again. By now he was directly behind the door opening of his cell; his buttocks still on his heels, his knees and thighs bent forward, his fists clenched and held forward in the handcuffs, waiting anxiously like a dog ready to jump at its prey. He listened to the loosening of the heavy padlocks outside, and then the small door creaked open. He could just make out two solid feet in a black leather boots outside the door, and as the owner of the feet bent down to push in the food, Ginny thrust his wrist and handcuffs forward like a cobra and struck the guard on the head.

The servicing warder gave a wild yell as Ginny forced the door open and crashed against him. The plate of beans flew up as he went down and knocked his head on the floor.

The guard who was escorting the servicing warder saw what was happening, and he hastily left the padlock of the cell he was checking. Oddly enough, the guard wasn't with his dog. The brute animal was sleeping when he was about to follow the service man and he had left her undisturbed. He still had about two or three cells to check before reaching Ginny's unit, but seeing what was happening, he abandoned what he was doing and drew his gun at alert.

Ginny noted the guard's movement as he sprang out, and almost immediately, he ran first to the left, then to the right, dived to the flour and began to roll on the ground towards the guard.

The guard stood motionless as Ginny spun rapidly towards him. Probably because he was too frenzied, or too careful to have a harmless shot at Ginny, he committed a fatal mistake. Two things happened at the same time; Ginny crashed into him and rapped the pair of handcuffs on his hands around his boots as the gun went off. The bullet ricocheted on the floor an inch off Ginny.

To Ginny's amazement, the guard had turned the gun upside down and was aiming the butt at his head. Ginny blocked the butt of the gun with a quick movement, wrapped his handcuff around the gun, jerked down the barrel and forced the guard to fall over him. As the guard fell over, Ginny released the handcuff around the gun and forcefully whipped him on the head with the chain on his hand. The chain made a deep dissection as it exposed the skin and brought out part of the white bone on the guard's forehead. Blood came out fast, dropping on Ginny's sweater as the guard rolled over. Within seconds, he was up on his feet with the gun.

Ginny knew how to handle guns. He had played tricks with guns all his life. He blew and split off the handcuffs with one quick shot. He lifted the rifle and fired at one end of the narrow flexible water pipe near the ceiling. As he ran forward to take aim at the other end, two guards, and three hefty dogs appeared. They were nosing around the lavatory when they were attracted by the booming noise of the gun. The dogs were coming so fast it seemed their legs were not touching the ground. Ginny saw them coming, and fired at the pipe again. The noise of his gun concurred with the noise of the gun fired by one of the guards. He was just in time to drop himself on the ground as the bullets fled past his ears. At the same time, he had succeeded in shooting out a cross section of the pipe and water was gushing out of the blown ends onto the floor but running into a stretch of underground drain along the jail hallway. He crawled forward and rolled the pipe off the drain area. He realized quietly that if he had to get away from the place, he would have to retreat the fast approaching dogs. He rolled over as another flash of gunfire appeared from the guards. Then like a tireless mercenary, he opened fire on the dogs and the guards behind them. The gun blasted for some seconds and forced two of the dogs to retreat instantly. The two guards threw themselves in different directions as the bullets crashed. Before Ginny could realize what was happening, the third dog was already on him. The dog attacked him straight with his fierce aggressive jaw, forcing him to raise up his gun as her horrifying teeth came close to his body. In a moment of struggle the gun dropped as he wrestled with the wild animal. He held his teeth as its paw sank in his flesh and turned him wild. He knew he must act fast to stop the animals menacing teeth from reaching his eyes. Then in one swift movement, his hands found the dog's neck. He tightened his grip and twisted her neck. There was a sharp crack of bone as the dog released his grip and went slowly to the ground.

Unfortunately for the two guards, they were so badly placed they didn't know what was happening between Ginny and the dog. They knew the two other dogs had been hit, and they weren't sure about the survival of the third. They saw water gushing out of the pipes along the wall and it appeared there was water everywhere. They felt there wasn't any way Ginny could escape except by going through the gate their position had already covered.

Suddenly, the other bandits in the cells began to shout and beat the doors. In the midst of the sudden uproar, Ginny quietly took the long water pipe and wiped off the water with the sweater he was wearing. With the gun in one hand and the pipe in the other, he began a long backward crawl. He had almost reached the end of the cells block where he could break into a run when three other guards appeared at the other far end with their dogs.

"Lie flat" One of the guards on the ground shouted frantically at his men." he's armed."

Ginny apprehended the command as the men fell to the ground. But their dogs didn't wait; they were heading fast for him. Two of the dogs suddenly slowed pace and stopped when they saw the body of the first three dogs lying helplessly on the ground. The third dog didn't give a damn. She wanted Ginny and wanted him fast. Ginny realized what might happen if he allowed the dog to reach him. He lifted the rifle and took a careful aim at the animal. The bullet hit and recorded another casualty. The guards saw what had happened, and one of them fired as the dog went to the ground. Ginny flattened himself on the ground and replied almost immediately. The guard who had fired almost had himself nailed, and he had to roll and shift into a safer position. Ginny studied the position of the men as they retreated and tried to find a safer cover. He wanted them to quiver before taking the last risk. On the flat ground, he slowly lifted his head, pointed the gun at their direction, and started shooting until the gun was empty of bullets. For a few seconds, he was bereft of reasoning. He gave the gun a long stare, not knowing what to do with it. He didn't want to attract the attention of the guards to what had happened, and he knew sooner or later, they'd guess he had no bullets left. He could just see the open field and the high prison walls behind him. Then with sheer confidence, he suddenly clasped his hands around the long pipe, hitched himself up, and started running towards the field. The guards started firing almost immediately. A bullet grazed him as he hurdled past the block that parted the cells and came out into the open field.

The guards still had about fifty or more yards to cover before they could come out into the open field. Ginny headed straight for the nearest wall, and after sprinting for about forty yards, he heaved up the long pipe and took a jump that carried him up in a single light movement. The guards came out as his body took a long journey to the air, riding higher with the long vertical pipe until it reached the edge of the fifteen feet wall. Bullets flashed across like lightening as he vaulted over the prison walls and sailed to the other side with incredible feat. As soon as he landed on the grass below, the problem of how to get to the kroon's junction as fast as possible was his main concern.

Chapter 14

Within the sight of land, but far away from public eyes and war of customs men, a large vessel trailed its course with unerring discretion towards one of the largest coasts of West Africa territorial waters. It's brilliantly colored staff, and other assorted features danced to the tune of the sea tide behind as she plodded steadily through the water to the Lagos sea port. The captain, a tall thin man with a bony face, watched the horizon beyond from the compass with unrestricted view; taking the bearings of shore objects and other ships, and observing the heavenly bodies for the purpose of calculating the compass error.

The water seemed untainted, expanded, and soft looking as the engine turned the propeller and drove the ship through the water, causing wave phases to beat back and paving the way for the ship and its entourage toward their destination.

As the vessel pursued her course, moving steadily, the captain and the watchman glancing at the compass occasionally, Charles Aduwo, Fredrick Akintunde, Segun Adio and John Osawe sat in a small isolated land about one and a half kilometer away from the ship. Surrounding the outstretched bank of the lagoon where they sat were tall grasses and scattered tropical shrubs which completely screened their position from view. The four men lay on two sizable planks that were thrown, overboard from wrecked ships. A small boat with four rowlocks on its side stood with its prow on the sand bank beside the men. Inside it were two big thwarts that made a firm support on each side, which in turn supported the oars that touched the water beneath. From where they were sitting, the kroon's junction was as visible as the noses on their faces. Although the small line of words on the flying flag that stood in the middle of the lagoon could not be clearly read from their position the white pole that carried the yellow flag was easily visible, and right now, not even a bird could approach the flag without being spotted by the watchful eyes of the four men.

"Our cargo might come into view any moment from now," Fred said, breaking the silence that had held the men for some few minutes.

The men with him glanced at their wrist watches and nodded in approval.

"As soon as it appears," Charles said authoritatively, "we get aboard."

"This is my first major job," Segun said, beaming with unusual enthusiasm,

"I pray it succeeds."

"It'll succeed alright," John said. "Just pray you don't get over excited when you see the stuff."

"Segun," Charles said, pausing to allow the air that swirled out of his mouth to get out. "You've got to handle that car very well. We'll go over the new bridge to avoid those cops we saw when coming. You'll take the old market road as soon as we left the bridge, and head straight for the hotel."

"Yes, sir," Segun said. "But we might run into a traffic jam in the market place."

"That's better than being maneuvered by an intrusive cop, Charles said. "This time, I'll go with you in the Mazda. Fred and John will use the beetle car." Unlike when they were coming, he had stayed with Fred in his beetle car, and Segun had come with John in the Mazda car. The Mazda had only two front seats with a covered back that usually housed their smuggled goods. It is reserved exclusively for their operations."

"I prefer this place than our former base," John said.

"It is really a nice place," Fred said.

"It's very private," Charles said. "We can now talk louder than the whispering voices we usually employed in our former base, and we only need about two or three minutes to carry our stuff to the cars. That's a real gain in time."

For some reason Charles couldn't explain why he had opted for a new place when they came to their former base today. Ten minutes of careful search had evolved where they now stood, and the new position was a lot safer than where they had been operating for the past two years. The tall grass surrounding them gave them a good cover, and except they moved out into the lagoon, they couldn't be spotted. The four men were still expressing their pleasure at the discovery of the place when a vessel appeared in the midst of the blurring dew of the horizon.

Fred was the first to spot it. "I think our people are coming," he said, blinking his eyes.

The other three stared for some seconds at the long distance, and then Charles said, "It is them. Let's move out."

John was the first to stand up. He ran quickly to the boat, righted its prow and got it floating. Within two minutes, the four men had climbed into the boat and sat on the thwarts. As they dipped the oars softly into the water and moved the boat away from the bank, they came under the watchful eyes of the Felony Boys who right in their former base had been lurking for them to come into view.

"Phew! They are here. Aren't they?" Bob said in a harsh whispering voice, flattening himself on the stuffy grass that covered where he was hiding with others.

"Shut up!" Pappy bawled. "Don't you have eyes? The wind carries sound faster, so stop asking questions."

"They are going to meet the ship alright," Hercules said scrappily. "I think we should follow them now."

"Can't you abide by instructions?" Pappy said irritably. "We only follow them if they take another course after getting the stuff. They are not likely to do that. I am positive they'll come back right to where they've just emerged. That's when we move out. Understand?"

Hercules didn't answer him. He was looking like the other men at the fast moving boat that nosed its way towards the flag in the middle of the lagoon.

"They are certainly going to beat us to it in that boat. I don't think our canoe could be as fast as that," Eddy said; referring to the canoe they had rented from some fishermen at the shore beside the port. The canoe was dragged out of the water hidden in front of them.

"Why then do you carry a gun in your pocket?" Pappy said still irritable. "Are you going to throw it into the sludge?"

Eddy suddenly grinned, thinking there wasn't much the men in the boat could do in the face of their automatic weapons.

Unlike Charles and his men, the Felony Boys were heavily armed. Each man had in hand a .45 automatic pistol with sufficient ammunitions in pocket. A sub-machine gun with 90 rounds of live ammunitions was also kept in the canoe in front of them. They were prepared and ready for any shoot out.

Before they left the club, the Felony Boys had anticipated trouble. They knew smuggling on the sea was a game of chance. It could go on favoring someone for years without a single trouble. But when it turned hot, it became so nasty that those who called themselves the anti-smuggling men would take to their heels.

It had taken them about thirty minutes before they could finally settle on where they now hide, unaware that where they had chosen was where Charles had been operating since he started his sea smuggling business. They weren't in any way suspicious, and they knew that somewhere around would be Charles and his men waiting for the ship to appear. They had come before time, and they were prepared to wait until they came out. Now that this had happened, they felt relaxed and thought only heaven could help Charles and his men when they began to attack them. The five men continued to peep at the men in the boat as they rowed along, juxtaposing themselves on the ground like guerilla warriors as they waited anxiously for them to come back.

Inside the coming vessel, Wale moved with quick short steps away from the crew accommodation. He walked past about two or three staff arguing over a broken bottle of whisky beside the cargo hatches as he moved further down and cornered the derricks with a light athletic movement.

The chief steward, Mr. Akim Odedele, was ordering some of the staff to complete their jobs before the ship berthed as Wale went past the catering department. The man saw Wale and both of them exchanged some meaningful glances. Wale respected Mr. Akim because he was an excellent chief steward and also helpful to most of the boys working on the ship. Without him, the diamond consignment wouldn't have passed through the pre-shipment inspection.

Mr. Akim allowed the diamond box to be included in some of the ship's foodstuffs by covering it with some green vegetables on a large steel crate. Carried by Wale and Olu and accompanied by Mr. Akim , the crate had gone unchecked by the customs lads. Mr. Akim had done it several times for Wale and Olu and he knew his tip for such jobs. Mr. Akim and Charles had been trained by the same master. Helping Wale and Olu meant helping Charles.

Mr. Akim preferred seeing Charles himself rather than getting a hand-out from the boys.

During the journey of the ship from Egypt to Lagos, Wale had carefully removed the diamond box from the large crate and transferred it to one of the empty wooden boxes among the ship's luggage. Now as he headed to the deck department for the box, he glanced hurriedly at his strap watch and noted excitedly that the ship still had about five minutes before it stopped for the port's signal. He increased his steps, and as soon as he stepped into the deck department, some body whistled to him from behind. He turned around quickly. It was Olu Abiodun. He whipped his index finger over his shoulder, telling him to meet him fast.

Running from the bottom of the engine room to the propeller underneath was a tunnel formed of steel plates. The tunnel housed the propeller shaft and it had enough room for one or two men to move at a time. Connected to the tunnel was a peak tank that ran passing the steering engine into docking bridge.

Wale and his colleague waited until the ship stopped. Then half-dragging, half carrying the diamond box, they moved it through the tunnel, passed the tank into the docking bridge. They stood on the deck line, allowing the large derricks behind to prevent them from being seen. Then they tightened two ropes to the shackles on the box, and waited hopefully for Charles and others to appear.

One minute later, Charles and his men propelled past the waiting ship as if they had no business with it. Satisfied they were safe, they turned around and rowed the boat skillfully towards the heavy vessel.

Wale and Olu were smoking as the men approached. They tossed their cigarettes into the water below and grinned widely at the four men as they eased the boat to the side of the ship. Within seconds, the two men had lowered the diamond box through a distance of about 16 feet into the boat below. The men in the boat loosened the ropes on the shackles of the box and then signaled for the ropes to be pulled up. They exchanged some secret gestures, and then the men in the boat pulled away from the side of the ship.

Charles and his men rowed back a few meters, turned and headed back towards where they had come from. Unaware of the danger that lay ahead of them, they increased the speed and rowed thirty strokes to a minute.

Thirty minutes after Sergeant Taiwo and his men had left the Central Casino; they arrived at the general uncovered area of the Lagos sea port. A little away from the port's gate, where a good number of crew men sat around some cafe tables, stood the investigation office of the Customs and Excise men. The same building, housed the security office of the same department.

From the way Taiwo jumped out of the front door of the Land rover, the three officers in the security office knew instantly that there was something at stake. One of the officers ran out to meet him. Without wasting time, Taiwo explained what brought them there.

"Did that man in front tell you all these?" The young officer asked, pointing to Folly who sat next to the driver.

Taiwo nodded in haste.

"It could be true," the officer said, looking curiously at Corporal Yemi and Sergeant Bolaji as they came to join them. "There is a ship waiting to berth right now at kroon's junction, which is about five kilometers from here. There are lots of sea-shores around the area, and any of these people you've mentioned could be hiding there. Although we have some of our men around the lagoon, most of them are not out to look at burglars attacking large vessels. The vessels themselves have competent detectives for such jobs and they'll notify us if they are confronted with any tricky situation. Besides, we have our men in all the main roads most of the smugglers cannot do without passing. So nothing can really happen in and out of the lagoon around here without our awareness."

"From the information I've gathered so far," Taiwo said unreservedly, "these men we are looking for could be staying in one of those numerous shores surrounding the lagoon. I believe there are so many routes around this area all of them could not be possibly discovered, so our men could have passed through your men unnoticed. These men I'm talking about are very dangerous criminals who can shut down the whole of your security set up in a minute. Right now, they are out for a big job, and the duty of all these men you are looking behind me is to prevent them from doing the job. I will therefore appreciate your action in providing us men who can take us to those areas.

Taiwo's words worked right in the ears of the custom officer. He looked wearily at his colleagues who seemed to know the right thing to do. As one of them turned and ran to the investigation office, a young navel officer emerged, fondling lovingly with his neat cap as he came out from one of the cabins. His smiling face suddenly turned into a hard frown when he saw the police Land rovers and the men around. With the type of dedication the men of the armed forces had for each other, he walked smartly to where Taiwo and his men stood and politely asked if he could offer a help.

Briefly, Taiwo explained what was happening to him. The man seemed to like taking part in trouble as he demanded how many of them could follow him on the motor boat that carried their experts to Sea emergencies. Taiwo and the other two with him couldn't believe their luck.

"What's your name, sir?" Taiwo asked.

"Mustafa Sanni, Ports Naval Foundation."

"That is nice of you, Mr Sanni," Taiwo said, offering his hand. Then he went to the Land rover and selected three good men among the cops. Corporal Yemi Benson was to follow him with the three cops, while Sergeant Bolaji was to lead the rest cops in search of the sea shores.

"You, come down here." Taiwo said, beckoning to Folly.

Folly came down and walked quickly to where he was standing.

"You are staying here until we return," Taiwo said. Then he turned to one of the customs men. "Please, officer," he said, "Can you keep this man under guard until we return? He's an important witness, and besides, he's not safe to be in the open now." The customs man nodded and then marched Folly to the security office.

The officer who had ran to the investigation office came out with two of their task force men. The men were holding two automatic rifles while he handled a .45 revolver. As soon as he came out, Taiwo explained the division of plan to him. They shook hands and wished themselves luck.

As Taiwo and Corporal Yemi ran with the three cops to meet the naval man who was already sitting behind the steering wheel of the motor boat, the drivers of the two Land rovers blared their horns, hurrying up Sergeant Bolaji and the three customs men who were still entering the two vehicles.

With his hard and sinful face staring at the road in front, Ginny squeezed the handlebars of his new found motorcycle with a deft of hands. His cloth was dirty and a tiny spot of blood showed on the chest of his crimson sweater.

The wind kept sweeping past his body with incredible speed, and his hair, now pressed flat on his head, flew up occasionally whenever he checked the speed of the Honda motorcycle he was riding. Right now, he had no idea whether the man he had hustled off the motorcycle was still alive or dead. It was a chance he had grabbed after rowing over the prison walls. The owner of the motorcycle had been very timely. He had waved him for a pick up, but the man, sensing his abnormal appearance, had increased speed. He had jumped deliberately on the road when the man was within reach, and the man, trying to avoid him, had skid off the road and crashed on the road side. He had dragged the motorcycle back on the road, and since then, it had been speed all along. He knew the road well and he was covering it fast. About a minute or so before he reached where he was going; a car suddenly appeared in the road ahead. He stamped his legs on the foot pedal and allowed the speeding car to pass. He slowed down, then lifting the front wheel; he climbed over the curbstone and moved to the sandy ground along the curb. He stopped the machine, jumped down and bent over the handle bars. He righted the front tire and pushed the machine until it entered the tall rows of grasses that lined the entrance to the bush. He pushed it further, then stopped and rested it on its side. He then ran out of the bush, cleaned the pattern the tires had made on the ground, straightened the bent grasses and went creeping past the motorcycle into the bush.

After moving for about six or seven meters, he saw the gloomy face of the heavy lagoon. Its edge was unclear and he could just see the swamps before him. He wanted to reach the edge and look all around. Sensing the couldn't do so without being submerged in the sludge, he turned co his left, crept again for some meters, turned to face the lagoon again and moved forward. This time, he was in a better position. He was nearer to the edge, but he couldn't see the lagoon properly. He could only stare at the water facing him. He decided he would jump over the small swamp in front of him into the clean water and swim out to see if there was anybody around. Then as he bent down and rolled up his trousers, a boat appeared in front, crossing over to the left. Inside the boat were four men, rowing with paddles. Ginny could just make out the shinning head of a grey steel box from where he was crouching. He knew instantly that these were the people the Felony Boys were after. Somewhere very near, he told himself, must be the Felony Boys. Then, he turned around swiftly and began to run, following the track of the boat as it whisked off.

As soon as the Felony Boys were satisfied that Charles and his men were on their way back, they prepared themselves for a devastating attack. From their location, each man took a cautious crawl to the canoe in front of them.

The canoe was fairly sized, solidly built and made of hard timber. It had enough space for the five men, and lying on the two thwarts inside it were four paddles. As soon as all the men had got in, Pappy sat in front and instructed the other four to take the paddles. They circled the canoe expertly and freed it from the shore. They could just see the boat they were going to attack coming at the far side, so they paddled along another direction; planning to make half a circle turn before they attacked the boat.

At the men came out Charles had seen them. Although he couldn't recognize the faces of the men in the canoe, but he was wondering about what the men were doing where they had just left. Since he started his notorious activities in the sea, it was unusual to see anybody emerging from where the men had paddled out. If at all a boat was passing, he thought concernedly, it was either the speeding boat of the naval men or that of the barely clothed fisherman who always rowed past without interference. But these people he was staring at, he thought uneasily, didn't appear like fishermen. They were fully dressed and they were paddling their canoe like strangers at sea. Just as he began to relax because the men were heading to another direction, Fred tapped his shoulder, startling him a bit.

"It appears someone is moving through the grasses," he said, pointing at the bush beside them. Charles stared at the rustling grasses for sometime. He thought he was beginning to see wonders.

"Relax the beats!" He shouted. "Who the hell could it be?"

The men slowed the pace of the boat, beating back the water gently. Almost immediately, the man who was running through the grasses stopped.

"So we are being shadowed," Charles said, grinning ruefully.

"He has stopped," Fred said.

"Well gentlemen," Charles said not looking at the men. "I've decided I won't tell you about the gun I have in my pocket until something forced me to tell you. I am sure somebody is after what we have here, and I won't hesitate to use the gun if he dared to attack us. So don't be surprised when I pull out the gun. I don't want any of you to start asking questions about where I got it. Just paddle on and let's see how we can get the stuff home safely."

As the three other men increased speed, Charles found his way to the rear of the boat. He looked up as he was about to sit down. To his surprise, he men he had seen coming out of their former base had turned back, and they were now directly behind them.

"I think we are in trouble," he said, surprised at his own calmness as he spoke. "Some pirates are following us, I've first seen them taking the opposite side, but now they have turned to follow us."

The three other men looked back as they paddled on swiftly.

"They look like pirates alright," John said.

"They must have spotted us when we were getting the box from the ship, but I'll stake my life none of them touch the box." Fred said.

"Just paddle on," Charles said, looking intently at the canoe behind them. "Move as fast as you can. I'll se how they'll beat us to it."

Although Charles wasn't feeling as confident as he spoke, he thought he was prepared for any offensive attack. These days, he said without spoken, it seemed he was being haunted around by violent. The memory of his recent encounter with Pappy and Bob was still fresh on his mind. Although he admitted he was a hard sea smuggler, he told himself he hadn't killed a single person since he started his business because he couldn't live with the conscience of killing someone to get money. He had limited his smuggling to the outmost part of the city, where he knew the exchange of gun fire was reduced to the barest minimum. That was why he operated every time without carrying arms. It was easy without arms if he was caught by the sea patrol men. He could claim he went out fishing. He always took violent as the last resort. But now, it seemed violent won't leave him alone. If violent meant you had to do whatever you needed to do to survive, however inimical to you assailant's objectives, then he was prepared to do just that at this moment. He looked once more at the men following them. They were moving closer with increasing strength. Then as his hands went down to bring out the gun in his pocket, the distance noise of a gun that banged in the air rattled his nerves.

The four men in the boat trembled slightly as the gun fired again. Someone in the canoe behind was shouting at them to stop or else he would kill the whole lot of them.

"Move on," Charles whispered. In a fraction of seconds, his fingers found the butt of the gun on his hand and he pulled the trigger.

"Phew!" Pappy shouted in the canoe behind as the bullet from Charles's gun whizzed past the head of the men in the canoe. "So the bastards are armed. We must approach them with caution."

"The least I expected was for them to be armed," Bob said, lowering his body as he paddled fiercely with the other men.

"I enjoy killing people," Pappy said coldly. "If they are as bad as I am, then you better be on the look out. I guess Charles is the one keeping them guard, so I'll make sure he's the first to get the bullet on the head. He's scaring us with the shot, but I'll surprise him just now." As he bent forward to take a careful aim at the man who was shooting at them from the boat in front, the sudden shouts of his name in the middle of the rattling grass beside the lagoon froze his finger.

Before the five men could register their surprise, Ginny had dived into the water and swam with short powerful strokes to the waiting canoe.

Sergeant Taiwo had nearly stepped off the motor boat into the waiting ship when the noise of a gun brought his legs back.

"There is a shooting down there!" The naval man exclaimed, "It could be them. The large ship was about to move off. They had raced to where it stood under five minutes. Taiwo stepped back quickly and waved to the ship's captain who waved back. Before he could settle down, the naval man had shifted gear and steered the boat free; perking forward, and aiming its prow at where the noise of the gun had sounded. As the sound of another gun fire came over the air Taiwo got himself into a comfortable position and watched as the rest of the cops sheltered themselves in strategic places.

The motor boat that was carrying Sergeant Taiwo and his men was covering the distance so fast that the cops could now see the men in the canoe and the other boat in front of them. Then from nowhere, just at the side of the sea-shore, a man dived into the water and joined the men in the canoe. It happened so fast it appeared it didn't. Sergeant Taiwo marveled at the expertise movement of the man who swam to the canoe and marveled at the movement of the men who pulled him in. The new man had scarcely settled down when one of the men in the canoe fired at the boat in front. Taiwo and the other cops saw a man thrown upward in the boat and pitched into the water, then it dawn on them that the Felony Boys were the one in the canoe. Carefully, Taiwo lifted his revolver and fired at one of the men in the canoe. It was a nice shot, and a long harrowing yell sounded in the air as the bullet hit.

Hercules caught hold of his arm as a bullet ploughed into his bicep. He stared grisly at the bundle of meat that was chopped off his arm, dropping the paddle as he did so. At the same time, the other men looked back, forcing the canoe to slow it pace. They saw the hard rims of police caps and gun barrels pointing at them from the motor boat behind.

"The bastards!" Eddy cried. "We've ran into a trap!"

'What's the matter with you?" Pappy shouted. "Are you crazy or what? Give way to fear and they'll sweep us off."

"Give me the machine gun," Ginny said coldly, fixing his eyes on Pappy.

Pappy looked under the thwarts, saw the heavy gun and heaved it out. He gave it to Ginny.

"You and you," Pappy said, referring to Bob and Eddy, "face the front and keep firing at those men. Make sure none of them survive to take that box away. I will face those cops with Ginny. We mustn't allow them to come near us. Sharafa, I want you to keep moving the canoe as much as you can." Then he threw a gun to Hercules and said, "Guide your body with that till the battle ends. Eh?"

Before Pappy could finish his orders, blast of gunshots came off the motor boat, forcing the six men to lay low. Ginny hitched up the sub-machine gun and leveled its barrel on the trim of the canoe. The butt of the heavy gun crepitated on his hands as he started firing, forcing the canoe to sway off course.

The policemen aboard the motor boat took cover behind the stern of the boat as the clamor of the sub-machine gun broke out. The bullets ripped off the woodwork of the boat's rudder, forcing the cops to flatten themselves on the floor. Another blast came and crashed below the steering wheel, forcing the motor boat to take another direction as the bullets struck.

"Hit out!" Taiwo snapped as the clamor of the guns died down.

An explosive sound of gunfire broke out as all the policemen returned fire for fire. In the midst of the uproar, Taiwo lifted his head and took a careful aim at the man behind the sub-machine gun. He was lucky as the bullets from Ginny's gun whistled past his ears as it moans down the side of the motor boat. At the same time, the bullets from his gun caught Ginny on the neck, pierced through his larynx and lodged in the cervical spine.

Pappy blanched as blood spilled out of Ginny's neck, watching in horror as he dropped the gun and slipped to the floor of the canoe.

Another blitz of bullets came and flung Sharafa off the thwart into the water as he was trying to steer the canoe on course. Pappy snatched the sub-machine gun from Ginny's sagging hands and started firing. One of the constables in the motor boat was caught with bullets and thrown overboard. The other cops lurked down, waiting for the noise of roaring gun to die down.

Inside the boat in front, Charles cringed at the sight of John's floating blood on the lagoon water. He was glaring at it without apprehension. Then the pelting smash of water on his body as a bullet swept past geared him back to his senses. He was just in time to position himself well as another bullet zipped past his head. He was the only one armed in the boat and there was nothing much his .25 caliber could do in the face of the tearing bullets that were coming from the heavy guns of the men firing at them. As he lifted his gun and prayed for a lucky hit, the recognition of the voice that was shouting at them to stop hit him. He was as startled as he realized who was shouting that he dropped the gun. It was Pappy; he belched, flattening himself to the floor of the boat. How on earth could it happen? He yelled, picking up the gun again with shaking fingers.

"Stop the boat and lie flat!" He cried again. "It's Pappy and his men. They could get you with their bullets under a minute."

Fred and Segun dropped the oars quickly and slipped to the floor of the canoe. They had hardly done so when the quivering noise of the sub-machine gun came on their ears. But to their surprise, the bullets of the gun were not coming to their direction. Charles wondered at what was happening. He lifted his head and looked out frightfully. Some men from a speeding motor boat were attacking the men behind them.

"It seems the police have been alerted," he said, his voice shaking.

"God help us," Fred muttered.

"How the heck did those rogues know we are out here?" Charles said.

"It's unbelievable," Segun said.

"Did you see what happened to John?" Fred asked.

"He's dead. There is nothing we can do for him now," Charles said. "Are we still far from the shore?"

"Not much," Segun said. "I think we have about two hundred or fewer yards to go."

"I think we have to swim the rest."

Are we leaving the box behind?" Fred asked surprisingly.

"I'll prefer that than being nabbed with it."

"Do you mean we should leave the golden box and run away?" Segun said.

"That's what I mean."

"No!" Fred bawled. "Let's find a way of paddling it to the nearest shore and ditch it somewhere."

"You can do that if you like," Charles said. "I won't loss my life because of some golden box. I am leaving."

"Okay, we are staying," Fred said. "I bet my life I will take the box out.

"It's okay with me. I'll take the risk to swim out. You have the gun. But don't say I didn't warn you," Charles said and tossed the gun to Fred. He waited impatiently for the noise of the shootings to die down. As soon as it did, he crawled up, raised his head slowly and peeped out. Some men were still firing at their direction. He waited again for their bullets to stop flying overhead. Satisfied he could go; he crept to the front of the boat, closed his eyes and plunged into in the water with edgy nerves. He expected some bullets to crash into this body, but nothing happened. He began to swim cautiously towards the shore.

Inside the canoe with Pappy, Bob could care less about what was happening behind him. His whole attention was centered on the boat in front. Eddy and he had been firing for sometime now, but none of the men in the boat ahead seemed hurt. He was just planning to tell Eddy to help the men at the rear when the bullets caught Ginny, Almost at the same time, Sharafa was thrown overboard and they were still staring at his helpless body when Charles dived into the water. Bob caught his movement, but he was too late. This was the man he wanted, he thought ruefully; the man who had plunged them into this trouble. And here was he, escaping under his nose. He had to follow him, he swore secretly.

"Eddy!" He suddenly shouted as if he was in a nightmare. "Charles had jumped into the water and he is swimming to the bank. I am going after him."

Eddy too had seen the man who dived into the water, but he was still trying to recover from Sharafa's assault when it happened. He was sure Bob had noticed it, but he decided he wasn't going to speak.

Pappy heard what Bob had said and stopped shooting.

"What the hell are you doing when he dived into the water?" He cried. "Just what are you doing with your guns? Nobody is going out until we are through with those cops. If any of you tried it, I'd hack out your brain!"

The three men were still glaring at each other when another hail of bullets came through and forced them to stay low. Within that brief moment Bob had shoved his gun into the leather case on his waist. Before another set of gunshots could come through, Bob leaned over the canoe and dived into the water.

A bullet grazed Bob's ear as he sank. He gave a sharp cry of pain as he began to swim beneath, swearing as he went.

"Why did you let that son of a bitch go?" Pappy shouted at Eddy, his eyes glaring.

"You want me to catch him in that storm of bullets?" Eddy said irritable." He took the risk and it favored him."

Pappy turned the barrel of the sub-machine gun to him.

"Drop your gun! You stupid idiot!"

Eddy studied his cold murderous eyes. He knew if he didn't, the gun on his hands will turn him to shreds. He allowed the gun to slide to the floor and then leaned back on the stern of the canoe.

"Stand straight!" Pappy cried raucously. "You are a traitor. You brought that mischievous fool to the club to ruin us. You think I don't know what you are planning to do. You want to leave us here and run away. That's impossible. Not with me still alive. I'll make sure I kill you first, and then get out and kill him."

"That's rubbish! You dare not accuse me like that! Even with you gun pointing at me, I still maintain there's nothing true in what you are saying."

"Go and say that to your grandfather in hell," Pappy said and squeezed the trigger.

Eddy saw the movement of his hands quite right, but he knew there was nothing he could do to safe himself. A bullet sank into his cheek, crashed through his face and rebounded out. Another bullet caught him in the lungs and he fell forward, dropping at the foot of his killer.

Pappy looked at Eddy for some time, his face gaunt and impious, and then he crept back to the rear of the canoe. He went to where Hercules was lying, touched him and found he had stopped breathing. He was now the only one alive in the canoe. With a strong determination to survive, he crept back to the front of the canoe with the sub-machine gun in hands and peeped out. To his surprise, the boat carrying the diamond box had started moving again. It wasn't moving as fast as before, and he could just make out about one or two hands gripping and pushing the oars. Cautiously, he placed the barrel of the gun on the trim of the canoe and began firing at the boat.

The sudden discharge of gun bullets from Pappy's gun forced Fred and Segun to hand off the oars quickly. Before they could realize what was happening, the boat was already on its side. Its trim was so badly upset that the two men only had a glimpse of the heavy box as it slid into the water. Another blast of bullets came. Fred caught his breadth and shuddered as Segun was caught by the heavy blast. He watched helplessly as his blood smeared on the body of the sinking boat, dropping the gun on his hand as his body began to shake. Then caring less for what might happen; he dived into the water, trembling slightly as the boat capsized and pushed him further down.

As the trigger of the gun snapped back thrice, Pappy knew that the sub-machine gun on his hands was empty. In a flood of fury, he threw it out into the water and listened indifferently as it sank. He crawled to where Eddy's body was lying and checked his gun. It was empty. He crept back to Hercules's dead body and checked his gun. That too was empty. Then he crawled up to Ginny who lay crumpled up at the rear of the boat with his head hanging down and his neck cut into half. Even with his dead body, Pappy respected him. On Ginny's feet was the double-barreled police special Pappy had snatched from Sergeant Taiwo at the beach. He picked up the gun and crawled up to the rear of the canoe. He knew the cops outside were still there.

Pappy wasn't hoping to fight them now. All he wanted was to jump into the water and swim away if he had the chance. He tried something to test the alertness of the men outside; he rose up one hand and quickly withdrew it. His hand had hardly gone down when a bullet sank into the floor behind him, scrapping the edge of the canoe before coming in. He knew that there was no way he could dive out into the water without being hit by bullets. He knew sooner or later, the cops would begin a move to get him killed or catch him alive.

For awhile, Pappy considered the harsh inglorious life he had been living since his father died. He had staged an unmatched cruelty. A cruelty inflicted out of pleasure and temerity. At one time or the other, several people had been victims of his misdeeds. He had dealt with every one of them without remorse; wounding or killing his assailants without mercy. Those he hadn't killed were either maimed or thrown into such perplexity that they dared not confront him again for life. Violent always inspired in him pleasure and excitement. Something unnatural and lugubrious in his sub-conscious always reminded him he couldn't enjoy life with virtues. He had examined himself in this premise and knew it was far from being bogus. He was born to be naturally cruel, and those who had tasted part of his cruelties knew truly that he was devoid of human feelings.

Pappy could still remember vividly well about that man he had killed when he was building up his reputation. What was the man's sin? He was moving with a girl more beautiful than his girlfriend. He had waited until the guy came to the Casino with the girl. Then he exhibited his shameless bravado by snatching the girl from the man. The man was unfortunate enough to protest. And what did Pappy do? He grabbed the man and stubbed the cigarette he was smoking on one of the man's naked eyes. On the second day, the man was found dead in the street. Pappy had done his work, and such was his nature.

Pappy do not know how to be good. He never had a conscience. But now, he thought regretfully, was his cruelty coming to an end? This same lagoon floated the dead body of his father. Would the same happen to him? Suddenly, the silence that had marred the roaring of the guns disappeared as the motor boat carrying the cops started again. His thoughts were cut off. His eyes quailed as he pressed himself flat on his position, waiting and ready to fire at the spur of the moment. Then above the roaring engine of the motor boat, he heard someone shouting, "Drop your guns and stand up!"

Augustine Pappillo, tell your men to surrender, or else you'll all be dead in a few seconds!"

As faint as the command came to him, Pappy knew who was talking.

"Mr Pappillo," the voice shouted again. "This is Sergeant Taiwo. Remember what you did at the beach. Well, there is no time for that here. Just come out and surrender yourself to us. We won't touch you, if you do just that."

How the hell? Pappy thought, terribly puzzled. The same cop who had prevented them from carrying out their plan at the beach, here doing the same. Was this expenditure arranged to trap them? Or was it just a tip off to hand them over to the law? He was still thinking when a bullet whizzed over his head and struck on a broken thwart below his feet. Quietly, he checked the gun on his hand. It had only three bullets left. Turning up the barrel, he fired two of the bullets into the air. The cops inside the boat replied with a long continuous shooting that turned the canoe to another direction entirely.

In that few seconds that the canoe turned around, Pappy's eyes had a glimpse of the policemen's caps inside the motor boat. He realized without fear that their onus aim was to kill him with any slightest chance they have. Perhaps, he thought, it would be more honorable to die by killing himself. Blinded by insanity, he lifted the gun, pointed the barrel to own head and squeezed the trigger.

CHAPTER 15

The two police Land rovers that went in search of the sea shores where so badly directed by the three customs men who went with them that had it not been for the sea intervention, Taiwo's plan against the Felony Boys would have been unsuccessful. The team was several minutes late, and it was only the clamor of the sub-machine gun which overturned the boat carrying the diamond box that brought them to the scene of the shooting. As soon as the Land rovers screeched to a halt, the cops dispersed themselves in different directions, covering the general area of the shooting scene.

While the men from the customs ran with some cops to where the noise from the guns was coming, Sergeant Bolaji and a young constable took to the opposite direction. The constable, Saidu Aliu, nosed his head forward as he crept and ran through the grasses glancing back occasionally at the sergeant, who kept waving him on. After a while, he came out into an open ground. He could see the general lay out of the lagoon as he came out, and just as he was waving his hand to attract the attention of some of his colleagues who had come out at the other end, the bubbling sound of the water in front stiffened him to attention.

Someone was under the water, and the person was swimming frantically towards him. As the water bubbled again, he ran back to the bush and took cover.

"What the crap do you imagine you are doing?" Bolaji snapped behind him.

Saidu explained what he had noticed. He had hardly finished when a man crawled out of the lagoon and ran forward with wobbling legs. Bolaji recognized who it was.

Mr. Charles, please stay where you are!" He snapped.

Charles stood motionless, his heart beating fast, his breathing coming in short gasps. Then he dropped to the ground like a deflated tire.

Bolaji ran to him, followed by the constable.

"So you are involved in this," Bolaji said, bending over him. "Well stand up. Let's join the rest."

Charles sat glaring at him, tired and exhausted. He wanted to say something, but stopped when the noise of another gun fire sounded in the air. The two cops looked at each other, and then looked out at the lagoon.

Bob was lucky. He had almost reached the shore to where the cops and Charles were standing. He slightly edged out his head to take in some fresh air and make sure he was going on the right direction. He saw two policemen bending over Charles and almost at the same time, the gun sounded. The noise of the gun completely stopped his movement. The two policemen didn't notice him. They were glaring overhead, turning their attention to where the noise from the gun was coming. He sank low, went deeper into the water and swam under the water to another side. Two minutes later, he came to a stretch of rough water at the shore, a little away from where the three men stood. He came out and crept silently to the bush, but his movement was not too fast for the eyes of the constable.

"Look out!" Saidu cried.

Sergeant Bolaji swiveled around and dropped flat, looking at the young cop as he crept quickly to the bush. He was in a very bad position. He was completely in the open, without any cover. He stared at the same direction the constable was staring. Then he saw a movement. He raised his gun and fired. Nobody yelled. He fired again, this time creeping up and running forward to take a cover in the bush.

Bob, who had removed his gun from the leather strap on his waist, saw the sergeant as he stood up. He fired once.

Bolaji staggered forward and fell to the ground as the bullet hit him. He dropped his gun and clutched his stomach.

Saidu felt a tickle of blood ran up his spine as the officer groaned. He saw Bob at the same time as he was trying to ascertain his position. Their eyes met and for some seconds the two men lay staring at each other, their hands closing up on the butt's of their guns. Then the two guns went off at the same time.

Bob was thrown into the air; and coming down, his face sank into a ridge of sand as he landed. He didn't for once leave the gun on his hand, and leveling it, blindly on the ground, he pulled the trigger again.

Saidu, who was already hit, tilted his head backward, and fell on his side as another bullet caught him on the chest.

Bob watched him as he fell over, and then he stood up, staggering to a standstill as he looked at the blood that was fast soaking his cloth from his shoulder. He staggered out of the bush and came out with the gin in hand.

With abrupt trepidation, Charles quickly changed his position, awakening himself from the hopeless grief that had paralyzed him. He rolled over and lay tummy flat on the sand. He was just planning to dive back into the water and swim to another part of the shore when a voice held him back. He looked up and saw the motor boat he had seen attacking the canoe coming towards him. The boat was running half its speed and somebody inside was shouting his name. He was still wondering who the hell it was when a voice barked at him from behind.

"Stay there! You fool!" Bob cried, fuming in fury.

Charles turned back and saw the barrel of a .45 automatic pointing at his chest. He began to shake so violently his legs found it difficult to support him as he saw the person pointing the gun at him. He gaped at Bob's blood soaked cloth, finding it difficult to breadth.

"You rogue! You twit! You bloody idiot!" Bob shouted, moving forward unsteadily as he spoke, "You think I won't catch up with you? You are a filthy pig. My wish is to see the end of your life. I live to plan your death and make you suffer for every single punishment I suffered in the prison. When I was going to jail, I promised you my revenge was going to be deadly. When I told you that you are going to regret your action against me, you thought I was joking. You now see what I meant. I'm a man of definite purpose. I believe in carrying out my wish, and that is why you are going to die today. I am going to kill you with the last bullet in this gun. You'll die first, so that when we meet in hell, we shall continue our quarrel," he paused, and suddenly grinned. As he leveled the gun and pointed the barrel at Charles's head drawing his fingers closely to the trigger, a barrage of bullets poured into his chest from the fast approaching motor boat, slitting across his face as he fell backward.

Charles flung himself clear off the ground and plunged into the water. He had scarcely landed when two cops dived into the water and dragged him out.

"You are foolish enough to be buried alive," Bola Thompson said, smiling at his friend. Charles had just finished telling him what happened three days ago.

Bola was a little tense. He was glad that his friend had not been killed.

Charles, back at home with his wife, felt he needed a year rest before venturing on anything again in his life.

"Darling," Shola said, resting her head on her husband's shoulder. "You are quitting that job. Aren't you?" This evening, she was wearing a cheap blouse over a transparent skirt and as she curled up beside her husband on the sofa.

Charles thought she was the most beautiful woman in the world.

"Yes, honey," Charles said, giving her his winning smile, "I've already I promise I will have nothing to do with smuggling again."

"You are like a square peg in a round hole on that job," Bola said, moving away from the window sill and coming to a seat in the centre of the room. "Hand off everything evil, and you'll enjoy your life."

"Thank you, Mr. Preacher," Charles said.

Someone knocked on the door. Before any of them could answer, the door opened and Sergeant Taiwo strolled in. This time, he wasn't in his uniform and he looked more civilian in the brown suit he was wearing. He had spent all day tidying up the mess over the weekend.

"I am here to give you a writ, Mr. Charles," he said as he walked around the three people and sat on a chair facing them, "You'll need a hard heart to tell the jury you went out fishing as you explained on Friday," he stretched out his legs, grinning at Charles.

"Honey, please get a nice cold beer for our great guest," Charles said, I think it's time we celebrate."

"Officer," Bola said, looking at the sergeant, "Charles told me of your wonderful job. I am proud to know you, sir."

"There is nothing to it. He was just lucky we arrived in time."

"Thank you very much for saving my husband's life," Shola said as she came back with a tray, and settled the bottles of beer on the stools beside the men. She filled the empty glasses and retired herself besides her husband.

"All said and done," Taiwo said, masking his face with frankness. "You are now back at home, safe and alive. There is no Pappy or Bob to haunt you around any more. After last Friday's operation, we scattered those bastards known as the Felony Boys. Additionally, Intelligence Officers have been assigned to the area to prevent gang reorganization. We have executed the necessary warrants to other local crime leaders to prevent their relocation."

"That is wonderful," Charles said.

"You should be glad we fished out your assistance, Fred before he could drown," Taiwo continued. "I also did my homework on you. I was aware your brother was a cop. He was a good man who died in the line of duty. I decide to give you a break and gave a story that completely rids you of suspicion to the superintendence," he paused, sitting bold right. "But don't let me kid you, for the next three months or so, you are going to be watched. So as from today, you are safe as long as you keep your hands on good things. If you really want us to be good friends, you have to be clean. You have to live a legitimate life. That's all I have for you."

"Sergeant," Charles said, concealing his gladness at what the officer had just said. "I must confess here that I owe you a lot. You are surprisingly great. Your have strength as hard as nail. If our entire police force can be made up of men with your type of courage, then our dear country will have less to talk about crimes. I want you to take it from me today that smuggling will be the last game I'll touch again before my life ends. I am speaking with honesty and integrity. I've already sworn to it. I gave you my word in the presence of my wife and my best friend. I won't betray you. I won't betray my people. I won't betray my country, and of course, I won't betray myself. I thank you once more for your help. May we live to reward the goodness you've done for us."

The sergeant relaxed back on his seat. "That's a brilliant speech," he said. "Well, I don't think you are going to get off that easy. I have spoken to a friend of mine who is one of the judges. He has agreed to give you one year probation. He wants you to be a good citizen, do some charity work, take care of the poor and feed the homeless."

"That is very kind of you. I will be very glad to appear before the judge and offer my civil services," Charles said.

"May I know what business you are now going to embark upon? The sergeant asked.

"I am going to be selling rice."

The three people with him burst out laughing.

THE END

978-0-595-45831-8
0-595-45831-9

Printed in the United States
93949LV00004B/394/A

9 780595 458318